Dark Memories Restored

THE CHILDREN OF THE GODS
BOOK FIFTY-FIVE

I. T. LUCAS

Dark Memories Restored is a work of fiction! Names, characters, places and incidents are products of the author's imagination or are used fictitiously and are not to be construed as real. Any similarity to actual persons, organizations and/or events is purely coincidental.

Copyright © 2021 by I. T. Lucas

All rights reserved.

No part of this book may be reproduced in any form or by any electronic or mechanical means, including information storage and retrieval systems, without written permission from the author, except for the use of brief quotations in a book review.

Published by Evening Star Press

EveningStarPress.com

ISBN: 978-1-957139-02-9

Mr. Wu

"Mr. Wu. It's so good to have you back." Doctor Wang dipped his head. "How was your trip?"

"Uneventful." Wu put his briefcase on the desk. "How did the meeting with the three prospective families go? Did they fill out the applications?"

"Not yet." The principal smiled apologetically. "They are very superstitious for Westerners. I wanted to reassure them that the school buildings are either new or completely renovated, so I made the mistake of telling them about the fire that destroyed most of the original structures on the property. When they heard that there was a fire, two of the mothers became concerned and wanted more details before making their decision."

"What kind of details?"

"Mainly, they wanted to know whether anyone died." The principal winced. "They are concerned about bad vibes imparted by the spirits of those who might have lost their lives in such a horrible way."

Superstitions were very common in the Chinese culture. If those ladies were of Chinese descent, they might have been influenced by their parents' or grandparents' beliefs.

Wu rounded his desk and pulled out his chair. "What did you tell them?"

He didn't invite the principal to sit down. If he wanted Wang to leave anytime soon, it was better to leave him standing. Doctor Wang was a charming guy and a great salesman, which made him perfect for the job he'd been hired for, but it also meant that he was overly talkative.

"I told them that I didn't know. They asked if it was possible to speak with the founder of the school."

The principal wasn't supposed to mention him to the parents of prospective students until it was time for the final interview. Regrettably, the man's excessive talkativeness was as much of a hindrance as it was an asset.

Wu stifled a groan. "I hope you told them that I don't meet with the parents or the students until after they pass the tests."

"I did, sir." The principal bowed. "But perhaps you'll be willing to make an exception for these families. They are planning on visiting other schools, and we might lose three potential students." The principal's lips lifted in a small smile. "I promise that it will not be a waste of your time. The three ladies are exceptionally beautiful. Mrs. Williams runs a modeling agency, and she looks the part.

She's very tall." He held a hand over his head to indicate her height. "Her sister is just as good-looking and perhaps even taller—a gorgeous woman who looks much too young to have a teenage son. The designer they work with is shorter and curvier, but she's also very alluring and seems feisty." He smiled lasciviously. "Naturally, they are all married, but it is not a crime to look and admire such fine ladies."

Wu pretended that he was not at all curious. "I will take your word for it, Doctor Wang."

"What should I tell them, sir?"

Three new potential students meant a lot of money for the school, and it would be a shame to lose them.

"Tell them that I can see them first thing tomorrow morning. Today, I want to rest from my trip."

"Of course." The principal inclined his head, his disappointed expression indicating that he'd hoped to secure an interview for the families for today. "I hope they won't mind prolonging their visit. I called their hotel, and the clerk told me that they were scheduled to check out later today."

Calling the hotel was sneaky of the guy, but smart.

"If they decide to stay another day to meet with me, it means that they are serious about the school, and if they don't, it means that they are not, and I will save myself the hassle of meeting with them."

The principal nodded. "Very astute, Mr. Wu. I will inform them of your decision."

"Make a big deal out of it." Wu waved a hand. "Tell them I had important meetings scheduled for tomorrow, which I had to reschedule in order to accommodate them. Hopefully, that will make them feel indebted, and they will not only stay, but also complete the applications."

"Very true, sir. I will call them right away."

"Hurry up before they check out of the hotel."

"Yes, sir." The principal dipped his head and pivoted on his heel.

When the door closed behind him, Wu pulled his laptop out of his briefcase, turned it on, and connected it with a wire to the school's network. Entering his ten-digit passcode, he accessed the school's surveillance network and searched for footage of the visitors.

Wang's comments about the three women piqued his curiosity. They most likely weren't the ones he'd been awaiting, but he was curious to see if they were indeed as impressive as the principal claimed. After all, he was a male, and not everything he did in life was about duty and honor.

Viewing the feed from Wang's office at ten times the normal speed, Wu didn't have to wait long before he found the relevant footage.

As the three couples entered the room, the incredibly tall guy with dreadlocks caught his attention first. He was wearing sunglasses indoors, which was strange, but since he was supposed to be a famous former star athlete, which made him a sort of celebrity, perhaps the shades were part of his image.

Wu had read the short profiles Doctor Wang had prepared about the prospective students and their parents, but he'd skimmed over most of it. To him, what mattered most was whether they had the means to pay the substantial tuition and board, and that the students had the minimum required academic qualifications and weren't troublemakers.

The athlete's statuesque wife was no doubt the model agency owner, and she was indeed magnificent. Tall for a woman, but elegant and graceful nonetheless. Her sister looked a lot like her, younger, less refined, but just as impressive.

The third one was partially obscured by her husband's broad back. From what Wu could see, she was much shorter than the other two and not of Chinese descent, as evidenced by her unruly hair. Even though it was gathered in a loose bun, it looked curly, and its ends were colored blond.

There was only one camera in Doctor Wang's office, and the way it was positioned, Wu couldn't see the woman clearly even when the couples sat down. The husband was still obscuring his view.

He could've switched to an earlier recording from the entrance camera but, curiosity aside, it wasn't necessary. Wu was more interested in the principal's sales presentation and the parents' responses to it than in the third woman's reported good looks.

During the presentation, the guy with the sunglasses made some disparaging comments about students cheating on their entrance exams, to which the principal's answer was perfectly worded. It was polite and yet encouraging.

"That's good to know," the guy with the glasses said. "It would be a shame to drag Junior out here only to get rejected."

The names of the three visiting couples had been included in the brief Doctor Wang had prepared for him, but Wu had glossed over them as well.

Williams.

That was the last name of the modeling agency owner and her husband, but he'd forgotten their given names. He should learn them before the meeting tomorrow.

Wang pulled out three folders and put them on his desk. "Would you be filling out the applications today?"

"We will take them with us," the modeling agency owner said. "We plan on touring several other schools, and we will only apply after we decide which one we like best."

"We would like to see the grounds," said the husband of the woman Wu was still waiting to see. "Our son is an athlete, and outdoor activities are important to us."

"I'm interested in seeing the dormitories," his wife said. "I'm more concerned with the living conditions."

Her voice sounded vaguely familiar, and Wu increased the volume to hear her better.

"Our son is used to luxury," she said. "I don't expect the school to provide him with the same level of accommodations as he's enjoying now, but I don't want him to spend the next three years in boot camp conditions either."

Wu had heard that voice before, the slightly nasal inflection grating on his nerves for some reason.

The principal gasped dramatically. "I assure you, Mrs. Furman, that our students enjoy every convenience and amenity. The main school building is relatively new. The dormitories have been completely remodeled to bring them up to the highest standards, and the new buildings were designed by one of the top architectural firms in Beijing according to Mr. Wu's exact specifications." He got up from behind his desk. "It's best, though, for you to see for yourself. Let me give you a tour of the school. Our classrooms are spacious, well-ventilated, and equipped with the latest and best educational tools. No other school on your list will come even close to ours."

When the parents rose to their feet, the shorter lady's husband finally got out of the way, and as she lifted her head and looked straight at the surveillance camera, the sight of her face was like a punch to his gut.

A growl started low in his throat. "You fucking bitch. Did you come to finish the job?" Baring his teeth, he banged his fist on the desk. "Not this time around, sweetheart."

"I apologize for my mother." Kian poured Dalhu a shot of whiskey. "She shouldn't have commandeered your house like that."

To give Geraldine the privacy she'd requested during the retrieval of her memories, Annani had taken over Amanda and Dalhu's place, practically throwing everyone out, including its rightful owners.

"It's fine." Dalhu offered him a rare smile. "I can understand why Geraldine needed to be alone with the Clan Mother. If it were me, I wouldn't have wanted a bunch of people whom I hardly know to hear my life's dirty details or even the not so dirty ones."

"We could have stayed in your backyard until it was done."

Dalhu lifted the whiskey glass in a salute. "Then I would have missed an opportunity to share a drink with you. I've grown fond of your whiskey and cigars."

Kian grinned. "I'm glad to have you as a partner in crime, but I bet Amanda isn't happy about it." He cast his sister a sidelong glance. "You hate the smell of cigars."

"Not true." Amanda rubbed a hand over her belly. "I hate the smell of cigarettes. I can tolerate cigars."

"Good to know." Kian saluted her with his glass.

She gave him a small smile. "I'm dying of curiosity. I can't wait to hear what Mother finds out."

"Me too." Syssi handed Amanda the cappuccino she'd made for her and sat on the couch. "I'm also worried for Geraldine. I know that Annani will handle her with the utmost care, but still. Geraldine's mind is fragile." She sighed. "Poor woman. I can imagine how frightening it must be for her to have a goddess prowling around inside her head."

Amanda lifted the cup to her lips, took a sip, and leaned back. "Do you remember how it felt when Kian released your memories?"

"How could I forget? I thought that my head was going to explode. That's why I'm so worried for Geraldine. When Kian released mine, I had only accumulated several days' worth of memories. She has a lifetime of them, and she won't be able to handle the onslaught."

"My mother is aware of that." Amanda sipped her coffee. "While we waited for Geraldine and Cassandra to arrive, she had time to think it through, and for a change, she asked my opinion." Amanda chuckled. "After all, I am a neuroscientist, so she figured I would know a thing or two about what the brain can handle. I advised her not to release Geraldine's memories all at once. Annani is going to bring them close to the surface so they can bubble up over time. But while she's at it, she'll take a look at them to find out what really happened with that immortal."

"I'm happy that she consulted with you." Kian walked over to the living room's sliding door. "I just hope that she'll actually follow your advice." He pulled the door open. "Dalhu and I are going out to the backyard for a smoke. If you hear from Annani or from Geraldine, let us know."

"Sure thing," Syssi said. "But I doubt we will hear anything anytime soon. Annani has years of memories to sift through."

Dalhu followed Kian outside. "I know the Clan Mother is powerful, but how can she access memories that are so old?"

"She can't, which is a good thing." Kian closed the sliding door behind Dalhu. "Otherwise, she would need to spend years inside Geraldine's head. She can only access recent memories and those that have left a lasting impression." He lifted the box of cigarillos off the patio table and offered one to his brother-in-law.

"Can you do that?" Dalhu asked as he pulled one out. "I mean with a human. Can you see old memories that left an impact?"

Kian shrugged. "Perhaps, but I don't have my mother's patience. I've only ever attempted to access recent memories." He lit Dalhu's cigarillo and then his own.

For a few blissful moments, he and Dalhu puffed on their cigarillos and sipped their whiskey in silence.

When Kian's phone rang, disturbing the quiet, Dalhu sat up. "That was faster than I expected."

Kian pulled the phone out of his pocket, but it wasn't Syssi's or Onegus's number on the screen. It was Arwel's.

"It's not about Geraldine," he told Dalhu before answering the call. "Good morning, Arwel. Or is it afternoon? What time is it over there?"

"It's eleven o'clock in the morning. I wanted to let you know that we are staying one more day."

"Why? Did Mey decide to give the echoes another try?"

"Since we are spending another night here anyway, that's the plan. We got an appointment with the head of school, but he could only see us tomorrow. The principal told me some crap story about meetings that had to be rearranged so Wu could see us, emphasizing over and over again how fortunate we were that he'd agreed to meet with us at all."

"Couldn't you just thrall him to schedule the meeting for today?"

"It won't help to thrall Wang when it's Wu that we need to talk to. Besides, Mey likes the idea of listening to more echoes. She learned a lot during the two previous nights."

They were perpetually short on Guardians, so pulling four of them for the investigation in China meant one less rescue mission each day that they were there. But finding out more about the Kra-ell was important. That being said, saving victims of trafficking was as important if not more so, and Kian hated to have to choose between investigating a potential threat to the clan and the trafficking victims.

The worst part of being the leader was making those kinds of calls.

"If you and the rest of the team don't mind staying another day, then I don't have a problem with that either. This investigation is important, and it's not like there is an emergency you need to take care of elsewhere. The trafficking cells, regrettably, will still be out there when you come back."

"I know." Arwel loosed a breath. "But I'm grateful that there are no emergencies. I tried to call Onegus earlier, and when his voicemail answered, it got me worried because he always answers his phone."

"He probably turned it off. He's dealing with family drama."

"Oh, yeah? What's going on?"

Kian didn't like to gossip, but since all the Guardians would soon learn about the immortal's portrait and Annani's suspicion as to who Geraldine had to descend from, there was no harm in telling Arwel the news now.

"I'll give you the highlights. Before Geraldine lost her memories in what we believe was a boating accident, her former husband saw her with a guy that Onegus suspected was the immortal who'd induced her. Onegus got Tim to draw his portrait from the ex-husband's memory, and he brought it over earlier today for Dalhu and Kalugal to take a look at. They didn't recognize him as one of the Doomers, but Annani knew right away who he was, or rather who he was a descendant of. According to her, the guy is the spitting image of the god Toven, Mortdh's younger half-brother. She summoned Geraldine and Cassandra and offered to retrieve Geraldine's memories of the guy. She's doing it as we speak, and Onegus is waiting with Cassandra to hear the results."

"That's big news, especially if Geraldine's guy is not alone. What if there is a community of Toven's descendants out there?"

"My thoughts exactly."

Shai

A steaming mug of coffee in hand, Shai walked into his and Geraldine's bedroom. She looked so peaceful, and after all the excitement of the previous day, she needed the rest. He would have liked to let her sleep a little longer, but William's guys were on their way, so he had little choice in the matter.

When they'd gotten home last night, Geraldine had been exhausted. The summons from the Clan Mother right after they'd returned from Oklahoma had been stressful enough. Then the emotional upheaval of the goddess's revelations sapped the rest of Geraldine's energy.

For the first time since they'd started spending their nights together, they'd gotten in bed but not to have sex. Shai had held Geraldine in his arms until she'd fallen asleep, but with thoughts and speculations about Orion swirling through his head, he couldn't even close his eyes, let alone relax enough to sleep.

"Wake up, love." He put the mug on the nightstand, sat on the bed next to her, and kissed her on the lips.

Murmuring something incomprehensible, she pulled the blanket up to her chin and turned on her side.

He tugged on the blanket. "The guys are going to be here in less than half an hour."

She opened her eyes. "Which guys?"

"William's crew is coming over to install the surveillance cameras and listening devices in the house. You need to get up and get dressed."

"So soon?" She reached for the coffee mug. "We only talked about it last night, and it's already happening?"

"After we left Amanda's place, Onegus made the calls and texted me to expect the crew today. I didn't know that they would be arriving so early, though. One of the guys called me half an hour ago to let me know they are coming."

Usually, Shai left for the village around that time, so it was good that they'd caught him home. Otherwise, he would have had to turn back to make sure that Geraldine was up and ready.

"What time is it?" she asked.

"Six-thirty in the morning."

"That's early." She took a sip from her coffee. "Can you stay until they are done? I don't want to be alone in the house with men I don't know."

It warmed Shai's heart that Geraldine considered him her protector, but she had nothing to worry about from William's crew, and he needed to get to work.

"You are perfectly safe with them, but I'll stay until they get here and make the introductions." He took her hand and lifted it to his lips. "If you want, you can leave them to do their work and come with me to the village."

"What am I going to do there while you are at work?"

"What did you plan to do here?"

"Think." She took another sip of coffee. "The Clan Mother said that the submerged memories she'd placed closer to the barrier between my conscious and subconscious mind would start to percolate, but I didn't dream of Orion last night."

Shai stifled a relieved breath. He would never tell Geraldine so, but he didn't want her dreaming of the immortal. He hadn't bought the story the guy had told her about them being related to each other—a family. He was convinced that Orion had been the one who'd induced her, and after the accident, he'd wiped out her memories of him because he'd decided to change the story and pose as her benefactor.

What Shai couldn't understand, though, was why.

Geraldine was beautiful, intelligent, and passionate, and that immortal would have been hard-pressed to find any female her equal, human or immortal. Why hadn't he wanted to continue their romantic relationship, but had still wanted to check in on her from time to time and take care of her?

So far, Shai had come up with three possible explanations, two of which painted Orion as a prick who deserved to be beaten into a pulp, and one that didn't.

The first one was that the immortal had something to do with Geraldine's near-fatal accident and stayed around out of guilt.

The second one was that Orion hadn't been involved in her accident, but upon finding out that she'd suffered irreparable brain damage, he considered her damaged goods.

And the third and least likely one was that he had never been romantically involved with her, and that he was a friend or relative of her inducer, and that for some reason, her inducer couldn't keep an eye on her and had tasked Orion with her care.

Geraldine lifted her hand to her temple, a reflexive move that usually signaled that she was nervous or that she'd forgotten something and was trying to remember it. "Perhaps I did dream about him and forgot?"

"It's possible." Shai rose to his feet and affected a neutral tone. "Dreams are difficult to remember, and I don't recall most of mine." He pulled the blanket off her. "Time to get up, my love."

The smile she gave him was enough to melt the thorny icicles around his heart. "I love it when you call me that." She took his offered hand and let him pull her against his chest but didn't let him kiss her. "I need to brush my teeth first."

"Fine." He turned her around and smacked her bottom to get her going. "Hurry up. I'm not moving from this spot until you come back and give me a proper kiss."

Turning to look at him over her shoulder, she cast him a sultry smile. "Do we have time for more?"

The answer was probably no, but he didn't care. The installation crew could wait outside the door until he let them in.

"We'll make time." He prowled after her into the bathroom.

Wu

Cloaked in darkness, Wu crouched behind a rocky outcropping and lifted the binoculars to his eyes. It was still early, only a little past eleven at night, and Stella and her companions didn't seem to be winding down for sleep anytime soon.

He didn't mind the wait. In fact, he'd arrived early to watch the way they interacted with each other. It was important to figure out who was the leader of the team, who was the second-in-command, and whether any of the couples were real romantic partners or just pretending for the sake of the recon mission.

It made a difference.

Love was a foreign concept to the Kra-ell for a reason. It caused people to make stupid mistakes, and knowing whom it affected improved his chances of success.

With the room's window facing the back of the hotel, they didn't expect anyone to be watching them. The window looked out onto a large open field that was sparsely wooded but still provided privacy. What they hadn't accounted for, though, was that it just as easily provided a watcher with the perfect hiding place. Perhaps they weren't professional spies, just murderers come to finish the job they'd started twenty-two years ago—an execution team.

Spies would have closed the opaque set of curtains and not just the sheers.

From Wu's vantage point, he could see them clearly, and with the help of his binoculars, it was like he was in the room with them.

He counted eight people, recognizing the three couples from the surveillance tape, and two additional men he hadn't seen before. Four of the males looked like they could give him trouble. Their muscled bodies and postures betrayed their military training. The fifth one seemed a little softer, a civilian perhaps.

The question was whether they were armed and whether they were as strong as the Kra-ell.

The females weren't, he knew that, but if any one of the males was his equal in brute strength, he couldn't take them on all at once. His best option was to wait for an opportunity to catch Stella alone or just with the one pretending to be her husband. Fortunately, that guy seemed to be the weak link in the chain, and Wu had no doubt that he could overpower him, provided the male was unarmed.

The only weapon Wu had with him was a hunting knife, and even that was considered dishonorable for a Kra-ell male to carry.

The Kra-ell were traditionalists for whom knives and swords were the females' weapons of choice. Males were expected to fight with their fangs and claws. Wu's nails were not nearly as hard and effective in battle as those of the purebloods, but his fangs worked just fine, and he didn't regret bringing the hunting knife.

He wasn't about to repeat the same mistake that had gotten the others killed.

Their stubborn adherence to tradition had cost them dearly.

When they'd been attacked, having firearms on hand might have saved them. But perhaps tradition hadn't been the real reason for the compound's lack of proper weapons. Jade's reasons for refusing to purchase contemporary weaponry might not have been about old-fashioned beliefs but about her continuous hold on power. She might have feared that the simmering internal unrest would eventually reach a boiling point and her tribe would turn against her.

Throughout the years, Wu had often wondered if the attackers had been his own tribesmen. Many of the hybrids hadn't been happy about the way they'd been treated—their second-rate status, their lack of access to Kra-ell females, and Jade's prohibition on them fathering children with humans.

They might have rebelled.

They might have gotten the weapons without Jade's knowledge.

Having guns and ammunition might have given them the edge they needed to overcome the superior strength of the purebloaded males and claim the females for themselves.

If not for the fire and the abandonment of the compound, that would have been the most logical assumption. But if the hybrids won, why would they leave?

Sitting back, Wu leaned against a smooth boulder and stretched his long legs in front of him.

Twenty-two years.

He'd been waiting twenty-two years for Jade and the other females to return, hoping against hope that they would escape their abductors, that he hadn't gotten all of them killed, and that he wasn't going to spend the rest of his long life alone, surrounded by humans who had no idea what and who he was.

It had been so long that he hardly ever thought of himself as Vrog anymore—a hybrid Kra-ell who was part of a tribe, who had a father and a mother, who had friends and cousins.

All gone, and it was probably his fault.

Since the rebellion theory had too many holes to be valid, only one suspect remained—Stella.

If he had never met her, had never revealed to her who he was, no one would have known his people even existed, and no one would have come to eliminate the supposed threat they posed.

A couple of months after his affair with Stella, Vrog had started suspecting that something was amiss, becoming concerned when his emails, phone calls, and voice messages hadn't been answered.

Even though he'd told no one about her, he'd assumed that Jade had somehow found out and feared that she'd decided to cut him off instead of giving him the whipping he deserved.

Hell, he had even been willing to redeem himself the old-fashioned way—dueling to the death with a pureblooded male. But when all his communication attempts had been unsuccessful, it had seemed as if the door had been slammed shut in his face and he could no longer return to his tribe.

Normally, Vrog wouldn't have dared to abandon his assignment in Singapore without Jade's permission, but after a week of utter silence, he could no longer stand the uncertainty. He had to find out for sure.

Incurring Jade's wrath was better than not knowing where he stood with her.

He'd booked a flight back home.

What he found was much worse than he'd expected.

Everything apart from the human living quarters, the barns, and some storage shacks had been burned down to the ground. His people, the humans, and even the livestock had all gone.

At first, he'd assumed that they'd left without him as punishment for Stella, his offense coinciding with the move, but not the cause of it. When relocating, it was a common practice for the tribe to eliminate all traces of themselves from the former location. However, after thinking it through and digging around for clues, he'd realized that something much more nefarious had taken place.

His first clue was finding the fireproof safes buried under the rubble, still locked, and given their weight, still full.

Using explosives to break in, Vrog had found gold, precious stones, money, and business files. Jade wouldn't have left those behind if the move had been voluntary.

Further inquiry into the tribe's bank accounts revealed that they had been emptied.

Only Jade and her second-in-command had access to the tribe's accounts, so either they had survived the attack and decided to cooperate with their abductors, or the information had been tortured out of them.

He'd even suspected a government raid, but no one in the adjacent towns and villages had seen soldiers passing through.

Searching for more clues, Vrog had kept on digging in the rubble for weeks, and what he'd found out painted a gruesome picture that he still didn't fully understand.

Lifting his hand, he looked at his father's ring.

Just like the other rings he'd found in the rubble, it was intact despite the fire that had turned his father's body into ash.

Vrog had found twenty-one rings, one for each of the pureblooded males they'd belonged to, each engraved with its owner's name and position in the tribe.

The males' rings were made from a dark blue stone that he suspected had originated on the Kra-ell's home planet, while those worn by the pureblooded females were made from a similar stone that was green. They too were engraved with their names and positions, but he'd found none of those.

His findings had led Vrog to believe that the pureblooded males had been slaughtered, while the females had either been taken or had escaped.

The males would have fought to the death to save the females, to give them a chance to escape, which was why Vrog still harbored hope that they would one day return to claim what had been left in the safes.

The hybrids didn't get the special stone rings, so he didn't know what fate had befallen them. The males had probably perished together with their pureblooded fathers. The females had either escaped or had been taken along with the pureblooded females.

The big question that he needed an answer to was who had done that and why.

After he had given it a lot of thought, Stella and her clan had become the prime suspects.

It couldn't have been a coincidence that the compound had been attacked mere months after he'd met her, and in his infinite stupidity, had let her walk away with the knowledge of his people's existence and the child he'd unwittingly planted in her womb.

Stella

Stella plopped down on the small couch in Arwel and Jin's room. "It was a fun day, but I'm exhausted, and I'm happy to stay here tonight and veg in front of the TV." She cast a suggestive glance at Richard. "Or take a long bath and go to sleep early."

To keep up the pretense of curious American parents who wanted their children to learn the Chinese language and culture, they'd spent the day sightseeing and doing touristy things.

Before Vlad was born, Stella had traveled extensively throughout the east, but she'd been more interested in visiting the big cities, not rural communities. It was a different type of experience, which she found surprisingly enjoyable.

Jin's mouth twisted in a grimace. "I'm tired as well, but I'm going anyway. I don't understand half of what they are saying on those Chinese soap operas you like, and watching Netflix on my satellite phone is just depressing."

"You can watch it on my tablet," Arwel offered.

Jin shook her head. "I'm coming with you, and there is nothing you can say to make me stay behind tonight. I can't sleep without you, and I end up waiting awake, anxious, and bored."

Being the smart man that he was, Arwel didn't argue.

"Watching Chinese television is a great way to learn the language," Stella said. "It's not for someone who doesn't know the basics, but you do, and it will improve your skills."

"I'll take your word for it." Jin opened the closet door and pulled out a pair of black yoga pants. "I just hate being useless."

"You're not useless." Arwel put down his tablet. "Tomorrow, we need you to tether the head of school so we can learn who he reports to, and you're the only one who can do that."

"You can learn all you need to know by thralling him. I'd rather not tether anyone unless there is no other way. You know how I hate the feeling of being weighed down by the consciousnesses of those I tether."

Mey turned to look at her sister. "Do you hate being tethered to me?"

"No, of course not. I know when to follow the string to you and when not to, so I don't catch you in embarrassing moments."

"I'm glad." Mey shoved a bottle of water into her backpack. "There is no reason for you to schlep with me tonight, though. I realized that I can't listen to the echoes and talk at the same time because it breaks my concentration."

It would have been a helpful piece of information to know before they'd invited Jin to join the team. The girl was a whiner, and sometimes she got on Stella's nerves. Then again, with Arwel as their team leader, they were stuck with Jin regardless of her usefulness.

Besides, she could still be helpful in some way. The head of school might be resistant to thralling, or he might be under someone else's thrall, and in both cases, Jin's unique talent would be invaluable.

Holding the pair of yoga pants in her hand, Jin sighed. "I know that you don't need me for that, but I want to come along nonetheless." She cast a sidelong glance at Arwel. "I can keep you company while you wait for Mey to be done. I know that if I stay, you'll insist on Jay or Alfie staying behind to guard me, which means less protection for Mey and Yamanu, who actually need it."

He nodded. "I can't argue with that logic. But since Stella and Richard are staying, I'm going to leave Jay to keep an eye on them anyway."

Richard shook his head. "Stella and I don't need a Guardian to keep us safe. This is a sleepy little town, and aside from the Kra-ell's compound burning down two decades ago, nothing happens here. In addition, the compound is located more than sixty miles away." His eyes lowered to where Arwel's holster was peeking out from under his windbreaker. "That being said, I wouldn't mind having a firearm under my pillow if you could spare one."

Stella chuckled. "Do you even know how to use it?"

Her mate looked offended. "I wouldn't have asked if I didn't. We got weapons training in the government paranormal program. I know my way around guns and rifles and even a rocket launcher."

She'd forgotten about that, and also about Richard and Jin being a couple during their time in the program. Maybe that was why she didn't like Jin as much as she liked her older sister?

Jealousy wasn't a pleasant feeling, especially when it was totally uncalled for. Richard and Jin hadn't been in love, and they had never become intimate. If not for Eleanor compelling them to start dating, they wouldn't have been together at all.

"What else did you learn in the program?" Arwel asked.

"Hand-to-hand combat, how to disarm an opponent, and a bunch of other stuff that I will probably never use. I don't regret getting the training, though. It might come in handy one day."

"True," Jin said. "I hated the self-defense class because the instructor was brutal, but I'm in great shape thanks to it, and I also feel more confident." She sat on the bed next to Arwel. "In retrospect, though, I don't think Simmons and Roberts were training us to become good spies. They just wanted to test our resilience so they would know what to expect from the super babies they wanted us to breed." She shivered. "I forgave Eleanor for everything else she compelled me to do, but not for pushing Richard and me to procreate." She cast an apologetic glance at Stella. "I'm so glad that my instincts fought so hard against it. On a subconscious level, I must have known that we were not meant to be together."

Looking like he would rather be anywhere but there, Richard pushed away from the wall which he'd been leaning against. "Let's go to our room." He offered Stella a hand up.

She turned to Arwel. "Are you sure that we can't be of help out there tonight?"

For a long moment, he didn't answer, looking as if he needed to think it through. "Frankly, I prefer not to split the team and to have everyone together, but it's not fair to drag you out there when there is nothing for you to do."

"We'll be fine," Richard said. "What about that gun, though? Can I have one?"

"I don't have one to spare, but I can give you a tranquilizer gun with some darts. I have two, and it doesn't seem like we will need any."

"That would be greatly appreciated." Richard looked relieved. "Do you have it here?"

"Morris has them in the van. When he gets here, you can come out and get it."

"Text me when he does."

"No problem."

"Good luck to you all," Stella said as they headed for the door.

Jin glanced at her watch. "What's your rush? We have at least two hours until we need to go."

Wrapping her arm around Richard's toned midsection, Stella gave Jin a conspirator's smile. "You said that you didn't like watching Chinese dramas with me, but if you don't mind, Richard and I can stay and watch them with you."

"Go." Smirking, Jin waved them off. "Let's pretend that watching television is what you have in mind."

Geraldine

Geraldine tried to stay out of Tyler and Aiden's way as they installed the cameras around her house. It seemed that the devices didn't even require wiring, but given how tiny they were, she wondered where the batteries went.

"Can I offer you something to drink?" she asked Aiden.

"Water would be nice." He came down the ladder.

"Can I ask you a question?"

"Shoot." He fell into step with her as she headed toward the kitchen.

"How do those cameras get their power supply?"

"They will be connected to your home's electrical wiring. But don't worry about power outages. We are putting a backup battery in your garage."

"I didn't see you installing wires."

"First, we wanted to find strategic spots for maximum visibility on the receiving side and minimum visibility on the recording side. After the cameras are all in place, we will run the wires."

"I see." Geraldine opened the fridge and pulled out two bottles of water. "So the big mess is still to come." She handed them to Aiden.

He nodded. "We will need to drill holes and patch them up, but we will clean up after ourselves. When we are done, you won't be able to tell where the cameras are or that anything was done in the house."

"Can you show me where you put them?" She smiled sheepishly. "So I will know where not to walk naked."

A blush creeping up his cheeks, he walked out of the kitchen. "I'll show you where they are. We didn't put cameras inside the bedrooms or bathrooms. We put them outside in the hallways pointing toward the doors, and outside on the windows and balconies." He chuckled. "Provided that Orion can't walk through walls, that should do."

"Got it." She smiled up at him. "So all I have to do is make sure I close the door and the curtains before getting undressed and remember not to leave the bedroom with no clothes on."

"Precisely." He started up the stairs where Tyler was working.

"Are there cameras on every window?" She followed him up.

"Not all of them, but on most. We wanted to cover all entry points. There are also several cameras monitoring the street outside and the backyard." He pointed to where Tyler was mounting a camera across from the master bedroom doors. "Do you want to see the one on your balcony?"

"No, that's okay. How long do you think everything will take?"

Tyler looked down from his perch on top of the ladder. "Hopefully, we will be done by the end of the day."

"I hope so too." She smiled up at him. "I should get out of your way and let you work."

That was much longer than she'd expected. Perhaps she should go out, call up one of her friends and see who was in the mood for shopping.

Shai had said that it was okay to leave the guys alone in the house, and even if he hadn't, she wouldn't have hesitated to do so. They were clan members, looking out for her and making her house safe, and they wouldn't touch anything they shouldn't.

Or so she hoped. Geraldine still remembered the house painters Cassandra had hired, whom she'd caught rummaging through her underwear drawer.

Some men were such creeps.

Were immortal males more respectful?

She wouldn't know unless she caught them, but Geraldine had no intention of wasting time or energy on that.

If Tyler or Aiden wanted to look at her panties, let them. She hoped they enjoyed it.

Downstairs, Geraldine took the cordless off the cradle and sat on the couch to call Gail. It started ringing before she had a chance to dial the number.

"Hi, Mom," Cassandra said. "I tried both your cellphones. Did you forget them in your purse again?"

"Oh dear." Geraldine bolted up. "I did. What if Shai tried to call me?"

"Relax. He would have called the home number like I did."

"Oh, right." She plopped back down.

"How is the work progressing in the house?"

"They won't be done until the end of the day. I was just about to call Gail and ask her if she wanted to go shopping."

"Good idea. You need to get out of the house more."

"I know. But what if you-know-who shows up?"

Cassandra cleared her throat, reminding Geraldine that she shouldn't mention Orion's name on an unsecured line. "Don't worry about it. Anyway, I spoke with Darlene, and we made plans for tomorrow. We are going out to dinner, just you, me, and her."

"What about Leo?"

"He's out of town. Something about getting antiques for the gallery he works for, and he'll be gone until Friday."

Geraldine twined a lock of her hair around her finger. "What are we going to tell her about Rudolf?"

"Can you get your cellphone and call me in a minute? Someone just walked into my office."

"Sure." Geraldine disconnected the call.

Wisely, Cassandra didn't want to discuss Rudolf and what they'd discovered over the landline.

Geraldine's purse was upstairs in her bedroom, and as she took the stairs, she hoped that Aiden was done installing the camera pointing at the master suite's door.

Thankfully, he'd moved his ladder to the other end of the hallway, and the coast was clear.

When Geraldine pulled both phones out of her purse, her old one and the one Shai had given her, she first checked for calls she might have missed. Other than Cassandra, though, no one had called her. Then she looked at the little bar indicating how much charge she had left and was relieved that there was still plenty.

The clan phone that Shai had given her was so much better than her old one. That thing needed to be recharged nightly regardless of whether she'd used it or not.

Everything the clan did was done better. The houses in the village were better insulated and soundproofed, the cars they used were a technological marvel, and the village was so cleverly hidden even though it was only a short distance from downtown Los Angeles, Beverly Hills, and Hollywood.

Sitting on the bed, Geraldine called Cassandra.

"Did someone really walk into your office?"

"No, I was just being careful. So back to Rudolf. We will tell Darlene the same story we told him about the brother our mothers supposedly had."

"What if she wants to see his picture?"

"I have it on my phone. Who knows? Maybe Orion is keeping tabs on her as well, and she'll recognize him."

"I haven't thought of that, but you're right. If he's been taking care of me throughout the years, he might have been helping Darlene too." Geraldine sighed. "I want to tell her the truth so badly. She deserves a chance at immortality, or at least to have the choice to attempt it or not."

"I want it for her as well. But we need to get to know her better first, and we need Shai to be there when we tell her, so he can thrall the memory of what we told her."

Geraldine switched the phone to her other ear. "What's the point of telling her if we make her forget right away?"

"So she can decide. She would have to leave Leo and hook up with an immortal male. That's not an easy decision to make."

"And yet you don't want to give her time to think it through. You want her to decide on the spot."

"That's why I said that we need to get to know her better and gently inquire about her true feelings toward Leo. The guy is a jerk, but he's been her husband for a long time, and she might really love him."

Geraldine leaned her elbow on her knee. "I don't think she loves him enough to give up immortality for him."

"I don't think so either, but we can't assume. We'll find out more tomorrow."

Vrog

When Vrog saw Stella and her partner leave their teammates in the hotel room, he stuffed his binoculars into his backpack and jogged the short distance from his hiding place to the hotel lobby.

Recognizing him, the clerk bowed her head. "Good evening, Mr. Wu. How can I be of service?"

He looked into her eyes, bending her will to his. "I need to know the room numbers for the Americans staying here. I'm particularly interested in the woman with the curly hair."

Her eyes glazing over, the woman opened her ledger. "Mrs. Furman and her husband are staying in room number six. Mr. and Mrs. Williams are in room number two."

As she continued listing the names of the American guests and who was in which room, he committed the information to memory. According to the clerk, the two single men shared a room adjacent to Stella's, which complicated things.

He'd counted on her partner being the weak link, but with two fighters sleeping in the next room over, that advantage might not be enough.

Vrog hadn't been trained as a warrior. His hybrid features and ability to eat human food allowed him to pass for a human, and since he was also fairly intelligent, Jade had groomed him for business instead of fighting. He might be physically stronger than the males guarding Stella, but he wasn't sure of that. These long-lived males could be even stronger than him, and they were probably better trained fighters.

If they were anything like the pureblooded Kra-ell males, he had no chance of overpowering them despite the hundreds of pushups and pull-ups he did every day.

His innate Kra-ell aggression wasn't nearly as explosive as that of the purebloods, but he still had to work hard to curb it while living among humans, and the only way he found effective was to exhaust his body with physical exertion.

Being fit and strong wasn't the same as being militarily trained, though, and those males looked like they were warriors.

Nevertheless, Vrog had no choice but to proceed. He needed answers, and that meant getting to Stella and forcing those answers out of her. He just needed to figure out how to get her alone. He couldn't thrall her partner, who was no doubt long-lived like her, so he needed to knock him out before either he or Stella could raise the alarm. Or maybe he should just put a knife to the guy's throat and scare her into talking by threatening to kill him.

Perhaps if he had more time, he could have planned it better, but it had to be done tonight. Tomorrow would be too late.

As soon as Stella walked into his office, she would recognize him, and if he canceled the meeting and refused to see her and her companions, she and the others might go home without him learning anything.

How would she react when she saw him?

Perhaps she'd come for answers as well?

If her people were responsible for what had happened to his tribe twenty-two years ago, then what did she hope to achieve by coming back and investigating the school?

His initial reaction to her had been fueled by anger and his assumption that she'd come to finish the job and murder whoever had survived.

But why wait so long to do that?

None of it made sense.

"Thank you." Vrog smiled at the clerk. "Forget that I was ever here and that I asked you anything."

Her eyes losing even more of their focus, she nodded.

The term his people had for what he had done had no equivalent in English or Chinese, but the literal translation was strong influence. Humans called it hypnotism or compulsion, while Stella had called it thralling, and he supposed that it was a combination of both skills.

Back in his hiding place behind the outcropping, Vrog pulled out the binoculars. He didn't need them to see who was in the room, but they were useful to detect details he might have otherwise missed, like the sidearm holster one of the males wore under his jacket.

If one was armed, it was safe to assume the others were armed as well, and that reinforced his belief that Stella had come to finish the job and eliminate the last of his people.

How had she found out that he'd survived?

And how had she found the location of his tribe in the first place?

He hadn't told her anything other than admitting that he was long-lived like her and that he was part of a group. She couldn't have followed him to the compound either, because he hadn't gone home until after the attack.

The only thing she or her people could have done was to find out the firm he'd been overseeing for the tribe and follow the money trail back to Jade. Supposedly, it was next to impossible to do, but Stella's people must have found a way.

Why kill the males and take the females, though?

Stella had seemed genuinely angry at the way Jade treated the males of his tribe, and she'd said that her clan's leader was a much more pleasant female.

It must have been all lies.

Her clan was probably just as short on females as his was, and if it was as small as his tribe, they were just as desperate for genetic variety to save themselves from extinction.

Perhaps after she'd told her people about his group's existence, they'd decided to fortify their numbers with the Kra-ell females. After all, five females were more precious than all the money and gold they'd left behind in those safes.

Hopefully, he would have his answers tonight.

Stella and her guy had gone to their room, but he needed everyone to be asleep before making his move, and the two couples he was watching weren't showing signs of retiring to their beds anytime soon. In fact, they looked as if they were waiting for someone to arrive or something to happen.

Richard

Usually after making love, Richard slept like the dead until morning, but this time he hadn't allowed himself to doze off. Instead, he spent the time waiting for Arwel's text, gazing with satisfaction at the blissed-out expression on Stella's beautiful face.

His ears, though, were trained on any noise coming from the street. He had plenty of time until Morris arrived with the van at two o'clock in the morning, but in case he made it there earlier, Richard would hear the old van's noisy engine and its rattling parts from a mile away.

So far, though, all he'd heard was nature in its nightly glory—rustling leaves, small nocturnal animals going about their hunt for food and mates, and the occasional hooting of an owl.

He should get dressed.

Taking one last look at Stella's rosy cheeks and puffed-up lips, he smiled and kissed her softly.

She sighed contentedly, but she stayed sleeping even after he gently extracted himself from her arms and got out of bed.

In the bathroom, Richard emptied his bladder, cleaned himself in the sink, brushed his teeth, and wetted a couple of washcloths with warm water.

When he walked back into the room, a slight noise outside the door froze him in place, but as a couple of moments passed with no other suspicious sounds, he figured it must have been a mouse scurrying down the hallway.

After cleaning Stella as best he could without waking her up, he went back to the bathroom and tossed the washcloths in the corner. Back in the room, he snatched his cargo pants and T-shirt off the back of a chair, got dressed, pushed his feet into a pair of shoes, and stuffed his wallet into one of his pants' many pockets.

Since he hadn't fallen asleep as was usually the case after a rigorous lovemaking session, Richard was experiencing the other kind of side effects, which were thirst and hunger. The fridge in their room was mostly empty by now, but there was a vending machine at the end of the hallway where he could get bottled water, some Chinese-made soft drinks, and snacks.

The vending machine accepted his credit card, which was good, but his luck was short-lived. The damn thing got stuck, the mechanical arm pushing the bottle out of its slot but not releasing its claws to let it drop. A bit of shaking solved the problem, but it made too much noise.

Fortunately, his team members were the only guests in the hotel tonight, and other than Stella, none were asleep. When no one came rushing to check out what was causing the ruckus, he repeated the operation three more times, getting another bottle of water and two bags of chips.

He stuffed the chips in his cargo pants pockets, tucked the bottles under his arm, and headed back to the room.

His phone buzzed with an incoming message at the same time he heard the van's engine.

Good timing.

He left the bottles by the door and jogged down the hallway.

When he reached Arwel and Jin's room, the team was already gone, but the door had been left open for him, and he left the same way they had—out the window.

The van was parked a hundred feet or so from the hotel, and as he jogged the rest of the way, it occurred to him that they weren't being very stealthy about their departure.

Then again, the town was more than an hour's drive away from the school, so the precautions weren't really necessary. The only reason for using the window as their exit point was the surveillance camera mounted in the hotel's lobby.

When he climbed into the back of the van, Morris handed him the tranquilizer gun. "Did you ever use one of these?"

Richard turned the thing in his hands. It looked like something from a Wild West movie or a Halloween prop and nothing like the autoloaders he'd trained with.

"What is this thing? It looks like a museum exhibit."

Jin smirked. "I thought that you were a weapons expert."

"I'm as much of an expert as you are. We took the same training."

"I should show you how to use it," Arwel said. "Close the door."

"Why?"

"Because I can't do it inside the van, and I can't demonstrate using a tranq gun on the sidewalk." He turned to Morris. "Drive to that wooded area at the end of the street."

Richard paused with his hand on the door's handle. "I don't want to leave Stella alone for too long."

Arwel shrugged. "It's up to you. You can leave now, but if you want the gun, you need to learn how to use it, which will take no more than five minutes including the time we are wasting talking about it."

"Fine." Richard closed the van's sliding door. "Let's do it."

Vrog

As Vrog heard a vehicle stop somewhere nearby at two o'clock in the morning, he wondered if that was what the two couples had been waiting for.

When a moment later the two single men entered the hotel room and then everyone left through the window, his suspicions were confirmed.

It seemed that Stella and her partner weren't joining them, which would be a tremendous stroke of luck for him, but he needed to make sure before making his move.

Running on stealthy feet, Vrog made it in time to see the six climb into an old beat-up van.

Where were they going?

Perhaps they were planning to attack the school again?

No, that was a stupid thought. They had no reason to go after the kids or the faculty. They were probably just after him.

Vrog smiled.

They wouldn't find him in his apartment in the staff quarters, and the joke would be on them because they were leaving Stella with only her partner for protection, and the guy didn't look like he would pose a challenge.

Vrog thought that his luck couldn't get any better when Stella's partner jogged to the waiting vehicle and climbed in.

Were they leaving her utterly alone?

That didn't make sense. If they suspected that there were more Kra-ell in the compound, they wouldn't do that. The van was just idling though, so perhaps not everyone on board was going, and someone would take his place guarding Stella.

If one of the fighters went back, Vrog's best option was to intercept him and cut his throat before he had a chance to make it back to the hotel.

Bile rose in his throat.

He wasn't a cold-blooded killer, and until he knew for sure that Stella and her people were responsible for his tribe's annihilation, he wasn't entitled to revenge. The Mother of all Life would not look kindly upon him killing without provocation and without giving his opponent a fighting chance.

Perhaps he could knock the male out instead.

No, that wouldn't work. The male wouldn't stay down long enough for Vrog to interrogate Stella. He would have to eliminate him permanently, which could damn him forever if he had no right to the kill.

The Kra-ell were brutal and unforgiving people, but they lived by a code of honor imposed upon them by The Mother of all Life and her earthly embodiment—their tribe's leader. Vrog had broken the code only once, and even that had been unwittingly.

Jade had forbidden the hybrid males to impregnate human females, and as the goddess's mouthpiece, she was the law. But Vrog had no way of knowing that Stella's body did not work like that of human females—she didn't need to be in her fertile cycle to conceive.

When he'd hooked up with her, he'd assumed she couldn't get pregnant because she hadn't been ovulating. If she had been, he would have detected it. Too late, he'd learned that with the right male, the females of her kind conceived on demand.

Why her body had decided that he was the most compatible male it had ever encountered was beyond him, though.

Perhaps it hadn't been what Jade had wanted, but it might have been the wish of a higher authority—The Mother of All Life.

It had occurred to him even then that The Mother's hand might have guided his encounter with Stella, and that the son they'd created together was destined for something great—something The Mother needed him to do.

That was why Vrog had let Stella go with his child growing in her womb.

Had it been the biggest mistake of his life?

When the van's door closed and it drove away with Stella's partner, Vrog lifted his head heavenward and thanked The Mother.

She must be smiling upon him tonight, guiding his steps.

He'd come with no plan and no weapons other than a hunting knife, his brute strength, and his fangs, and yet he would succeed.

He had to move fast, though.

As the van neared his hiding spot, Vrog sprinted away, using the shadows to cover his retreat.

When the van stopped right where he'd been a moment ago, shameful fear gripped Vrog, and he ran even faster while keeping his footfalls as silent as he could.

They had guns, and he couldn't outrun a bullet. His only hope was that they hadn't seen him.

Reaching the back of the hotel with no sound of pursuit, Vrog climbed inside through the window that Stella's people had left open, and then rushed out of the room.

Not knowing how long they would be gone, he sprinted to the end of the hallway, careful not to make any noise.

It didn't matter whether Stella was awake or asleep. He had the element of surprise on his side, and she was no match for him. But if she heard him coming, she might call her people back, and he had to get to her before she had a chance to do that.

Richard

After the explanation and demonstration Richard had gotten, he doubted the usefulness of the dart gun, or rather of the darts themselves.

The tranquilizer just didn't work as fast as a bullet to incapacitate a perpetrator.

Morris had assured him that William's tinkering with the gun mechanism and Merlin's magic touch with the paralytic inside the ballistic syringe made the thing a highly effective non-lethal weapon. But the tranquilizer needed a few seconds to work, and if a perpetrator had a gun, he could kill him and Stella in the time it took for the chemical to enter his bloodstream.

Arwel had shown him how to load the syringe and had given him one more to put in his pocket. Apparently, Charlie, the other pilot, had gotten one into Emmett's neck without the help of a gun just by throwing it.

Richard had a decent aim with darts and a strong throwing arm, so if push came to shove, he could use that option. But since anyone attacking him or Stella in the little sleepy town was such an unlikely scenario, Richard carefully tucked the gun into one of his pockets, the extra syringe into another, and headed back to the hotel.

His pockets were so overstuffed with the potato chips he'd bought, his wallet, the vials with the sleeping potion that he'd forgotten to take out, and now the gun and the additional syringe, that they were stretched to bursting and uncomfortable to run or even walk fast in, but he did anyway, a sense of foreboding urging him to get back to Stella as soon as possible.

It was probably nothing. All that thinking about potential perpetrators must have gotten his adrenaline pumping.

When he found the door to their room slightly ajar, his anxiety increased tenfold, the adrenaline rush swelling his muscles, readying them for a fight.

With his mate sleeping in the nude, it was unlikely that he'd forgotten to close the door, but he tried to reason with himself that the lock might have not latched properly. He'd been careful not to wake her, so he might have closed the door too softly for it to lock.

Except, glancing at the two bottles of water he'd left on the floor, he knew that he would have noticed the door not being closed when he'd put them down.

Richard pulled out the tranquilizer gun.

Softly nudging the door open with his foot, he thanked the merciful Fates when it didn't make any sound and entered.

What awaited him was a scene from his worst nightmares.

A tall man held the terrified and naked Stella in front of him, an arm wrapped around her middle, right under her breasts, pressing a knife to her neck with the other.

"Don't move or I'll slash her throat," he bit out. "Put the gun down."

"Please, don't hurt her. What do you want? Do you want money?" Richard put the gun on the dresser. "I'm going to take out my wallet. You can have it all." He reached into his pocket.

The guy hissed, revealing a pair of razor-sharp fangs. "Not another move, or I make her bleed."

A Kra-ell male.

Richard's blood froze in his veins. He was no match for the male's strength, and the guy was holding a knife to Stella's neck.

The gun was useless and so was the extra tranquilizer dart.

Other than that, all Richard had were his wits, the wallet in his left pocket, two bags of chips, and the useless sleeping potion vials...

Or perhaps not so useless.

Could he use the sleeping potion to distract the guy? Perhaps the Kra-ell weren't immune to the chemicals?

It was worth a try.

One vial was enough to put a couple of teenagers to sleep, two vials were enough to knock out an adult male. He didn't need to knock the guy out. He just needed to disorient him while not making one single threatening move.

Feigning terror, which wasn't hard, his hand closed on the bag of chips and the two vials in his left pocket.

"Why?" Stella whispered.

"Why?" The male dipped his head to look at the side of her face. "You slaughtered my people, and you are asking me why?"

The guy was insane. What the hell was he talking about?

As a small trickle of blood started where the knife was pressed against Stella's carotid, Richard's hands started shaking. "Don't hurt her, please." He made his voice tremble and his teeth rattle while crushing what he held in his hand.

The crunching noise of the chips covered the sound of breaking glass, and Richard stifled a wince as the glass shards cut into his fingers, focusing instead on the wet liquid sliding down his leg.

The male's head snapped to him. "What did you do?"

"I'm sorry." Shaking violently, Richard looked down at the stain forming on his sweatpants.

The male sneered. "Did you wet yourself?"

Richard didn't have to work hard to force blood up into his face and feign embarrassment. The rage inside him was boiling the blood in his veins and painting his vision red.

"I've never even met your people," Stella whispered, tears sliding down her cheeks. "Don't do this. We have a son, Vrog. His name is Vlad, and he looks just like you."

This was Vrog? Vlad's father? He looked nothing like Vlad, but Stella was smart to say that.

Talk about a shocker.

He would think about the implications later. Right now, Richard's entire focus was on the hand holding a hunting knife to Stella's throat.

Something passed over the guy's eyes, something that looked like uncertainty and remorse, and he lowered the knife but didn't let go of Stella.

Regrettably, it seemed like the sleeping potion had no effect on him, but at least he was no longer holding Stella at knifepoint.

He still had the knife in his hand, though. He could still change his mind and kill her.

The guy sniffed. "What's that smell?" He swayed just a little, enough for Richard to realize that the potion was working after all.

Stella must have realized the same thing, or perhaps she just took advantage of the guy's arm around her slackening a fraction. Dropping to the floor, she slipped out of his hold, exposing him to Richard.

There was no time to grab the gun.

As Vrog bent down to grab Stella, Richard delivered a powerful kick to the guy's head, sending him flying backward, pulled the syringe out of his pocket, jumped on top of him, and stabbed him in the neck.

That wasn't enough, though. Despite the sleeping potion, the kick to the head, and the tranquilizer dart, the guy wasn't out and managed to deliver a punch to Richard's face that would have knocked him out if he were still a human.

Hell, it might have knocked an immortal out as well, but Richard's rage and need to protect his mate gave him the boost of power he needed.

Ignoring his broken cheekbone, he returned the favor, delivering one punch after the other to Vrog's face until the combined effort of his fists and the tranquilizer finally weakened the guy and then knocked him out.

In case Vrog was just feigning unconsciousness, Richard kept punching. He might not be able to kill the Kra-ell with his bare fists, but he was going to smash his ugly puss into a pulp.

"Stop!" Stella caught his arm. "He's already out. Let's tie him up before he regains consciousness."

Richard freed his arm from Stella's hold and delivered one last punch to the guy's bloodied face. "He's not going to wake up anytime soon."

"If he's like us, he will."

Arwel

As Arwel's phone rang, everyone's eyes turned to him. They'd left the hotel no more than fifteen minutes ago, and people back home knew that he was on a mission and wouldn't be calling him.

Arwel pulled the device out of his pocket. "Richard. What's up?"

"You need to turn around. We have a Kra-ell male tied up in our room. He's out cold, but I need something better to tie him up with than my belt, and I need to get more of those sleeping potion vials. I stabbed him with the tranquilizer, but I don't know how long the effect will last and if it's safe to stab him so soon with the other. Stella doesn't want me to accidentally kill him."

"The sleeping potions will probably not work on him."

"They do to some degree. I used the two I had on me to disorient him."

Arwel had so many questions, but he didn't want to keep Richard from doing everything he could to secure the guy before they got back. "I have more vials in my room. They are in the backpack inside the closet. But be careful. He might not be alone."

Morris slowed down and looked at him through the rearview mirror for approval.

Arwel nodded and made a circling motion with his finger.

"He is. The mysterious Wu, the head of the school who we were supposed to meet tomorrow, is actually Vrog, Stella's old flame. Just get here as soon as you can and bring handcuffs or a strong rope. The guy is a damn gorilla."

"We will be there in less than ten minutes."

"Good. I need to hang up. I'll tell you the rest when you get here."

Shaking his head, Arwel put his phone back in his pocket. He'd had a number of surprises during his life, some good and some bad, but Stella's old boyfriend showing up at their hotel made it to the top of the list.

"So instead of us finding the Kra-ell, one has found us," Jin said. "And not just any random Kra-ell, but Stella's Vrog."

"Do we have jumper cables in the van?" Yamanu asked. "We don't have reinforced handcuffs, and a regular rope won't be enough to hold him if he's as strong as Emmett. The jumper cables might do the job, though."

Arwel had never used those cables to do anything other than jump-start his car, and he doubted they were flexible enough to tie up a prisoner. "Our best option is to tranq him all the way to the airport and get him to the jet as soon as possible."

"We don't have jumper cables," Morris said. "And even if we did, I don't think we could use them for tying up a prisoner, but a good rope might be enough to hold even a gorilla."

"We can't leave yet." Mey twirled the end of her braid over her finger. "I need to listen to more echoes."

Arwel gave her a smile. "We captured a Kra-ell male, and he can tell us all we need to know. You no longer need to listen to echoes."

"I think that's a mistake, but you're the boss, Arwel."

She hadn't said it angrily, only factually, and she might be right. "If necessary, we can come here again. The walls are not going anywhere."

Jin snorted. "Unless someone sets them on fire."

With Morris pushing the old clunker to its limit speeding down the road toward the hotel, they made it back in much less than ten minutes.

Arwel didn't bother with stealth as he jogged through the lobby to Stella and Richard's room. With Yamanu no longer needing to preserve his energy, he could cast a shroud around them, hiding them from the woman at the front desk.

Later, they would tamper with the surveillance feed from the lone camera in the lobby. Thankfully, it was the old kind that wasn't connected to an outside server.

Richard waited for them with the door open. "Remind me to thank Merlin for his potions."

His face had taken a beating, but Arwel knew that it looked worse than it was, and it was already on the mend.

Mey winced. "Is your cheek broken?"

"It was." Richard put his hand over the side of his face. "I hope I pushed it back in place correctly. I don't want to have it re-broken to fix it."

"It must have hurt like hell," Yamanu said.

"It did, but the other guy looks worse."

Inside, Stella sat on the floor next to the unconscious male, her eyes red-rimmed as if she'd been crying for hours.

The Kra-ell was on his belly, hands tied behind his back with a leather belt. It was a good makeshift restraint, but anyone with minimal training and a bit of muscle strength could break free from that.

"Oh, sweetie." Jin rushed to Stella's side and wrapped her arms around her. "Were you frightened?"

Stella nodded.

"Did he hurt you?"

As Stella shook her head, Arwel released a relieved breath.

"Then why are you crying?" Jin asked.

"He hates me."

Mey frowned. "Who hates you?"

"Vrog." Stella's chin wobbled. "He thinks I'm responsible for slaughtering his people."

For a long, shocked moment, no one spoke.

"The Kra-ell were slaughtered?" Yamanu asked.

She nodded. "That's what he said. And he thinks I did it."

"Why would he think that?" Jin helped Stella up.

"I don't know." More tears slid down Stella's cheeks.

"I think I can explain," Richard said. "As some of you know, Vrog and Stella have a history. He's Vlad's father. He's also Mr. Wu." He tossed a wallet to Arwel. "I found this in his pocket."

Arwel flipped the thing open and looked at the identification card. "This is written in Chinese. I can't read it."

"Neither can I," Richard said. "But Stella can, and it says that his name is James Wu."

Arwel closed the wallet, put it in his pocket, and looked at Stella. "Can you think of any reason for why he blames you for his people's demise?"

Looking distraught, she shook her head.

"Maybe because he told Stella about them," Richard said. "The fire happened about the same time they hooked up. So, he might have assumed that there was a connection."

As the guy on the floor groaned, Richard pulled out a vial from his pocket and snapped it open over the male's head. "I was lucky to have two in my pocket." He looked at Arwel. "They were enough to distract him a little, but even after I stabbed him with the tranquilizer and beat the hell out of him, he still wouldn't stay down. By the way, when I went to get more vials from your room, I didn't want to waste time going in through the window, so I forced the door open. We will have to cover the cost of the repairs."

"That's fine. You did very well." Arwel patted Richard's shoulder and then crouched next to the prone Kra-ell male.

Richard jingled the vials he still had in his pocket. "We have five left, which doesn't give us much time. We also have more darts, but I'm not sure how many we can use on him safely. We still need to interrogate him, and I don't mind knocking him out the old-fashioned way." Richard shook out his hand. "Now that I heal so fast, the bruising is not a big deal."

The guy was obviously enjoying it, but Stella wasn't.

"I'd rather use as few as possible of the tranquilizer darts, but I will if the sleeping potion is too weak to hold him down." Arwel checked Vrog's pulse. "We need to get him out of here."

Holding a rope in his hands, Morris walked in through the open door. "I found this in the hotel's storage room."

"Good. Tie him up." Arwel rose to his feet. "We are all leaving. Jay and I will load him into the van and head to the airport. The rest of you pack up and take the limo." He turned to Yamanu. "Before you leave, take care of the surveillance footage and leave money on the front desk to compensate them for the broken door and for cleaning up the mess in here."

"I'll clean up the blood." Stella lifted her gaze to him. "Just try not to hurt Vrog. He's not a bad guy. He's angry because he thinks that I had something to do with his people's fate." She shook her head. "It's so sad. All this time we thought that they'd just moved on."

Stella

Stella squirted hand sanitizer on the bloodstained carpet and attacked it with the spare toothbrush she'd sacrificed for the task. "You were amazing, Richard. But did you really need to beat him up so badly?"

She still couldn't believe that the two of them had managed to overpower a Kra-ell male. Richard had been magnificent—cool-headed, fast, strong.

While they'd been waiting for the team to arrive, Stella had told him as much, and since then he'd been strutting around like a peacock, wearing his bruised cheek like a badge of honor.

Nevertheless, she was so proud of him. He was entitled to a little strutting. What she didn't like, though, was his attitude toward Vrog.

Vrog wouldn't have hurt her, she was sure of that, but he'd held her at knifepoint while she was naked, and her mate would never forgive and forget that.

Richard closed his suitcase. "I didn't hit him hard enough, and you should leave that bloodstain alone." He lifted his suitcase off the bed and set it down next to hers. "We need to get going."

"It's not coming out." She scrubbed even harder.

"And it's not going to. Arwel said to leave money for the repair and for the cleanup. We don't have time for this."

Leaning back on her haunches, she looked up at him. "It's not a coffee stain, Richard. It's Kra-ell blood, and it can be analyzed. This place looks like a crime scene. What if someone calls the authorities?"

"You're right, and I have an idea how we can solve it. I'll be back in a minute." He strode out of the room.

When more scrubbing only diluted the brownish red splotches and spread the stains further, Stella let out a sigh and sat back. It seemed that the only way to get rid of the evidence was to cut out the affected area, and maybe she should do that. Who knew what could be found in Vrog's blood. The last thing they needed was for someone to analyze the stain and find abnormalities.

A few moments later, Richard returned with a bottle of bleach. "This should take care of it."

"Smart. Where did you find it?"

"In the hotel laundry room. Step aside so I don't get any of it on you."

She pushed to her feet and moved away from the spot. "The bleach is going to ruin the carpet."

"That's less of a problem than leaving traces of Vrog's blood behind." He removed the cap from the bottle.

"Careful. If you pour from up high, the bleach will splatter all over your clothes."

Richard looked down at the cargo pants he'd been wearing for four days straight. "Not a big loss." Nevertheless, he crouched next to the stain and poured the bleach directly over it.

She'd given him so much grief about wearing the same pair of cargo pants since the start of the investigation, but he'd insisted on roughing it, and in the end, those damn pants might have saved their lives.

The first night they'd gone to the compound, Arwel had given each of them two vials of Merlin's sleeping potion in case Yamanu's thrall didn't work on some of the students or faculty, but they hadn't used any. If Richard wasn't such a slob, he would've given the vials back to Arwel instead of keeping them in his pocket.

Lifting a trembling hand to her neck, Stella ran her fingers over the spot Vrog had nicked with his knife. What if she was wrong about him? What if he would have killed her if Richard hadn't stopped him?

Was Vrog capable of murdering the mother of his son?

Fates, what a mess.

Stella had spent long years feeling sorry for Vrog, wondering what other hardships his bitch of a leader had forced upon him, and during all that time Vrog had been fanning the embers of hate and plotting revenge for a crime she hadn't committed.

"What smells so bad?" Mey walked into the room.

"Bleach." Stella looked at the carpet that had turned white and yellow. At least the bloodstains were gone.

"We are ready to go," Mey said.

"So are we." Richard hefted both of their suitcases.

"I need to wash my hands and dispose of the last bit of evidence." Stella took the nearly empty bottle of bleach, tossed in the toothbrush she'd been using, put the cap back on, and gave it a vigorous shake.

That should take care of any traces of Vrog's blood.

After washing her hands, she lifted her purse off the nightstand, took one last look around the room to make sure they hadn't left anything behind, and followed Richard out.

Mey, Jin, and Alfie were already waiting for them in the limo, but Yamanu wasn't there.

"Where is your mate?" Richard asked Mey.

"He had to wait for you to be out before tampering with the surveillance footage. He also needs to thrall the front desk clerk."

Thankfully they hadn't thralled her too often, so hopefully the poor woman wouldn't suffer irreparable damage.

"I can't believe that they were all slaughtered," Jin said softly. "Why spare the humans and kill the Kra-ell?"

Stella had been pondering the same thing. "Maybe they are not dead. I didn't have a chance to ask Vrog why he thought they were."

It was wishful thinking, and Stella was well aware of that. Vrog wouldn't have been so filled with hate if he hadn't had a good reason to believe that his people had been killed.

"He probably found their bodies," Alfie said.

Stella shook her head. "Whoever did that burned them to destroy the evidence. They wouldn't have left bodies of aliens lying around." She lifted her eyes to him. "That's why Richard and I bleached the carpet in our room. We had to destroy all traces of Vrog's blood." She cast Richard an accusing glance. "Richard broke his nose and he bled all over the place."

"Who could have attacked them?" Mey murmured, looking out the window. "And what is taking Yamanu so long?"

"Perhaps it was the Chinese government," Jin suggested. "They could have discovered the Kra-ell and eliminated them, or rather most of them. I bet they took a few to interrogate."

A shiver rocked Stella's body. "I'm glad that we are leaving. I don't feel safe here."

Richard wrapped his arm around her shoulders. "I'm glad to be out of here as well, and I can't wait to interrogate that son of a bitch."

"Don't insult his mother," Mey admonished. "She might have been a good woman."

"She must have been." Stella leaned her head on Richard's arm. "Despite what he did tonight, Vrog isn't a bad guy, and given what Emmett told us about Kra-ell fathers, it wasn't his father's doing."

"I disagree." Richard tightened his hand on her shoulder. "A good guy doesn't attack a defenseless woman while she's sleeping naked in her bed. Whatever he imagined you did to his people is no justification."

"He lost his mother and father," Stella whispered. "His friends and relatives are all gone and probably dead. Would you have been as forgiving if you thought some ex-lover of yours was responsible for your people's annihilation?"

When Richard didn't respond, she let loose a sigh. "That's what I thought."

Annani

"Merlin." Annani opened her arms and embraced the lanky doctor. "I love your new look."

"Thank you." He straightened, but not to his full height, remaining in a slightly hunched position, probably not wanting to tower over her. "I was delighted to receive an invitation from you. It has been ages since we had tea together."

"Indeed." She sat back down and motioned for him to join her on the couch. "I enjoyed our talks very much." She smiled. "But you have been busy lately."

He dipped his head and sat next to her. "I'm never too busy for you, Clan Mother."

"That is so nice of you to say." She tucked her legs to the side and smoothed her skirt. "How many couples have joined your conception expediting experiment?"

"Since Kian and Syssi, only four more are participating in my program." He sighed. "I wish more would join, but even if all of the mated couples participated, my sample would still be too small to qualify as a scientific study."

Annani waved a hand in dismissal. "What you are doing is part science and part magic. In the end, it is up to the Fates to decide who will be blessed with a child and when."

As Merlin nodded in agreement, Onidu arrived with their tea.

"Tea is ready, Clan Mother." Bowing, the Odu put the tray down on the coffee table.

"Thank you."

"Should I pour for you, Clan Mother?"

"Yes, please."

Annani waited for Onidu to pour the tea into both cups, lifted hers, and turned to Merlin. "You are probably wondering why I invited you here today."

Merlin's eyes sparkled with mischief. "I guessed it has something to do with Ronja and her acquiescence to consider attempting transition."

"You guessed it. Am I correct in assuming that despite her acquiescence, things have not progressed much in the romantic department?"

His smile wilted. "Ronja needs time. In her mind, it would be disrespectful to her husband's memory to get romantically involved so soon after his death."

"Yes, I am aware of that." Annani took a sip of her tea. "The reason I wanted to talk to you is that I am going home, and I do not want you and Ronja to start anything without me here. My blessing is absolutely crucial to the success of her transition. I will return to the village in one month to be with Amanda when she nears full term, but in case Ronja relents sooner, you do not have to wait with romantic activities, but you will need to use precautions until I arrive."

Annani had expected Merlin to be dismissive of her so-called blessing, but his expression was somber as he nodded. "I will wait for your return, Clan Mother. Ronja needs time not only to mourn her husband but also to strengthen her body, and that cannot be done overnight."

Did he suspect what her *blessing* really was?

Merlin was very bright, and he might have guessed, but as long as he did not know for sure and did not mention it to anyone, there was no harm in him speculating.

Annani refilled her cup from the carafe and lifted it to her lips. "Ronja told me about the exercise program you suggested. What else is included in the rejuvenation regimen you put her on?"

"Some dietary changes, mainly the elimination of sugar and the inclusion of large quantities of greens and herbs, including medicinal herbs from Gertrude's garden." He smiled sheepishly. "I do miss Ronja's amazing cakes, but I can't expect her to bake them and not eat them. Once she transitions, though, I hope she'll bake me a new cake every day." He smacked his lips.

That sounded like a good healthy approach, but it did not sound like a miracle in the making. "Is that all it would take to make her younger from the inside out?"

"I also remind her to drink plenty of water, and I'm dialing in a perfect combination of substances for her potion. Every person is different, and what works for one might not work for another."

"That is very true." She put her cup down. "Geraldine's older daughter is forty-nine, which up until recently was considered too old to transition. So far, she has not been told about us or her special genes, but I believe that at some point in the near future her mother and sister will tell her everything and offer her the option to attempt transition. You might have one more person in your biological health experiment. It would be interesting to see what things work on both women and what will work on one, but not the other."

Merlin reached for the carafe and refilled his own cup. "I will do whatever I can for Geraldine's daughter. Is there any news with the facial recognition program finding Orion?"

Annani laughed. "How did you hear about that so soon?"

"I saw Amanda in the café this morning. She told me about the mysterious Orion. Was it supposed to be a secret? I told Ronja, but I can ask her not to tell anyone else."

That was how rumors spread so fast through the clan.

"By now, Onegus has probably shown the pictures to so many people that it no longer matters."

"Maybe Kian should call a village meeting and let everyone know about Orion," Merlin suggested. "Instead of people having to rely on rumors, which have a tendency to distort the original story, they would get it without all the embellishments."

"That is a good idea." Annani sighed. "William ran the portrait through his facial recognition software, but it did not flag anyone. It seems that Orion knows how to effectively obscure his features."

Merlin nodded. "Another option is that he is limiting his travels now that the technology makes it difficult to hide. He might reside in another country that doesn't have cameras on every corner."

Annani lifted a brow. "Where would that be?"

"Many places in the world are still safe in that regard. Most of South America, Africa, part of the Middle East, and even some of the Far East, the Caribbean and other islands. There is no shortage of places to hide." He smiled. "For now."

Arwel

Arwel sat in the back of the van, watching the Kraell male sleep. He would have liked to wake the bastard up and find out what he'd hoped to gain by attacking Stella, but he couldn't risk it.

Pointing a gun to his head might keep him in line, but Arwel didn't know enough about Vrog to risk it. The guy might decide that committing suicide via Arwel's gun was better than getting captured and later interrogated.

Arwel had seen his share of misplaced heroics. For all he knew, the guy could have a poisoned tooth ready to deploy.

"How are we going to get him to the jet?" Morris asked.

"Good question." Arwel's lips twitched with a suppressed smile. "Do you think we could stuff him inside a suitcase?"

Vrog was at least six feet four inches tall, but he was slim. If he was flexible, they could stuff him in a crate and carry it into the jet, but it wouldn't be necessary. Arwel wasn't a great shrouder, but he could probably manage the twenty-minute walk with the guy slung over Jay's shoulder.

"He's too tall," Morris said as if Arwel's comment had been serious. "We will have to wait for Yamanu to arrive and shroud us. It's better to wait another half an hour than risk dragging the dude through the airport with his bloody face on display."

"He already looks better. Besides, Jay can carry him while I shroud the three of us, but you'll have to thrall the officials on the way."

"No problem. But I still think that we should wait for Yamanu to make it as smooth as possible. It's a busy airport, and Chinese officials are suspicious bastards. We might get delayed, and you'll run out of shrouding juice. If you're worried about pretty boy waking up too soon, I have more tranquilizer darts back in the jet, and I can bring them back to the van."

"That's an option." Arwel pulled out his phone and called Yamanu.

"Hello, boss," the Guardian answered. "Cleanup is complete, and we are on our way."

"Good. Tell Alfie to put pedal to the metal. We might need you to shroud Vrog as we carry him through the airport, and I don't like waiting while we don't have him properly secured."

"No problem. With the piece of junk Morris is driving, we will catch up to you in no time."

"How is everyone doing?" And by everyone, Arwel meant Stella.

Understandably, she had looked shell-shocked when he'd left. The woman was tough, but she was a civilian, and waking up to a crazed guy holding a knife to her neck must have been traumatic.

"Everyone is fine. We are brainstorming ideas about what might have happened to the Kra-ell. Do you think that the Chinese government did it?"

"It has crossed my mind, but I'd rather wait for our guest to wake up and give us more information to work with."

"Mey says that she should go back and listen for more echoes. Now more than ever, it's crucial to learn what happened to them."

"Right now, we are going home. I can't risk detaining Vrog in China. We might come back, though. I'm going to call Kian, give him an update, and check what he wants to do."

"Good deal. See you later, boss."

It was nearly four o'clock in the morning Beijing time, but given the time difference it was only about one o'clock in the afternoon in Los Angeles.

Kian answered on the second ring. "Trouble?"

"Yes and no. We've gotten ourselves a Kra-ell male, and we are taking him to the jet. Hopefully, no one will try to stop us." Arwel continued with the rest of the story, which didn't take long since he didn't know much.

Kian let out a long breath. "Talk about a twist. So let me get this straight. Vrog met Stella and fathered Vlad in Singapore twenty-two years ago. When he returned home and found that the compound was deserted and most of it burned down, he assumed that Stella had something to do with it because of the timing."

"That seems to be it. We will know more once he wakes up. If I had reinforced handcuffs, I would have interrogated him on the way to the airport, but without them, I don't want to risk waking him up before we get him on the jet."

"How strong is he?"

"Strong. He fought Richard even after getting hit with a tranquilizing dart. Richard kept beating him up until the drug took effect, but after that, he kept the guy down with Merlin's sleeping potion. Frankly, I'm surprised that it worked on Vrog, even if the effect is short-lived. It has no effect whatsoever on us, and we are supposed to be distant relatives of theirs."

"Perhaps we are not related to the Kra-ell after all."

"We certainly share a common ancestor." Arwel pushed his fingers through his hair. "The Kra-ell seem to be an older version though, less enhanced than the gods.

Perhaps whoever created all of us kept improving the design."

Kian chuckled. "I hate to think that there is an even more enhanced humanoid version than the gods out there, but I wouldn't be surprised if there were. Hundreds of thousands of years have probably passed since the gods created humans, and probably millions of years since the gods themselves were created. That's a lot of time to experiment and improve on the model."

Stella

As the limo hit yet another pothole, Richard gripped the handle above the window. "I'm glad that we are immortal." His arm around Stella's shoulders tightened.

Alfie was driving the thing like a bat out of hell and grinning like a kid who'd gotten permission to go wild.

"Relax." Yamanu crossed his massive arms over his chest and smiled at Richard. "Guardians get race car driving lessons, and with our enhanced senses and faster response times, we can handle speeds that even professional race car drivers would be hard pressed to surpass." He leaned closer. "You're no longer human. Stop thinking like one."

"I can't help it. These country roads are not meant for speeding limousines."

That was true.

Stella didn't doubt Alfie's driving skills, but they couldn't compensate for the road condition. At the speed he was going, a deep pothole could send the limousine tumbling into a ditch.

Thankfully, the limo's seats were incredibly cushy. As they kept hitting one pothole after the other and getting jostled from side to side and up and down, their backsides didn't suffer too badly.

The one good thing about the rollercoaster ride was that it helped take her mind off Vrog and the rabid hatred she'd seen in his eyes.

"Here is the van," Alfie said. "I told you that I would catch up to it in no time."

"You're insane." Richard huffed. "We left almost an hour after them, it should have been impossible for you to catch up. I didn't even know that a limo could go that fast."

"Live and learn, buddy. Live and learn." Alfie flashed his headlights to alert Morris that he was right behind him. "You can relax. It's going to be a slow ride from now on."

Stella's heart started hammering in her chest.

Soon, they would board the plane, Arwel would let Vrog wake up, and she would have a chance to talk to him, tell him about the son they shared, and what a wonderful man Vlad was.

Reaching into her purse, she pulled out her phone and searched for pictures of Vlad. There were so many, and those she had stored in her phone were just the recent ones. Vlad with Wendy, Vlad and Wendy together with Richard and Stella, Vlad and Richard—

The pictures told a story—a story of a family. How would that make Vrog feel?

Angry, most likely.

He'd lost his family and had been alone for the past twenty-two years, while she'd had a son, had been surrounded by her clan, and had found her true-love mate.

Perhaps she shouldn't show him the pictures.

"I like this one," Richard said. "Wendy is making a goofy duck face and Vlad is laughing. He doesn't laugh often enough."

She turned to look at him. "It's not that he's unhappy. Vlad is just shy and introverted."

"I know. I just wish he'd let loose a bit."

The quintessential extrovert, Richard was the opposite of reserved. He was easy to laugh, easy to befriend, and easy to love.

She smiled. "You want him to be more like you."

"Is that a bad thing?"

"Not at all." She kissed his cheek. "You are wonderful, but Vlad can't be you. He has a different personality."

"Like his father's?" There was a distinct note of jealousy in Richard's tone.

"I don't know Vrog well enough to answer that. From what I remember, he was somewhat reserved, but that was probably because he was hiding who he really was."

"He's insane." Richard's fingers dug into her shoulder. "Living alone and hiding for all these years must have messed with his head. You've heard what Emmett said about the Kra-ell males. They revere their females. It should have been impossible for him to attack you, and yet he did."

That was only partially true. Given what Emmett had told them about the Kra-ell sexual practices, a male had to fight the female, and if he wasn't able to subdue her, she wouldn't grant him the right to father her child. But what was sanctioned during sex was not tolerated at any other time.

Vrog might have been her lover at one time, but nothing about their encounter tonight had been sexual. Perhaps his Kra-ell half was less dominant than his human half.

"I'm not Kra-ell, and Vrog is half human. He might have absorbed human attitudes toward women."

That was a poor excuse, and she knew it. Just a small percentage of human males mistreated women, and it wasn't fair to condemn the entire male gender because of the misdeeds of the few. The immortals and the Kra-ell might have had it hardwired into their psyche, but humans had a choice, and Vrog had chosen poorly.

"Don't excuse his behavior," Richard bit out. "I just want you to be careful, and I don't want you to take to heart the unfounded accusations he'll no doubt throw at you."

"I'll try." She sighed. "You know me. I'm not as fragile as I might seem, and I don't give up easily. By the time we land in Los Angeles, I'll have it all sorted out."

Shai

When Shai pulled up in front of Geraldine's house, William's guys were loading their equipment into their van and blocking the driveway, where he usually parked.

For some reason, he still didn't use the garage even though there was enough space next to Cassandra's old car. Geraldine joked that he wanted the neighbors to know she had a boyfriend so no one would get ideas. But the truth was that he still treated her place as a temporary arrangement even though he'd de facto moved in. His clothes were hanging in her closet, his shaver was on her bathroom counter, and the only reason he still stopped by his house from time to time was to pick up more things to take to her place.

Shai would have preferred for things to be the other way around, but he wasn't complaining. He was with the female he loved, so it was all good.

For now.

One day, Orion would show up, and everything might go to hell.

With a sigh, Shai killed the engine, stepped out of the car, and walked over to the van. "All done?"

Aiden nodded. "Do you want me to show you where the cameras are?"

"Good idea."

Aiden laughed. "Your lady wanted to know where they were so she wouldn't walk by one in the nude. Is that what you are worried about?"

Shai stifled a growl. Geraldine's flirtatiousness was frustrating even though it was harmless. Such a remark would have given human males ideas.

Hell, it could have given Aiden and Tyler ideas as well.

Without the bond, Geraldine was theoretically fair game, and immortal males were desperate enough for mates to try to seduce a female who was already in a relationship with another.

To keep his anger down and his expression neutral, Shai had to remind himself that many couples stayed loyal to each other without being forced by a chemical or hormonal bond.

"It hadn't even crossed my mind." He affected a smile. "How many feeds are going out?"

"Eighteen. I don't envy the Guardians monitoring all that. They'll have long hours of boredom staring at nothing."

Shai cringed. "How many walls did you have to patch up after the wiring was done?"

"Not many. Since the cameras are installed at ceiling level, we ran the upstairs wires through the attic. Downstairs we needed to get a little more creative, but we managed with very few holes to patch up."

"I'm glad." Shai opened the front door.

As the cooking smells from the kitchen filled his nostrils, his belly rumbled, reminding him that he hadn't had lunch.

"Shai." Geraldine's smile was radiant as she took the apron off and walked toward him. "You're early."

"I couldn't stay away." He pulled her into his arms and kissed her on the lips despite Aiden watching, or perhaps because of it. "What are you making, love?"

"Butternut squash soup and curry." She looked at Aiden and smiled. "Are you sure that you guys can't stay for dinner? I cooked enough for four."

"Thank you, but we need to get going." Aiden looked at Shai expectantly.

If he was waiting for an invitation, he would be disappointed.

"You probably have plans for later this evening," he told the guy.

"Oh, I'm sure they do." Geraldine smirked. "Two handsome men like you would not be spending your evenings alone in front of the TV." She winked, making Aiden blush.

He needed to have a talk with her about that flirting. She might not mean anything by it, but others might, and it was grating on his nerves.

"Show me where the cameras are," he told Aiden.

Less than ten minutes later, they were done with the short tour.

"Thank you for doing this for us." He walked them out. "And thank William for me."

"It was our pleasure," Tyler said.

When the van pulled out of the driveway, Shai let loose a breath and thanked the merciful Fates that they were finally gone.

Schooling his expression, he walked back into the house. "I'm starving." He leaned against the kitchen counter and crossed his arms over his chest. "Is dinner ready?"

"Almost. But we can start with the soup, and by the time we are done, the curry will be ready."

"I'll ladle it." Shai filled two bowls to the brim and brought them to the table.

"Did you see how well they hid those cameras?" Geraldine asked.

He nodded. "That was the easy part. The tricky part was the wiring and making as few holes in the walls as possible. That was what impressed me the most."

Now that they were gone, Shai had calmed down enough to appreciate the incredible job they'd done.

He took another couple of spoonfuls. "William's squad is the best. If Rhett were an immortal, I bet he would have wanted to join them." Thinking of his son, Shai smiled. "Unlike his father, the kid is good at math and he finds programming fascinating."

Geraldine got up to check on the curry. "Is that what he's studying?"

"He studies computer engineering at Berkeley," Shai said with no small amount of pride.

It was one of the toughest computer programs in the entire nation to get into.

She brought the dish to the table and put it on a trivet. "That's not far from Los Angeles. Do you visit him a lot?"

"Not lately," he admitted.

"Is it because of me?"

Shai could lie and say that it wasn't, but he didn't like doing that, even to spare her feelings. Instead, he said,

"Would you like to come with me to visit him? We could drive up there this weekend."

Her eyes widened. "I would love to."

"Great. We can take Pacific Coast Highway and stop for lunch in Monterey. It'll be like a mini vacation."

"How long is the drive?"

"With the stop for lunch, probably eight hours."

Her excitement dwindled. "That's way too long. We won't be able to make it there and back the same day, and I can't be away from the house for so long. Can we fly to Berkeley?"

"If we take a commercial flight, it will take almost as long to fly as to drive there. We will need to get to the airport at least an hour before the flight, and the drive there will take about an hour. The flight itself will take about two hours, and we will need to rent a car when we get there and drive to Berkeley. We won't be saving much time if at all, and the trip would be much less fun."

She put a generous heaping of curry onto his plate and then on hers. "I assume that you can't ask Kian for the clan's jet. He would want to know why you're flying to Berkeley, and you can't tell him."

"I could say that I want to take you on a romantic vacation, but that wouldn't justify borrowing the jet and it would be an outright lie. If I'm forced to lie about Rhett, I prefer to lie by omission."

Geraldine

Geraldine felt guilty. Shai hadn't visited his son since they'd become a couple, and now she was keeping him from going because of Orion.

"Let's take a red-eye flight to Berkeley. We can leave Friday night, get there early in the morning, and then fly back in the evening."

Shai smiled. "We could also drive there Friday night and drive back Saturday evening. If we don't stop on the way, it'll take almost the same time, and our schedule would be much more flexible."

"Sounds good to me." She leaned over and took his hand. "I can't wait to meet Rhett."

Shai had shown her pictures of the boy, and they looked a lot alike. Same blond hair, same vivid blue eyes, and they were about the same height. In fact, if someone who knew Shai met Rhett, they would wonder about the resemblance.

"I don't think it's fair of Kian to issue such draconian rules. I understand that the human children of the males can't be told about immortals, but to prohibit contact with them is just cruel."

Shai smoothed a hand over his hair. "It's the smart thing to do. I'm risking a lot by having close contact with Rhett, but I just couldn't turn my back on Jennifer when she got pregnant. I wasn't in love with her, but she needed financial and emotional support, and it was important to her that my name was on the birth certificate." He chuckled. "Naturally, it was a fake name, so I didn't object. I planned to leave after the baby was born, but the moment they placed him in my arms, I fell in love. So I told myself that I would stay around for his first year of life and then disappear, but I just couldn't do that."

"Of course not." She pushed to her feet, walked over to him and sat in his lap. "You're a good man." She cupped his cheeks and kissed him softly.

"I strive to be," he murmured against her lips.

Leaning away, she looked into his eyes. "You are. Never doubt that."

He sighed. "Sometimes the line between good and bad isn't clear. I'm breaking clan rules to follow my heart, which some might regard as bad and others as good. Some would view a man staying away from his child as a shitty person, while others would appreciate his sacrifice. Clan rules allow for financial support, but for me that wasn't enough. I love my son."

"Of course, you do. As you should." She rested her cheek on his chest. "Immortality is a blessing and a curse." She sighed. "A memory of Orion surfaced while William's guys worked on the electrical wiring, and it was so sad."

The muscles in Shai's arms and chest contracted. "What was it about?"

"Every time Orion came to visit me, he released some of the memories he suppressed so I would recognize him. One of those times he told me about a woman he loved. He told me that he was grateful that she was barren and hadn't given him offspring. He said that it had been difficult enough outliving her, and he couldn't imagine outliving his children."

"He shouldn't have gotten involved with a human female. That's asking for heartache."

"Maybe he didn't know that he was immortal yet?"

Shai frowned. "That's impossible. I mean for a male, it's quite obvious. Where did he think his fangs came from?"

Geraldine rubbed a hand over her temple, willing more of that memory to surface. Orion had told her how he'd discovered that he was immortal, but he hadn't given her a time frame. Was it before or after he'd met the woman?

Could that memory be false?

It was possible that she was mixing up real memories with fantasy.

"I'm not sure when he was turned, and he didn't tell me how." She smiled sadly. "Although even if he was immortal when he fell in love with her, leaving her might have been impossible for him. As you know, the heart doesn't always listen to logic."

Shai nodded. "Indeed. Perhaps he knew, but with no guidance, it would have been difficult for him to hide what he was from his sex partners. Thralling needs to be learned and practiced, but then we know that he can also compel, and I believe that's an inborn skill. I know four compellers, and all of them became aware of their ability at a young age. I just wonder what Orion thought he was, and who induced him." He rubbed his hand over the back of his neck. "Inducing a male also requires biting, and that's something he should have remembered. The other option is that he was fathered by Toven, who as a pureblooded god could sire an immortal child with a human female. The mother most likely didn't know who the father was."

Geraldine chuckled. "Maybe he thought that he was a vampire. Back then, it was a very popular myth."

"When was back then?"

She chewed on her lower lip, debating whether she should tell him what she thought she remembered but wasn't sure that it hadn't been a dream. "I might be making some of his story up, but I can't tell which parts he really told me and which I imagined. It could be that he told me none of that."

Shai's eyes softened. "That's okay. Just tell me what you think Orion said."

"He discovered that he was immortal on the battlefield, when he sustained an injury that should have killed him. He talked about swords and shields, so it must have happened a long time ago." She lifted her eyes to him. "Do you think the Clan Mother would agree to take another look at my memories? I think she can tell which ones are real and which are not."

Shai shook his head. "Annani is leaving today, and she won't be back for another month. But you can talk to Vanessa. She might be able to help you figure out what's real and what's not."

The idea of talking with a shrink still terrified her, but not as much as it had before Annani verified some of her memories. Perhaps the clan therapist would be okay.

"Will you come with me?"

"Of course. I can schedule an appointment for tomorrow."

She winced. "Damn my stupid memory. I forgot to tell you that Cassandra and I are meeting Darlene for lunch and then we are going shopping, and after that we're having dinner together as well. It was supposed to be just dinner, but Cassandra thought that we would need more time with Darlene to get her to open up to us, so she added lunch and shopping. Thankfully, Darlene doesn't work, so she had no problem with the change of plans."

He arched a brow. "Can I at least join you for dinner?"

"I'm so sorry, but it's girls only. Cassandra and I want to get Darlene talking about her relationship with Leo. She won't do that with you and Onegus around. That's why Cassandra is taking half a day off. It's that important." She kissed his cheek. "You know that I would have preferred for you to be there. I hate being apart from you."

"Same here." He let out a breath. "But that's fine. It's a good opportunity for me to stay late in the office and catch up on work."

"Tomorrow morning, I'll pack lunch and dinner for you so you don't go hungry." She gave him a mock stern look. "I know that you don't take breaks for food so you can finish earlier and come home to me."

Shai smiled. "Are you worried about me?"

"Of course. I love you."

"I love you too." He kissed the tip of her nose. "Back to Vanessa. Is Wednesday okay?"

"I guess. But maybe we should wait until we come back from Berkeley."

"There is no reason to wait. I'll give her a call tomorrow and check when she's available."

Vrog

Vrog came to with a pounding headache, a vile taste in his mouth, and a rough rope tied around his wrists and ankles.

He'd been captured, and he was no longer in Stella's hotel room.

Keeping his breathing even and his eyes closed, he let his other senses assess his environment. Given the steady engine noise, he was on an aircraft, a private jet most likely. They couldn't have transported him hog-tied and bloodied on a commercial flight. Surprisingly, though, he hadn't been dumped on the floor or in the cargo bay. He was lying in a comfortable, reclining seat, and other than the beating he'd gotten from Stella's partner, he hadn't incurred new injuries.

His mistake had been to underestimate the guy.

Stella's partner might not be a trained fighter, but he performed well under pressure and was a damn good actor. The act he'd put on had been so convincing that Vrog had ignored what should have been an obvious warning sign.

He remembered hearing a crunching noise and wondering why the guy was squashing a bag of chips in his pocket while shaking in fear and wetting his pants.

Now he knew.

The wet stain hadn't been urine. The guy had crunched a bag of potato chips to cover the sound of him breaking a container with an anesthetizing liquid that had turned into a gas. Somehow, Stella and her partner hadn't been affected by the fumes, but he surely had been.

Had they formulated it to work only on the Kra-ell and their hybrid offspring?

They must have experimented on the females they'd taken twenty-two years ago and found a way to incapacitate his kind without harming themselves.

The fumes hadn't rendered him unconscious though, so the formula must have been off. But it had been enough to disorient him and weaken his muscle control. Then the guy had kicked him in the head with much more force than Vrog had thought him capable of. That one kick had nearly finished the job, sending him flying away from Stella.

When he'd landed on the floor, the guy had pounced on him and stabbed him in the neck with something stronger, a tranquilizer of some sort. Vrog had kept fighting for as long as he could, but eventually the drugs and the beating had knocked him out.

Given the taste of his own blood in his mouth and the tingling in his nose, Stella's partner hadn't stopped once Vrog was out and had gone to town on his face.

"I know that you're awake," a woman said softly.

Stella.

For her to detect that he was conscious despite his efforts to appear the opposite, her senses must be just as sharp as his.

A vile curse at the ready, he opened his eyes and cast her a baleful look.

She lifted her hand to stop him. "Before you say things that you are going to regret later, I want you to know that I had nothing to do with what happened to your people. My team and I thought that they'd moved to a different location, and we have no idea what happened to them. I hope that you can help us figure it out."

Her lies were not convincing.

As the guy sitting next to him activated the seat's mechanism, lifting Vrog to a sitting position, a wave of nausea hit him so hard that he struggled to keep the contents of his stomach down. Except, with how empty it was, all that would come up was bile.

Perhaps he shouldn't have. Covering the bitch with vomit would serve her right.

"Are you okay?" She sounded concerned. "You look like you are about to barf."

"I'm fine," he bit out, refusing to show weakness.

"Perhaps you should put the blanket up as a shield," the team's leader said without looking up from his tablet.

He was sitting across the aisle from Vrog, next to the sister of the modeling agency owner, who Vrog assumed was sitting behind him. His bindings didn't allow for much maneuvering, but he could smell a woman's perfume and a man's cologne coming from that direction.

Between what he could see and what he could hear and smell, only the eight team members from the hotel were with him on the jet. Naturally, there was also a pilot and possibly a copilot.

"I'm sure Vrog can hold it down," Stella said. "Some water might be helpful, though." She turned to her partner. "Can you get him a bottle?"

"He didn't ask." Glaring at Vrog, the guy crossed his arms over his chest.

At least he was honest and not faking concern like Stella. Were they playing the good cop/bad cop game with him?

Ignoring the guy's glare, Vrog trained his gaze on Stella. "How did you know where to look for my people?"

She glanced at the team's leader for approval, but the guy was still reading on his tablet as if the conversation was of no interest to him.

Vrog doubted that was the case.

Shifting in her seat, Stella adjusted her skirt over her knees. "A hybrid Kra-ell who'd left your tribe thirty-some years ago joined our clan recently. He told us where his old compound used to be."

Vrog had never heard about a hybrid deserting their tribe, but that didn't mean that there had been none. It wasn't something that Jade would have wanted to be known, and she would have compelled everyone's silence on that so the others wouldn't get similar rebellious ideas. What gave Stella's story credence, though, was that Vrog had never told her how old he was. She could have perhaps guessed, but if she wasn't sure, she would have just said that the hybrid had left a long time ago instead of providing a narrow and easily challenged time frame.

Not giving anything away, he said, "I don't know of anyone who has ever left the tribe—hybrid, human, or pureblood."

"You were probably a young boy when he left, so you don't remember him."

The hybrid children had stayed with their human mothers, and they had been pretty much ignored by the purebloods as well as the adult hybrids. The guy wouldn't have remembered him, but he should have known the hybrid.

There hadn't been that many of them.

"What's the guy's name?"

Stella winced. "He calls himself Emmett Haderech. He hasn't told us his Kra-ell name."

On the one hand, knowing what his people called themselves added more credence to her story, but on the other hand, if she'd been involved in abducting the females of his tribe, she could have gotten the information out of them. She could also have learned how old he was, and that he'd been away from the compound when her clan had sacked it.

"Did you ask him if he remembers me?"

"He doesn't."

Vrog pinned Stella with a hard stare. "How convenient."

"You don't believe me."

"Why should I?"

"Because she's telling you the truth, moron." Her partner leaned over and slapped him over the head, but since there had been no force behind it, the slap was meant as an insult.

Vrog stifled the growl rising up his throat. To a Kra-ell, that was an invitation to a duel, but even if he weren't bound like a hog, responding with aggression would have done him no good. His damn Kra-ell instincts had to be subdued or they would get him in trouble.

"Don't hit him," she admonished. "Can you get Vrog a bottle of water, please? He really doesn't look good."

In his anger, Vrog had forgotten to eat, and with how fast his hybrid metabolism worked, he was probably anemic by now. Blood wasn't necessary for his sustenance like it was for the purebloods and some of the hybrids, but he needed to eat plenty of meat to compensate for its lack.

The guy frowned. "If you barf on my mate, the beating I gave you before will seem like gentle patting."

Despite the threat, he opened the side compartment next to him, pulled out a bottle, and tossed it to the male sitting next to Vrog. "I'm not helping him drink."

The male removed the cap and held the bottle to Vrog's lips. "I'll give you just enough to wet your lips. Too much and you will barf for sure."

"It must be a side effect of the sleeping potion," Stella said. "Didn't Merlin test it on humans before assuring us that it was safe?"

"He did," the leader of the team said. "Maybe it has that effect only on the Kra-ell." He pushed to his feet. "I'll check the first-aid kit for anti-nausea medication."

Vrog turned his face, signaling that he was done drinking. "Don't bother. I'm not going to take any medication from you."

The guy shrugged and sat back down. "You're wasting your energy on hating the wrong people, Vrog. We are not your enemy."

"I don't have enemies. No one else had anything to gain from slaughtering the males of my tribe."

Stella's eyes widened. "Just the males were killed? Not everyone?"

As if she didn't know.

"I can't be sure of that," he admitted. "But the evidence I found suggests that the females were spared." He narrowed his eyes at Stella. "What did you do with them? Are your people using them as breeders?"

Stella

To convince Vrog that the clan had nothing to do with what had happened to his tribe was going to be much harder than Stella had expected.

The 'introduction' he'd gotten probably didn't help matters.

Richard had broken his nose and probably one of his cheekbones as well. Vrog was fast-healing, but not as fast as an immortal. His face was no longer swollen, and the cut on his upper lip was almost fully healed, but the bones were probably still knitting themselves back together. He had dried blood on his cheeks and on his black T-shirt.

He looked exhausted, physically and mentally.

Vrog needed someone to blame, and it would be hard for him to accept that his own people had done the unthinkable.

Now that she knew that only the males had been killed, the Chinese government seemed like a less likely suspect, but it was still possible that they'd killed the males and taken the females to interrogate or to experiment on. The other suspects were the hybrid males. Tired of being denied access to Kra-ell females and not allowed to father children with humans, they'd had good cause to rebel.

From Emmett's descriptions and from what she remembered Vrog telling her, the Kra-ell females didn't sound like such a coveted prize, but they were the only ones who could provide the hybrid males with long-lived offspring.

Jin chuckled. "From what we know about your females, we wouldn't take them even if they begged us. They are vicious."

One side of Vrog's mouth twitched in a barely-there smile. "That might be true, but when your people face extinction, five extra breeders with new genetic material are welcome no matter what their attitudes are."

"We are not facing extinction," Stella said.

They had faced it up until not too long ago, but then the merciful Fates had taken pity on them, and suddenly after thousands of years of nothing, Dormants had started popping up left and right. It was only a matter of time before the next generation arrived—a generation that would not suffer from the same limitations as their clan mothers and fathers. With the new matrilineal genes introduced into the genetic pool, their numbers would soon start increasing more rapidly.

Hopefully, the trend of incoming Dormants wouldn't end anytime soon, not until every clan member was blessed with a mate, preferably a true-love match, but any love match would do.

There was something to be said about free will and choosing to stay with a partner instead of being compelled to do so by the mate bond. There was nothing wrong with loving a mate without the mystical bond to tie them together for eternity.

Trying to come up with a succinct way to explain it to Vrog, Stella started to lean forward, but Richard pulled her back. "Don't get too close to him."

With how tightly Vrog was bound, he couldn't do much, and even if he tried, Jay would stop him. But he was supposedly super strong and could possibly snap the bindings. Not that she believed he would do that. It would be extremely stupid to attempt anything on board a jet flying at thirty thousand feet, and with five males who would overpower him in seconds. But she didn't want to worry Richard.

As it was, her mate was having a difficult time with the situation.

She leaned back in her seat. "We don't have the same problem the Kra-ell have. We have nearly an equal number of males and females."

"I have no choice but to take your word for it." Vrog released a resigned breath and closed his eyes.

Obviously, he didn't believe her, and the truth was that given Kalugal's men tipping the gender balance, what she'd told him wasn't entirely true. But the clan had other problems that the Kra-ell didn't have or had to a lesser extent. The clan might be made of a nearly equal number of males and females, but since they were forbidden to each other, it didn't matter as far as producing the next generation went. They were on the right track, but it would take a long time.

Nevertheless, the Kra-ell females wouldn't be helpful in that capacity because they couldn't produce Dormants. The pureblooded females could produce hybrids, but the longevity ended with them. A hybrid female's offspring was human no matter who the father was. Or so they assumed.

Emmett had left the community a long time ago, and during that time, they might have found out that the hybrid females could have hybrid children with humans as well as the pureblooded males. It was also possible that pureblooded Kra-ell females with immortal males and immortal females with pureblooded Kra-ell males could produce a whole new breed of offspring.

Vlad, Mey, and Jin were the offspring of hybrid Kra-ell males, and they were definitely different from other immortals. What would their lifespans be?

Since they'd inherited the godly gene of immortality from their mothers, they would most likely be immortal.

Or so she hoped.

Stella pulled out her phone. "Don't you want me to tell you about our son? I can show you pictures."

Vrog's eyes snapped open. "Show me."

As she tried to lean forward again, Richard snatched the phone from her hands and handed it to Jay. "You can do that."

She cast him a reproachful sidelong glance. "What can he possibly do to me?"

"I don't know. But if you care enough for him not to see him beaten to a pulp again, he'd better not touch you."

She wondered whether Richard was motivated by concern for her or by jealousy, but this was not the time to have a talk with him.

"Fine."

Jay lifted the phone to Vrog's face. "This is Vlad. Handsome fellow, isn't he?"

Vrog tried to keep his expression impassive but failed. His eyes softened and he leaned toward the small screen as much as his bindings allowed. "He does look like me. I thought that you were just saying that to get me to release you. Who is that pretty girl next to him?"

"That's Wendy," Stella said. "His fiancée."

Vrog lifted his head. "He's about to get married? He's too young even in human terms."

"They are in love, and they want to get married. The wedding is scheduled for a couple of months from now."

She cast him a bright smile. "Vlad would be thrilled to have his father attend his wedding."

Next to her, Richard stiffened. "Vrog is not Vlad's father. He's only the sperm donor." He glared at Vrog. "A father is the man who raises a child, or at least contributes financially to their upbringing. You planted the seed and then ran like a coward back to your mistress."

"You're not helping," Stella hissed at him. "Vrog didn't plan on getting me pregnant. It was just a fling, and it's not his fault that he wasn't part of Vlad's life. He could not have been there for Vlad even if he wanted to."

"Why not?" Vrog asked. "My mistress was gone. I could have acknowledged my son."

"How was I supposed to know that?" Her eyes misted with tears as she shifted her gaze to him. "Remember the vow you made me take? I didn't tell anyone who fathered my child. Everyone assumed that Vlad had been sired by a random human."

Vrog

Vrog had forgotten about the vow. Even when he made Stella take it, he hadn't believed she would keep it, and the truth was that he'd just used it as a loophole to sidestep his own oath to Jade.

The Mother of all Life demanded the most from her chosen children—the Kra-ell. Stella was a non-believer, and as such, she wasn't expected to uphold the code of honor the Kra-ell lived by. She wouldn't have been punished as severely for breaking her promise, if at all.

He, on the other hand, was still bound by that damn oath of loyalty to Jade, awaiting her return, making the most of the money left in those safes, and accumulating profits on her behalf.

Only her death would release him, but until he had proof that Jade was gone, he wouldn't dare break it. His own mother was probably dead, so he no longer had to uphold the vow to protect her life, but he still needed to do so for the sake of his son—the only remaining blood relative Vrog cared for.

The Mother of All Life could punish him for breaking his vow by hurting Vlad.

Had Vlad inherited Stella's longevity?

He prayed to The Mother that he had.

"How long have you kept the secret?" he asked.

"I kept it until a few months ago when we discovered your tribesman running a cult in Oregon. Then other things started surfacing, and I knew that I could no longer keep the secret." She turned to her partner. "I didn't break the vow even then, though. Richard connected the dots and figured out that Vlad must have been fathered by a Kraell. Technically, that doesn't count as breaking my oath."

Vrog ignored the comment about his tribesman running a cult. He was curious, but he was even more curious about how Richard had figured out that Vlad hadn't been sired by a human. Was he clairvoyant?

"How did you know?" He addressed the male directly.

Richard shrugged. "It's a long story and one that you need to earn the right to hear. Right now, I'm not in the mood to indulge you."

"Fair enough."

Vrog could understand why the male was still enraged. It seemed that Stella and her kin followed human traditions of couples' exclusivity, and Richard regarded her body as his property.

She'd been naked when Vrog had attacked her, and even though his intent hadn't been sexual, it might have been interpreted that way.

"I apologize, Stella." Vrog bowed his head as much as his bindings permitted. "Once I realized that you were naked under the blanket, it was too late to retreat. I wanted to force answers out of you, not to violate you. That's not the Kra-ell way."

Richard snorted. "You think that's what I'm angry about? You held the woman I love at knifepoint, threatening to cut a major artery that could potentially kill even an immortal. You made her bleed. You're lucky my fangs are not fully developed yet, or I would have torn your throat out."

Vrog frowned. "What's wrong with your fangs? You are a fully grown male."

The guy grimaced. "I transitioned only about three months ago, and it will take another three for them to become fully functional."

What the hell was he talking about?

"Transitioned from what?"

Stella put a hand on Richard's arm. "He doesn't know what transition is."

"Right." Richard sent him a pitying look. "I forgot that they don't have Dormants."

"What are Dormants?"

Stella turned to look at the team leader. "Can I tell him?"

"Not yet."

"I'm sorry." She smiled apologetically. "That's privileged information. If you join our clan, you will become privy to it."

He sneered. "Is that an invitation?"

"It's not up to me to invite you. The head of our clan needs to decide what to do with you."

Vrog swallowed. She would probably order him to be tortured. That was what Jade would have done. But Stella had told him that her leader was a kind female.

Besides, what could she want from him?

"Let's assume for a moment that I believe you, and that your people had nothing to do with the slaughter of my tribe's males or with the fire. If not you, then who?"

"I hoped that you would know more and help us solve the mystery." She glanced at those sitting behind him. "So far, we've come up with two possible theories. Mey thinks that the Chinese government discovered your people and decided to eliminate them. Perhaps they spared the females thinking that they would be easier to interrogate." She closed her eyes and sighed. "It's also possible that they took them to experiment on. Even though your females sound vicious, I wouldn't wish that on anyone." Her eyes popped open. "Were there any children in the compound?"

He winced. "Human, hybrid, and pureblooded. I hope that whoever did that at least spared the children."

"They let the humans go," said the woman sitting behind him.

"How do you know that?"

"Mey has a special paranormal ability," Stella said. "She can listen to echoes of conversations that were imbedded in walls, but only the highly emotional ones leave echoes. That's how we were searching for clues. She listened to the old walls, but since only the human quarters were left still standing, she only heard echoes from emotional events involving them."

That was a paranormal talent Vrog had never heard of, but as someone who could enter human minds and manipulate them, he was not as skeptical as those with no paranormal abilities would have been upon hearing of such an outlandish ability.

He strained his neck, trying to look behind his shoulder. "What did you learn from the echoes?"

Taking pity on him, the woman got up, took a couple of steps, and then sat on the armrest of their leader's seat. "I hope you don't mind." She smiled at him.

"Not at all." The guy just scooted sideways, giving her more room.

Apparently, these people didn't believe in formalities. Jade would have snapped the neck of anyone daring such disrespect. Then again, maybe Mey was the leader, and he was just the military commander who took his orders from her.

"I don't only hear echoes, I also see them." She crossed her legs at the ankles. "What I see is not the actual people speaking but the way others see them, so it's far from accurate." She pushed a strand of her long hair behind her ear. "A male, who might have been a hybrid Kra-ell, walked into the humans' kitchen and told them to pack their things and leave as soon as they could. That's why I think the humans were spared."

The relief Vrog felt was tremendous, but then the guilt came. He'd assumed that his mother had been killed along with her Kra-ell masters, but if the humans were spared, she might still be alive. He'd wasted twenty-two years during which he should have been looking for her.

But why hadn't she stayed around?

She'd known that he was in Singapore at the time, and that he survived.

Perhaps the human females had been taken along with the Kra-ell?

If his theory about the hybrids rebelling was true, they might have taken some of the human females with them. They wouldn't have killed the humans, only the purebloods whom some of the hybrids hated with a passion even though their hatred had been misdirected.

The pureblooded males obeyed Jade and the other pureblooded females. If the hybrids had needed someone to hate, they should have directed their hate at the females, and especially at Jade.

Except, the vows of loyalty tied them all to her. No one would have dared to harm her and risk the lives of everyone they cared for.

Still, he could understand the hybrids wanting the females for themselves, but why leave the compound?

Who had they run from?

As far as he knew, he'd been the only one absent from the compound when the place burned down, and the hybrids wouldn't have feared him. There had been enough of them to overpower him even if he decided to avenge his father and the others they'd slaughtered.

"What did the male look like?" Vrog asked the woman who heard and saw echoes in addition to supposedly running a modeling agency. Even though she looked the part, that was probably just a cover story.

"He was a tall and slim Eurasian. His looks weren't particularly distinctive. He had a commanding attitude, though." She folded her arms over her chest. "He spoke good Chinese, but he had a slight accent that I thought sounded Russian, but I'm not sure of that. It could have been some other Slavic accent. He didn't talk for long enough for me to get a better grasp on it."

A chill ran down Vrog's spine. "None of the hybrids had foreign accents. Our first language was Chinese because that was what our mothers spoke. And later we learned the Kra-ell language and some of the Western ones, but none of us spoke Chinese with a foreign accent."

Richard

It seemed that Stella had achieved what she'd set out to do.

She'd sorted things out, albeit partially, but she'd made a lot of progress in a short time.

Vrog no longer looked at her with hatred in his eyes, and now Mey had offered him a new suspect to ponder.

Richard didn't like where Stella's head was going. Did she really expect Kian to welcome Vrog into their village with open arms?

The problem was that Kian might do just that. The guy was an unknown, so there was a risk in that, but he was without a community, and Kian might take pity on him. The big boss seemed gruff, but he had a soft heart.

Richard didn't want Vrog in the village.

He finally had a family to call his own, and he wasn't going to share it with a guy who hadn't done anything for Stella or for Vlad aside from reluctantly contributing his sperm.

Richard hadn't done much either, but that was only because he hadn't been in their lives for long enough. Still, he had been there for Stella when she needed him, and he'd been there for Vlad when the kid needed to face Wendy's jerk of a father. He'd earned his position as the honorary dad in their small family.

Vrog didn't deserve even the title of an honorary uncle.

A small vicious voice in Richard's head whispered that Vrog was a temporary nuisance. He was long-lived but not immortal, so Richard wouldn't have to tolerate him for eternity.

"How do I know that you are telling me the truth about what you've heard?" Vrog asked Mey. "You could have made it up."

"Why would I?" She leaned close enough to breathe in the guy's face. "We have no interest in your females. And we don't go around slaughtering people. That's not what and who we are. I can spend hours telling you about all the good the clan has done for humanity, while your people treated humans as breeding stock and free labor, keeping them as slaves. And don't get me started on all the babies your people had gotten rid of, the ones fathered by hybrid males and born to human females before your leader forbade it."

Richard stifled the urge to applaud Mey's bold words. Everything she said was true, and as one of those babies who had gotten discarded, she had every right to rain on Vrog's holier-than-thou parade.

"Did the hybrid who joined your clan tell you about that?" Vrog asked.

"Some of it," Mey said. "The rest my sister and I experienced ourselves." She smiled, revealing her tiny fangs. "We were two of those discarded babies."

Vrog seemed stunned, looking at Mey as if she had grown a pair of horns.

"You are Kra-ell?"

She shook her head. "My father might have been a hybrid and my mother a human. My sister and I were given up for adoption and were lucky enough to be adopted by a wonderful couple."

"So you are both human," Vrog stated. "Not immortal."

"No, we are both immortal."

"How?"

Mey smiled, but it was a cold smile. "That information is on a need-to-know basis, and right now, you don't need to know." She stood up and returned to her seat.

Vrog shifted his gaze to Stella. "Did your clan find a way to turn regular humans into immortals?"

She shook her head. "No, and I can't say any more on the subject."

He let out a breath. "Is there a chance you can unbind me? I really need to use the bathroom."

Jay pushed to his feet. "I'll take you." He glanced at Arwel. "Can I untie his legs?"

Arwel leveled his eyes on Vrog's. "If you vow on your honor that you will not try anything stupid, I'll let Jay untie you."

Richard arched a brow but didn't say anything. Arwel was the boss, and to question his authority was bad form even for a civilian.

"I vow it," Vrog said. "We are on a plane. Where would I go?"

"Nowhere but down," Arwel said. "But there is no limit to people's stupidity. I want to make sure that you are thinking with your head and not your heart."

Vrog let out a breath. "Frankly, I don't know where my heart is right now. Everything Mey said was true, and it shames me to admit it. Not that I could have done anything about it. As a hybrid, I had no say in how things were done. But they were still my people, and now I have no one. I don't know what to do or think anymore."

"What did you think before we showed up?" Jay started on the knot at Vrog's ankles.

"I hoped Jade and the other females would come back to get what they'd left behind. I thought that I was holding the fort for them, so to speak."

"Twenty-two years is a long time to wait." Jay removed the rope from Vrog's ankles and pushed up to his feet. "If it were me, I would have given up hope after a year." He motioned for Vrog to lean forward so he could untie his hands.

"It's not like I spent that time idly, just waiting. I founded the school with the money Jade left behind in a safe, and I've been actively involved in managing it throughout the years. I only used a small portion of the profits for what I needed to live on. The rest was deposited for Jade to claim when she returned."

Such loyalty to the queen bitch.

Richard wondered what she'd done to earn it. Perhaps she had used some alien supernatural talent of persuasion, or maybe tethering of a different sort than Jin's. Who knew what powers these Kra-ell had.

When Jay freed Vrog's hands, the guy pulled his arms forward and rubbed at his chafed wrists. "Thank you." Pushing up to his feet, he looked at Stella. "Once again, I apologize for attacking you."

"So do you believe me now that I had nothing to do with what happened to your people?"

He nodded, but Richard could tell that the guy wasn't convinced. There was doubt in his eyes, but it wasn't as strong as it had been before.

Perhaps Stella was right, and by the time they landed in California, they would have everything sorted out.

"The bathroom is in the back." Jay took Vrog's elbow. "You can go in by yourself, but leave the door open so I can see you. I'll close the curtain to give you privacy."

Vrog nodded. "I understand."

Kian

Kian couldn't remember ever having so many people in his office since he'd moved into the village. Onegus, Turner, Bridget, Shai, and the eight-person Kra-ell investigative team had taken up all of the twelve chairs surrounding the conference table. Shai had to roll over Kian's desk chair so he would have a place to sit.

The team had returned from China early in the morning, depositing the Kra-ell male in the keep's dungeon before heading to the village.

"Who did you put in charge of guarding Vrog?" Kian asked Onegus.

"Alec and Vernon." The chief shifted his gaze to Alfie and Jay. "These two will take over after they get some sleep. They have experience taking care of a Kra-ell."

Alfie's lips twisted in a grimace. "I'm not looking forward to being cooped up in the keep again or getting blood for the leech from the Chinese market."

"Did you check with Vrog if he drinks blood?" Stella asked.

The Guardian shrugged. "I didn't, but I assume that his nutritional needs are the same as Emmett's."

"Not necessarily," Bridget said. "It is true that both Vrog and Emmett are half human and half Kra-ell, but one's metabolism might have taken after his human mother, while the other might have taken after his Kra-ell father."

Onegus pulled out his phone. "I'm sure that Alec and Vernon will sort it out with Vrog." He started typing on the screen. "But I'm texting them just in case."

Richard huffed. "The bastard is getting the royal treatment as if he were an honored guest and not a prisoner awaiting trial." He folded his arms over his chest. "I hope Edna sentences him to a whipping."

"Stop it," Stella hissed. "Revenge is stupid, and it will achieve nothing."

Kian lifted a hand to stop the argument from escalating. "Vrog is a guest. Other than his attack on Stella, for which he got pummeled by you, he hasn't done anything to us. We are actually the ones in the wrong in this situation—we had no right to abduct him, and we have no right to keep him imprisoned—but we need to interrogate him, and that couldn't have been done in China."

"The same can be said of Emmett." Richard unfolded his arms and braced his elbows on the table. "He hadn't done anything to us either, and you kept him in the dungeon for months."

Kian cast him an incredulous look. "Emmett abducted Eleanor and then Peter. He planned to take Peter to his leader to be used as a breeder and an inducer. I think that justified his imprisonment."

Refusing to back down, Richard held Kian's gaze. "I don't see the difference. If the clan hadn't sent a team to investigate Safe Haven, Emmett wouldn't have done anything to threaten or harm the clan. It could be said that we were in the wrong in his case as well."

It seemed that Richard was no longer intimidated by him, and Kian wondered whether he'd lost his edge after Allegra's birth and had become too soft. More likely, though, Richard's anger over Vrog's attack on Stella had obliterated his healthy self-preservation instincts.

"Emmett is dangerous. I don't get the sense that Vrog is." Kian signaled that he was done with the discussion by turning toward Arwel. "Is there anything you would like to add to what you've told me about him so far?"

Arwel nodded. "During the flight, Stella successfully engaged Vrog in conversation, and we learned a few more details, but perhaps I should start from the top for the benefit of those who haven't heard my previous report yet."

Kian nodded. "Go ahead."

Those present who hadn't been part of the team had been given a brief summary of what Arwel had told him, but it was likely that Kian had omitted details that Turner might find important. Having the guy attend the meeting without giving him all the relevant information would be counterproductive.

Throughout Arwel's retelling of Vrog's attack, capture, and what the team had learned from him, Turner scribbled on his yellow pad and asked the other team members to elaborate on a few points.

When all was said and done, Turner put his pen down and leaned back in his chair. "Frankly, based on what I've heard from you all, I don't think the coup was perpetrated by the Chinese government or by rebelling hybrids. In my opinion, Vrog's tribe was attacked by another group of Kra-ell who were after their females. But I admit that we don't have enough information for me to conclude that with any level of certainty."

The same thing had occurred to Kian. The hybrids would have stayed in the compound or at least taken the money Vrog had mentioned his leader leaving behind. A Chinese task force wouldn't have left the money either, and they would have taken the humans instead of telling them to leave.

"We need to brainstorm this with Vrog." Kian let out a sigh. "I just hope that he's cooperative."

"Let me know when you plan to interrogate him," Turner said. "I would like to be there. I want to know what he's basing his assumptions on, and why he thinks the males were killed while the females were taken."

"The Russian accent Mey detected in the echoes is a clue," Kian said. "I assume that you remember David's theory regarding the Tunguska event?" He glanced at Shai. "If you don't, I'm sure Shai can refresh your memory."

Jin pursed her lips. "I don't remember hearing anything about it, but my memory leaves a lot to be desired, so I might have been told and forgotten."

Shai smiled. "I can summarize it for you in under one minute. The Tunguska event was a massive explosion that occurred at the beginning of the twentieth century over a sparsely populated Eastern Siberian Taiga. It was attributed to a shock wave produced by an air burst of a large stony meteoroid entering the atmosphere. But even though the shockwave flattened about eighty million trees, there was no impact crater, suggesting that whatever had exploded had disintegrated at an altitude of several miles above ground. Since then, hundreds of scholarly papers have been written about the event. A recent one published in 2013 included an analysis of micro-samples taken from the area, which showed fragments that might be of extraterrestrial origin."

"Okay..." Jin cast a sidelong glance at Kian. "What does this have to do with the Kra-ell?"

"According to Emmett's best educated guess, the Kra-ell arrived on earth at about the time of the event. Their mothership might have malfunctioned and entered the atmosphere, which a craft that big had no business doing. It was destroyed over Siberia, but smaller landing crafts or perhaps escape pods might have been deployed before the explosion or there would have been no Kra-ell survivors. Some pods could have landed in China, while others could have landed in Russia."

Jin nodded. "If that's what happened, why did it take those who landed in Russia nearly a century to find those who landed in China?"

Turner tapped his pen on his yellow pad. "The landing crafts or escape pods might have lost communication between them when the mothership exploded."

"Then how did they find them twenty-two years ago?" Stella asked. "Vrog's tribe kept a very low profile. We didn't know that they even existed, and we've been actively monitoring every bit of news about alien sightings and the like."

"We might not have known what to look for." Kian leaned back in his chair. "Perhaps the Kra-ell have a tell."

"Yeah," Richard snorted. "Their tell is humans disappearing in the vicinity of their compounds, especially young, attractive females."

Bridget sighed. "Regrettably, the Kra-ell are not the only ones who prey on young women and girls. As we know, there are enough human predators who contribute to that abhorrent phenomenon."

When a long moment of silence stretched across the table, Stella lifted her hand. "If it's okay with you, Kian, I would like Vlad to meet his father."

"Not yet. I need to question Vrog first."

Stella wasn't happy to hear that. "He's not going to attack his own son."

"I don't think he would either." Kian crossed his arms over his chest. "In fact, I'm counting on Vrog desperately wanting to meet Vlad. Withholding visitation rights might motivate him to talk."

"Good luck with that," Richard spat. "The guy is as stubborn and as suspicious as they come."

"What do you plan to do with him?" Stella asked Kian. "Are you going to invite him to join the clan like you did with Emmett?"

Kian nodded. "Possibly. He's all alone."

Richard huffed out a breath. "I knew that you would feel sorry for him."

Kian arched a brow. "Shouldn't I?"

"He attacked Stella and held a knife to her throat. He should be punished, not rewarded with an invitation to the most exclusive club on the planet."

"I forgave Vrog," Stella said. "And so should you. Try to walk a mile in his shoes. He was distraught, thinking that I was responsible for his people's fate, which made him feel guilty for letting me go all those years ago. He wanted answers, but he was outnumbered and desperate, so when he thought that I was alone, he made his move. He wouldn't have hurt me. He just wanted to get the truth out of me."

"You're naive and softhearted."

Kian lifted his hand to stop the argument between the two from taking over the meeting. "I'm not inviting him yet, and he will probably spend as long in the dungeon as Emmett did, which is punishment enough."

"Right." Richard snorted. "As if staying in that fancy apartment is such a hardship."

Kian was in no mood to go down that path again.

"Enough," he snapped. "I suggest that all of you get some rest." Leveling a hard stare at Richard, he added, "You are tired and irritated."

Richard was smart enough to clamp his mouth shut, and as the team left the room, Kian let out a breath. "I can't blame him. If someone attacked Syssi, I would have done much worse. There would have been nothing left of Vrog to scrape off the rug."

Onegus chuckled. "It reminds me of Amanda and Dalhu in that cabin, and your heroic rescue attempt. You thought that he was hurting her, when what he'd been doing was the exact opposite of that."

Kian rolled his eyes. "I'd rather forget it ever happened." He shifted his gaze to Turner. "I'm planning on visiting Vrog around four in the afternoon today. Does that work for you?"

"I'll make it work. I'll meet you at the keep."

Onegus

Onegus left Kian's office and took the stairs down to the lobby. Pulling out his phone, he checked the two messages he'd received during the meeting. Since they had been at least half an hour apart, he'd assumed that they weren't urgent, and he'd been right.

One was from Bhathian, asking for authorization to reorganize two of the Guardian teams that needed shoring up, and the other was from Andrew, asking Onegus to text him when he was free to receive phone calls.

He typed his responses to both messages while walking toward the pavilion.

Andrew wouldn't call him from inside the government building where he worked. There were cameras everywhere, and every word said was being recorded. If he had information that he thought Onegus needed to hear, he would drive out of the building and call from one of the nearby coffee shops.

Onegus was back at his office when Andrew finally called back. "Do you have a moment?"

"For you, I have all the time you need." Onegus pushed the chair back and propped his legs on the desk. "What's up?"

"I did what you asked and checked who was still monitoring Roni's parents. Just as I thought, up until Cassandra told Darlene and Leo about Roni contacting her, the only surveillance remaining was a tap on their phones. The landline and both their cellphones. My next suspicion was that one of them had said something over the phone that had raised a red flag, so I pretended to compile data about potential hackers in connection to a case I'm working on. When I looked into Roni's, I found out that his damn father had called in and reported that Roni had resurfaced."

"I'm going to kill that asshole." The rage rising in Onegus's chest refused to obey his command to stand down. "Slowly."

"Do you need help?"

Onegus's smile was vicious. "Actually, I do. Since I can't actually murder him, I will have to be satisfied with making his life hell. From what I hear, you're the perfect man for the job."

Andrew could access the government database and flag Leo as a suspected terrorist, have his credit cards canceled and his bank accounts frozen.

"I have a few tricks up my sleeve, but Roni can do the same. I think it should be his decision what to do about his father."

"True." Onegus put his feet down. "Why did he do that? Is there a big prize on Roni's head?"

"You've got it. Half a million dollars if the information leads to his capture. Roni was a very precious asset that our government did not like losing, especially if he crossed over to our nation's enemies."

"Bastard. Selling out his own son is lower than low."

"I know. He's either a sociopath or he hates Roni."

Remembering the guy's comment during their meeting, Onegus uttered a vile curse. "I think Leo suspects that he's not Roni's father."

"Suspects or knows?"

"I'm not sure. Cassandra and Geraldine are meeting Darlene today without her husband. They might be able to get her to talk."

"You can do that with a little thrall. Why leave it to chance?"

"When the clan's security is not on the line, I prefer not to resort to thralling."

"Roni is an important asset to the clan and to its security. It may be argued that any information you collect in connection with him is a security matter."

Onegus chuckled. "I don't think Edna would be impressed with that argument."

"If you want, I can help. What I do is not thralling and it's not against clan rules. You can ask Darlene questions and I will tell you if her answers are truth or lie."

"Thank you. If all other methods fail, I might ask you to do that. We could also get into their house, collect a few hairs from Leo's comb, run it through a DNA testing machine, and compare the results to Roni's."

"True. But before you do anything, I suggest that you talk to Roni."

"I will right now. Thank you, Andrew."

"Anytime."

Onegus ended the call and rose to his feet. Roni's lab was two minutes' walk from his office, and what he needed to tell the kid required face-to-face.

With a heavy heart, he made the short walk to the lab and entered through the open door.

As usual, Roni sat in his enormous black swivel chair that dwarfed his slim frame, the side wings making it look like a bat mobile.

"Onegus." He swiveled the monstrosity around. "What brings you to my lab?"

"I have upsetting news."

When Roni's eyes flared with alarm, Onegus raised his hand. "No one got hurt. The news is upsetting on an emotional level." There was no gentle way to say it. "Your father betrayed you to the government."

Roni frowned. "What do you mean? How?"

"I couldn't understand why and how the snoops showed up, so I asked Andrew to dig around if he could. He found out that your father called the office to tell them that you've resurfaced. Apparently, there is a big prize for any information that will lead to your capture."

"Bastard," Roni spat out. "I knew that he was a piece of crap, but I didn't know how pestiferous."

"Do you want to deal with him yourself? Or do you want Andrew to make his life hell?"

Roni closed his eyes. "I need to think about it. If I destroy him, my mother will suffer too, and I don't want that."

Onegus put his hand on Roni's shoulder. "It's up to you. Whatever you decide, just know that Andrew and I are ready and willing to help in any way we can."

Roni nodded. "Thank you."

Stella

It was almost noon when Stella left Richard sleeping at home and headed out to the café. In half an hour or so, Vlad would be back from his shift at the bakery, and he would stop by the café to have lunch with Wendy.

There was no perfect time or place to tell him about Vrog, but this was as good as any, and the sooner she did it, the better. The news about Vrog's capture and what he had done leading up to it would soon spread throughout the village, and Stella didn't want Vlad to hear what had happened from anyone but her.

She'd texted him on the way from the airstrip, telling him that they were back and that she and Richard were having a meeting with Kian and then going home to catch up on sleep. But telling him about Vrog in a text message or even a phone conversation seemed wrong.

Fates, how was she going to break it to him? Perhaps she shouldn't tell him about the attack. Or maybe she should tell Wendy first?

Or should she tell them together?

Wendy might be a calming influence on Vlad.

Or maybe the right thing to do was to tell just Vlad and let him decide if he wanted to share the news with Wendy.

What was she thinking? Of course, he would want to tell his mate.

She was overthinking it. Vlad was a resilient young man, and he could handle the news. Then again, given Richard's response, Vlad might be enraged by what Vrog had done to her. She could tone it down, but he would hear about it from Richard anyway.

When she entered the café's enclosure, Wendy waved at her. "Welcome back, Stella. How was your trip?"

"Interesting." She walked up to the counter and leaned over it to kiss the girl's cheek. "How were things here while we were gone?"

"Busy as usual. Can I get you a cappuccino?"

"Yes, thank you. I haven't had a decent cup of coffee in days."

"Awesome. I'll make myself one as well, and you'll tell me all about China. Did you enjoy your trip?"

Had she? More than anything, it had been stressful.

"It was full of surprises." Stella sat on the only barstool available and glanced around the crowded café.

Perhaps it hadn't been such a good idea to tell Vlad about Vrog in a public place. Not every member of the clan knew about the Kra-ell, and perhaps she shouldn't be telling Wendy about it where she could be overheard.

"Did you get to do any sightseeing?" Wendy put a cup of cappuccino on the counter in front of her. "Or was it all work and no play?"

"We did some touristy things, but that was only to support our cover of being parents searching for a good international school for their kids." She leaned closer to Wendy. "I'd rather we talked somewhere private. I have interesting news."

The girl's eyes sparkled with excitement. "Oh, yeah? We can talk behind the café. I just need to wait for Wonder to come back from her break."

"How long?"

She lifted a hand with splayed fingers. "She should be back in less than five minutes."

When Wonder returned, they took their cappuccinos with them to a neat little hiding spot tucked between the back wall of the café and the tall hedge forming the café's enclosure. There were no more than five feet of space between the two, but it was shaded, and there were even two bar stools to sit on.

"That's Wonder's and my makeshift break room." Wendy sat on one of the stools. "When we need a break, we hide back here."

Perching on the edge of the seat, Stella took a sip from her cappuccino. "So here is the big news." She was just going to pull the Band-Aid off. "We brought Vlad's father back with us. He's in the keep."

Wendy's arm froze with the cup midway to her mouth. "What do you mean, you brought Vlad's father? From where? How did you find him?"

Stella told her most of the story, omitting only the gruesome details of how badly Richard had beaten up Vrog. "I didn't tell Vlad yet. I'll tell him when he gets here."

"Oh, wow." Wendy finished the rest of her cappuccino in one gulp. "Is Vrog excited about meeting his son for the first time?"

"Very. He tried to play it cool, but I know he cares. Regrettably, Kian isn't allowing Vrog to have visitors yet. He wants to interrogate him first."

Wendy tilted her head. "It has just occurred to me that the names Vrog and Vlad both have four letters and start with the same one. Was that why you chose the name Vlad for your son?"

Stella nodded. "I couldn't tell Vlad about his father, but I wanted him to have something of Vrog. People thought that I was nuts, calling my child after the most psychotic immortal ever born, but it had nothing to do with the Prince of Darkness."

Wendy had heard the stories about the infamous Vlad and who he'd really been, so she wasn't shocked to hear that.

Lifting her hand, she looked at her watch. "Vlad should be here any minute now. Do you want to wait here? I can send him over."

Stella nodded. "Do you think Wonder would mind if you took a longer break? It might be a good idea for you to stick around."

"She won't mind at all."

"Here you are." Vlad strode toward them. "Wonder told me that you were both here." He kissed Wendy's cheek and then Stella's. "Is this a secret meeting or can I join?"

"It's not a secret from you." Stella got up and motioned for him to take her seat. "Actually, what Wendy and I were talking about has to do with you. There is something I need to tell you."

His smile turned into a frown. "How bad is it that you want me to sit down for it?"

"It's not bad, but it might come as a bit of a shock. Your father is in the keep."

He looked confused. "Do you mean Richard? And why is he in the keep?"

A warmth spread through her. "I'm thrilled that you think of Richard as a father figure, but I meant your biological dad. We brought Vrog back with us from China."

For a moment, Vlad just stared at her with his mouth gaping. "How did you find him? Or did he find you?"

"He found us." She repeated the story, omitting the same details she'd chosen not to tell Wendy.

Threading his fingers through his long bangs, Vlad pushed them back. "I don't know if I want to see him. It's not like he wanted me. He asked you to abort me."

"He wants to see you. I showed him your pictures, and he got very emotional when he saw you with Wendy."

Vlad arched a brow. "Are you trying to make him sound better than he is? From what you've told me about him, I don't think Vrog is the kind of guy who gets emotional."

"Oh, he is. He tries to hide it behind a veneer of machismo, but I see right through it. Vrog is a good man who's been dealt a bad hand in life. Cut him a little slack."

Vlad shook his head. "What does Richard think about all this?"

Stella sighed. "He's not happy. I think he's a little jealous, not so much about me as about you. He doesn't want Vrog to become a father figure to you."

"There is no chance of that. Richard had my back when I needed him." Vlad put a hand over his chest. "He might be too young to play the role of my father, and I don't think of him in those terms, but he's been doing his best to support me whenever I needed it. I'm not going to forget that anytime soon, or ever."

Geraldine

"A Brazilian grill." Geraldine read the sign embossed on the restaurant's window. "I've never had it. Is it the same as Argentinian?"

Cassandra pulled the door open for her. "They use a different breed of beef, but frankly, I can't taste the difference. I've never dined in this one, but the place was highly rated, so it should be good."

Nothing Cassandra had said was upsetting, not now and not on the way to the mall, but Geraldine knew her daughter well and she could detect the sharp edge in Cassandra's tone, which she'd been trying to soften without much success.

Perhaps someone at the office had upset Cassy. It wouldn't be the first time her daughter's explosive temper had gotten the better of her. But when she'd asked, Cassandra had said that she was fine and to stop bugging her.

Geraldine had no intentions of doing that. After lunch, when Cassy was more relaxed with a full belly, she might fess up to whatever was bothering her.

"Two for lunch?" The hostess pulled out two menus.

"Three," Cassandra said. "My sister is joining us."

"Maybe she's already here." Geraldine craned her neck to look over the tables. "I don't see her."

"I hope she doesn't bail on us." Cassandra followed the hostess. "I took half a day off to spend time with her, so she'd better be here."

The place didn't accept reservations, but it was conveniently located inside the galleria, where they planned to go shoe shopping after lunch.

Geraldine was looking over the menu selection when Cassandra got up and waved. "Over here."

Darlene rushed over, a big shopping bag swinging from her arm. "I'm sorry I'm late." She huffed as if she'd been running. "There is a big sale at Bloomingdales." She hugged Cassandra and then leaned over to hug Geraldine. "I got here earlier to catch the bargains before they were all gone. I found two gorgeous outfits at fifty percent off." She put the bag on the floor, pulled out a chair and plopped down.

Perhaps it was the excitement of getting new clothes, or maybe the freedom to be herself without the oppressing presence of her husband, but Darlene looked like a different woman. There was a sparkle in her eyes, and even her skin looked more radiant.

"You look lovely," Cassandra said. "Did you lose weight since the last time we met?"

Darlene beamed happily. "It's the outfit. Black is slimming." She winked at her sister.

As the waitress came to take their orders, Geraldine kept staring at her older daughter. Without the worried and pinched expression, Darlene was beautiful. It was astounding the kind of transformation a simple mood change could achieve.

Once the waitress left, Cassandra leaned back and regarded her sister from under lowered lashes. "Forgive me for saying it, but you look much happier without your hubby around. What's the deal with that?"

Geraldine nearly choked on a piece of bread. That had been the least diplomatic way to phrase the question.

Darlene winced, her good mood vanishing as if a dark fairy had waved a nasty-smelling magic wand over her face. "I can finally breathe. There is no pleasing that man, and I'm tired of trying and walking on eggshells when he's around."

"That's not a healthy way to live," Cassandra said. "Why do you put up with him?"

"Leo is not that bad." Darlene sighed. "And I'm too old to look for a new adventure. The devil you know and all that."

Cassandra cast a sidelong glance to Geraldine. "What do you think? Should Darlene stick with what she knows, or should she strive for something better?"

"The second one. Definitely."

As the waitress came back with their drinks, Darlene reached for the glass of wine with a hand that trembled slightly and drank it in one gulp.

"It's easy for you to say." She waited until the waitress left. "You are both young and beautiful. I'm an overweight, forty-nine-year-old woman who doesn't have a job or friends. If I leave Leo, I would be alone, and I'd rather suffer his mood swings than have no one to talk to. Besides, we've been together for so long that I wouldn't even know what to do with another guy."

"Were you always like that?" Cassandra leaned toward her. "Or were you a wild party girl in college?"

A small smile lifted Darlene's lips. "I wouldn't call myself wild, but I partied a little." She chuckled. "Coming to Los Angeles after growing up in Oklahoma, I had to let loose, right?"

"Of course." Geraldine sipped on her wine. "I never went to college. Was it fun?"

"For me it was. How come you didn't go?"

"Life happened." Geraldine put her glass down. "I just didn't get the chance. But maybe I still will. It's never too late to learn, right?"

"What do you do now?"

She couldn't tell Darlene that she was retired, and if she said she was quilting and selling her creations, Darlene might ask her where and how, and she wouldn't have an answer for that. What else could she claim to do?

"Geraldine works for me," Cassandra said. "She's my assistant."

That was a quick save.

The answer seemed to satisfy Darlene, and what was even better, it had shifted her focus to Cassandra. "You work for Fifty Shades of Beauty, right?"

"I'm their marketing director."

"That's an impressive job for a woman as young as you."

"I'm not that young." Cassandra lifted her wine glass. "I'm thirty-four."

Darlene scrunched her nose. "You don't look it."

"You don't look forty-nine either," Cassandra returned the compliment.

"Thank you." Darlene tucked a strand of hair behind her ear. "Even if it's not true, it's nice of you to say."

As the waitress put the plate in front of her, Geraldine leaned back. "That smells delicious, but how am I going to eat ribs smothered in barbecue sauce without getting it on my blouse?"

"Like this." Cassandra lifted a napkin and tucked it in her décolletage. "Dig in, ladies, and forget about all those good manners. Ribs are meant to be eaten with hands." She grabbed a rib from both sides and bit down.

"Well, when in Rome..." Darlene tucked a napkin the same way Cassandra had and lifted the rib. "*Bon appétit*, my lovely cousins."

Cassandra

After Cassandra had demolished the two ribs that came with her combo plate, she attacked the steak on her platter with an unprecedented enthusiasm, imagining that it was Leo she was cutting into little pieces.

Damn, she needed to calm down or things would start blowing up.

With Sylvia's help, Cassandra had been practicing controlling her power, and she was getting better at focusing it, using it like a well-honed weapon. But sometimes it still boiled over.

Hopefully, concentrating on the food she was consuming would distract her enough to diffuse the buildup.

How the hell was she going to tell Darlene what her husband had done?

And what if Darlene knew about that and hadn't warned Roni? Or worse, what if she was just as guilty as Leo?

Selling out her son because of greed or fear or a combination of both?

Regrettably, neither she nor Geraldine could thrall the truth out of Darlene, but once Cassandra told her sister what Leo had done, her response should be telling. Would Darlene look shocked? Angry? Or guilty?

The problem was that Cassandra couldn't say anything without implicating Andrew. Onegus had warned her against sharing what they'd learned from him.

Geraldine would have been too upset to keep quiet, or she might have forgotten why she shouldn't tell Darlene about Leo's treachery.

Perhaps the best way was to approach the subject from another angle, to find out whether Roni's father was a sociopath who didn't care for his son, or whether he resented Roni because he wasn't really his.

Putting down her fork and knife, Cassandra lifted a corner of the napkin she'd tucked into the neckline of her blouse. "What's the deal with Leo wanting to see Roni's DNA test? Does he suspect that Roni is not his?"

Darlene nearly choked on a piece of shrimp. Going red in the cheeks, she coughed and reached for her glass of water.

Cassandra didn't relent, waiting patiently for her sister to regain her composure while not taking her eyes off her.

"You're awfully blunt, Cassandra."

"I know. But I'm not going to apologize for it. We are your family, Darlene, and if you need to get something off your chest, we are here for you, and we are never going to betray your trust. And if you want to leave Leo, Geraldine and I are also going to help you in any way we can, which is quite a lot. You are not going to be alone. I can promise you that."

Darlene regarded her with wide eyes and a slightly gaping mouth. "Why are you pushing so hard for me to divorce Leo? Did my father say anything to you about him?"

Geraldine put a hand on Cassandra's arm. "Stop pestering your cousin. Not everyone is as assertive and as independent as you."

Cassandra let out a breath. "You are right." She looked at Darlene. "I'm sorry. It's just that Leo got on my nerves the last time we met. But then I don't have to like your husband, right? It's enough that I like you and your son. I even like your father, and I didn't expect that after what you told us about him."

"I even liked Niki," Geraldine said. "I don't know why you don't like her."

Darlene grimaced. "She's a loser who found herself a sugar daddy. But whatever. If he's happy with her, who am I to object."

"He seemed contented," Geraldine said. "He's still hurting, though. He loved your mother very much."

As a tear slid down Darlene's cheek, she wiped it away angrily. "I don't know why I still get upset when I talk about it. I guess one never gets over the death of their mother, no matter how many years have passed, or how old they are." Darlene smiled apologetically through her teary eyes. "I'm not telling you anything you don't know, though. You lost your mother as well."

Under the table, Cassandra gripped Geraldine's hand for support. "We might have an uncle who's still alive," she told Darlene, to cheer her up.

"We do?"

As Cassandra and Geraldine took turns weaving the story about the uncle who was meeting with Sabina in secret, Darlene listened intently. When they got to the part about the forensic artist drawing his picture from her father's memory, her eyes widened.

"Do you have it?" Darlene asked.

"I do." Cassandra pulled her phone out of her purse and scrolled through her photos. "He looks a lot like Geraldine, so I assume he also looks a lot like Sabina and our mother." She handed Darlene the phone.

The truth was that the resemblance was superficial, but she wanted to plant the suggestion in Darlene's mind.

"He's gorgeous." Darlene stared at the picture. "Am I the only ugly duckling of the family?" She handed the phone back to Cassandra. "Our mothers were beautiful, you two are stunning, our uncle looked like he belonged on the cover of a men's fashion magazine, and I'm just a plain Jane."

"You are not plain." Geraldine reached for her hand. "You are beautiful. When you smile, you light up the room. You just don't smile enough."

Vrog

"I can eat regular food." Vrog took the cup of blood the guard handed him. "And by that I mean meat that is not overcooked." He removed the lid and took a sniff. The blood was fresh. "But thank you. I'm not averse to blood either."

The guy let out a relieved breath. "I would gladly skip the butcher shop and get you hamburgers from now on."

"Steaks would be better, but sure. Hamburgers are fine."

To his great surprise, Vrog was being treated like a visiting dignitary. The apartment they'd put him in was much fancier than the one he had in the school compound, and the guards assigned to him served him like a couple of fussy butlers, bringing him a fresh change of clothes and making sure that he approved of their selection. They'd also gotten raw meat and blood for him, which they believed was what he preferred to eat.

If that was how they treated their enemies, he wondered how they treated their friends.

It could all have been an act, but why go to so much effort to convince him that they were the good guys?

He had nothing to give them. Perhaps they thought that he did?

Or maybe Stella hadn't lied about her leader being a kind female, and maybe she also hadn't lied about anything else.

Would she come to visit him?

Richard would probably try to prevent her from doing so, and if he allowed it, he would most likely tag along.

Sometime during the flight, Stella had told Vrog that they weren't married, but that they were mated, which supposedly was a bigger deal than human marriage. According to her, the bond between immortal mates was so strong that no official ceremony was needed to ensure their eternal commitment to each other.

That was taking human attitudes toward sex and reproduction to a whole new level, and Vrog wondered whether it was the result of a belief system or something biological that was unique to this particular breed of long-lived people.

Stella had kept referring to herself and the others as immortals, though, not long-lived, so perhaps their lifespans were even longer than that of the Kra-ell.

He'd tried to ask the guards about it, but they'd refused to answer, saying that he would need to save his questions for the big boss's visit.

The time of that visit was approaching fast, and with it Vrog's apprehension.

What did they want with him? Why did they bring him here?

He knew that he was somewhere in Southern California, but not precisely where. As soon as he'd been seated in the bus that had picked them up from the airstrip, Arwel, the team's leader, apologized and then tranquilized him once again.

The next time Vrog opened his eyes, he found himself in this lavish underground apartment, with a metal cuff around each of his wrists and two new guards who explained what the cuff was for.

They contained trackers and were impossible to remove, but that wasn't the only thing they did. They also contained explosives that would blow his wrists up if he crossed the threshold of his apartment or tried anything stupid.

His guards could activate the explosives remotely.

But that hadn't been the most shocking thing Vrog had learned. When he'd asked if the cuffs could malfunction and blow his wrists up for no reason, the guard named Vernon told him that it wasn't likely, but even if it happened, it would be painful, but he shouldn't worry because he could regrow new hands.

Apparently, Stella's people could regrow limbs. The Kraell healed much faster than humans, but Vrog didn't know whether they could do that. He had never lost a limb, and as far as he knew, neither had any of the purebloods or the hybrids.

The lack of information about their origins had been one of the major reasons for the hybrids' discontent. It hadn't been as critical as being denied access to pureblooded females and the chance of producing long-lived offspring, or any for that matter. They weren't allowed to father children with humans either. But it had been one more way the purebloods lorded over them and reminded them of their lowly status.

Vrog didn't even know how long he was expected to live. A few centuries? A thousand years? Perhaps he was immortal like Stella but didn't know that?

When the door mechanism activated with a whizzing sound, Vrog pushed to his feet and mentally readied himself for the clan leader's visit.

He would show her the proper respect, but if she expected him to grovel at her feet, she would be disappointed. He'd obeyed Jade, but he hadn't groveled to her, and he wouldn't grovel to Stella's leader either.

Kian

"It will only take a moment," Vernon said as he opened the door to Vrog's cell.

The Guardian insisted on following protocol and securing the prisoner before letting Kian and Turner walk inside.

It wasn't necessary because he had Anandur and Brundar with him and also because Vrog wasn't a threat. For some reason, Kian wasn't as worried about Vrog stepping out of line as he'd been about Emmett when they'd first brought him to the dungeon.

From what he'd heard so far about the guy, Vrog didn't seem dangerous. Richard, who wasn't a Guardian and had gotten only minimal combat training, had managed to overpower him with relative ease.

On the other hand, Kian might have been underestimating Richard, and Vrog could be as dangerous as he'd believed Emmett to be at the time.

Emmett had grown on him, though. The guy was selfish and opportunistic, but he also had redeeming qualities. He genuinely believed that he could help people, especially those who had trouble fitting into mainstream society, and it wasn't total crap. Some people didn't do well in one-on-one relationships or were just too awkward to secure a partner, and for those, Safe Haven's free-love philosophy was a good match. It was a place they could call home, a community of like-minded people who accepted them for who they were.

There was something to be said for that.

There had also been some lines that Emmett hadn't allowed himself to cross, which meant that most of what he had done couldn't be regarded as criminal activity, or at least no more criminal than what clan males did to hide their venomous bites.

The problem was that Kian still wasn't a hundred percent sure that Emmett hadn't used compulsion and drugs to seduce his partners. The guy claimed that he'd never needed to resort to unsavory methods to secure bed partners, and that he'd used those methods only to hide who he was.

Margaret had confirmed his claims, but she might have been protecting him. The guy had taken her in when she'd had nowhere else to go, and in his own twisted way, he'd protected her from her deranged husband.

She probably felt indebted to him.

When Alec stepped out and gave them the all-clear sign, Kian motioned for Turner to go ahead. "After you."

Holding his Mulberry black leather briefcase in one hand and his thermos in the other, Turner followed the two Guardians into the dungeon apartment.

Kian entered last. "Good afternoon, Vrog." He walked up to the guy and offered him his hand.

"Good afternoon." The Kra-ell gave him a tight smile and looked at the door as if he was expecting another person to come in.

"Please, sit down." Kian motioned to the couch.

Vrog glanced at the door again. "She isn't coming?"

"Who? Stella?" Kian sat in the armchair closest to the door.

Gingerly, the guy lowered himself to the couch. "Your leader. I thought the meeting was with her."

Did he mean Annani? Why would he expect her to come?

"What gave you that impression?" Turner asked.

Vrog shifted his eyes to Alec and Vernon, who were sitting at the small dining table together with the brothers. "They said that I would be visited by the big boss. I assumed they meant your clan's leader."

Understanding dawning, Kian smiled. "The head of our clan is my mother, but she leaves the day-to-day management to my sister and me."

He doubted anyone had told Vrog about Annani being a goddess, but given the way Vrog's society was structured, it was natural for him to assume that the big boss was a female.

In a way, it was refreshing. Human society was still largely patriarchal, and when someone said 'boss' and didn't clarify by saying 'lady boss,' people usually expected a man.

"I see." Vrog still looked as if someone had pulled the rug from under his feet. "Stella told me that the head of your clan was a kind female."

"My mother is indeed very kind, and so is my sister." Kian crossed his legs at the ankles. "I'm not as nice, but I'm a reasonable male. If you cooperate, you'll find me a very generous host. But if you don't, you'll see a side of me that you won't like."

It was a very vague threat, but Kian didn't want to scare Vrog. After all, the guy was Vlad's father, and Stella insisted that he was a good male despite his attack on her.

"What do you want with me?" Vrog asked.

"We just want information. You had time to investigate the crime scene so to speak, and we want to know what you found out."

"Why?"

Richard had been right. The guy was stubborn and suspicious.

"Let's start with introductions. My name is Kian, and this is my advisor, Victor Turner."

As Vrog dipped his head, Turner opened his briefcase and pulled out a yellow pad and a pen. "If you don't mind, Kian, I would like to ask Vrog a few questions first."

"Go ahead."

Turner clicked his pen open. "Do you know about any Kra-ell communities outside of yours?"

Vrog frowned. "There are no other tribes."

"You mean to say that you don't know of any other Kra-ell. You might not have been told."

Vrog cast Kian a questioning look. "Do you know of any?"

"We know even less than you do," Kian admitted. "But our leading theory is that your compound was sacked by a different group of Kra-ell. We are basing this assumption on what Mey heard and saw in the echoes."

Vrog lifted his hand and pinched his temples between his forefinger and thumb. "The hybrids weren't told much by the purebloods. I thought that the precautions they were taking were meant to defend against discovery by humans, but perhaps they feared their own people."

Kian nodded. "Emmett said the same thing."

"Stella told me about the Kra-ell hybrid who joined your community. I would like to meet him. Perhaps we could compare notes."

"That can be arranged at a later time," Turner said. "I understand that you believe only the pureblooded males were killed and the females were taken. Did you find their bodies when you returned?"

Shaking his head, Vrog took in a deep breath. "The fire destroyed the evidence. All I found were their rings." He lifted his hand. "This was my father's." He took off the dark stone circle and held it up between his thumb and forefinger. "Each of the purebloded males had one, engraved with their names and their rank. I found all twenty-one of them. The purebloded females had different-colored rings, a dark shade of green instead of blue, and I found none of those. The hybrid males and females didn't get rings, but given what happened to the purebloods, the hybrid males were most likely killed as well, and the hybrid females were taken."

"Who did you think did that?" Turner asked.

"I didn't know what to think, but Stella was a prime suspect."

"Why did you think that she had anything to do with that when you never told her the location of your tribe?"

"I assumed she or her people followed me and found the businesses I was overseeing for Jade. I thought that they might have found some correspondence, or that they followed the money trail and that's how they found my tribe."

"Makes sense," Kian admitted. "But it wasn't us. The way I see it, those who did that are a threat to us as much as they are to you. They might be Kra-ell, but that doesn't make them your friends. They are still your enemy. They are our enemy as well, or at least a threat that we need to protect ourselves from."

Vrog

Vrog had often wondered whether there were more Kra-ell out there. When he asked his father, the answer he'd gotten had been cryptic.

"We are all that's left of our people, at least in this corner of the universe," his father had said. "I don't know about other worlds. There might be more out there."

There had been pain in his father's eyes when he said it, and when Vrog opened his mouth to ask more questions, his father stopped him by lifting his hand. "That is all I'm going to say. Don't ask me any more questions."

At the time, Vrog had had a feeling that his father had already said more than he'd been allowed to. Out of all the purebloaded males, his father had been the least dismissive of his hybrid offspring, but the rare displays of affection he'd shown Vrog had always been done in private where no one could see them.

Jade would have frowned upon that, would have called it coddling, and would have made it her mission to make Vrog's life miserable. The hybrids needed to know their place, which was serving their superior masters.

Not that the few pureblooded children had it any easier. They trained twice as hard as the hybrids to satisfy Jade and their mothers' demands.

There had been no room for weaklings in the Kra-ell society.

"There is one more option that we need to consider," Victor Turner said. "Perhaps the pureblooded males rebelled against your leader, and they tossed the rings aside as a symbolic gesture."

Vrog shook his head. "That's not possible. They were bound by oath and honor to protect Jade, the other pureblooded females, and the children." When the guy looked doubtful, Vrog added. "The Kra-ell take their vows very seriously. Without his honor, a male is no better than an animal, and to break a vow is nearly the most dishonorable act possible, second only to killing a female."

"What about the hybrid males?" Kian asked. "Could they have rebelled? Weren't they also bound to your leader by oaths of loyalty?"

"They were bound by the same vows." Vrog shifted his gaze from Kian to the four guards sitting at the dining table and listening to every word. "But as hybrids, perhaps honor was not as essential to the self-perception of some of them. It wasn't such an integral part of who they were." He looked down at the cuffs on his wrists. "We were regarded as second-tier members of the tribe, and some of the purebloods treated us with derision."

Victor Turner leaned forward and braced his elbows on his thighs. "So do you agree that it was possible for the hybrids to rebel?"

Vrog nodded. "Personally, I would have never done that. I took my vows seriously. But perhaps the others didn't feel the same way."

Kian pinned him with his intense gaze. "Did you keep your vows out of loyalty or out of fear?"

"Both," Vrog admitted. "Not fear for myself, but for those I loved. They would have been punished by The Mother of All Life for my crime."

"Do you still believe that?" Turner asked softly.

Vrog swallowed and then nodded. "Mey said that the humans were spared, so my mother might still be alive. I also have a son who I need to protect."

Kian let out a sigh. "It's just superstition, Vrog. You seem like an intelligent guy. Why would you believe in such utter nonsense?"

"Because the stakes are too high to risk testing the belief."

"I understand that," Kian said. "But if another hybrid broke his vows and nothing happened to his loved ones, would that shake your belief?"

"Maybe."

"The other Kra-ell hybrid who joined our clan had left your tribe, which I understand meant breaking his vow. Did his loved ones suffer as a consequence?"

"I wouldn't know," Vrog said. "No one ever spoke of a hybrid who deserted. Perhaps he was excommunicated and just claims to have left of his own accord."

"Have you heard of such a hybrid?" Turner asked.

"I have not," Vrog admitted. "But Jade threatened it often enough. That was why I at first thought that they left without me. I thought that Jade had somehow learned about Stella and the baby I put in her womb, and my punishment was excommunication." He rubbed a hand over the back of his neck. "Although I should have known better. Jade would have made a spectacle out of it. She wouldn't have missed an opportunity to make an example out of me."

Kian smiled. "And yet, even though you broke your oath, none of your loved ones suffered for it."

Vrog winced. "I thought that I found a loophole, but shortly after that my entire tribe vanished. Maybe that was my punishment."

Kian regarded him with pity in his eyes. "It was just a coincidence. You need to talk to Emmett and get his take on this. I'm sure he had loved ones who he cared about when he left your tribe."

"Do you know how old he is?" Vrog asked.

"Over seventy. Why?"

"And when did he leave?"

"Thirty-some years ago."

"If his mother was no longer alive and his father was one of the meaner purebloods, he might not have cared who suffered because of his actions."

"Gentlemen." Victor Turner lifted his hand. "Arguing about religion is futile. Beliefs are not rational, and they cannot be changed with rational arguments. We need to concentrate on the investigation. What else did you find in the rubble?"

As Vrog listed all the things he had found and then all the important things that had been missing, like money in the tribe's bank accounts, Victor Turner wrote everything down on his yellow pad.

"I assume that you kept the files, correct?"

Vrog nodded.

"I would like to take a look," Turner said. "Maybe we will find clues that you missed. Were the files written in Chinese or in the Kra-ell language?"

"Both."

The guy turned to Kian. "We will need Emmett's help going over those."

Vrog lifted his hand. "I didn't agree to hand them over yet. What are you looking for?"

"Other Kra-ell," Kian said without hesitation. "The bastards who killed your males and took your females." His blue eyes blazed with inner fire. "Don't you want to find them and avenge your people?"

"I do."

"Then work with us, not against us."

"When can I see my son?"

Kian smiled. "When you tell us where we can find those damn files."

Vrog crossed his arms over his chest. "You claim to be on the same side as I am, and yet you treat me as a prisoner. If you want me to hand the files over, you will let me see my son first."

For a long moment, the two of them played chicken, staring each other down and waiting to see who would blink first.

"You can see your son whenever you want," Victor Turner said. "But if you renege on your promise, it will be a long time before you see him again."

"I can live with that." Vrog released Kian's gaze. "When can I see Vlad and Stella?"

Kian leveled his eyes at him. "You know that she's mated, right?"

"I'm not interested in her that way. I just want to hear more about Vlad growing up. She promised to show me more pictures of him as a baby and a little boy."

Kian's eyes softened. "I'll tell Stella that she can see you whenever she wants, but it's up to her and Vlad to actually show up."

Vrog nodded. "Are you going to send someone to collect the files from China?"

"Not yet." The guy rose to his feet. "It's not urgent. These fuckers murdered your people twenty-two years ago. Another week or two will not make any difference."

That was a strange reversal.

A moment ago, the guy wanted those files badly enough to deny him seeing his son, and now he was in no hurry?

"Why the change of heart?" he asked.

Kian shrugged. "Since you don't know much, Mey needs to go back and listen to more echoes, but the team needs to rest for a few days. When they are ready to go, I'll have you call the principal and ask him to make the files and the facility available to my team."

"Which brings the next issue I wanted to discuss." Turner put the yellow pad in his briefcase. "You need to send an email to your principal, explaining why you had to leave suddenly." The blond pushed to his feet. "We wouldn't want the esteemed Doctor Wang to think that you met an untimely demise." The guy made a step toward the door, stopped and turned around. "By the way. How did you explain your youthful looks?"

"Good genetics and good nutrition." Vrog smoothed a hand over his cropped hair. "The age listed on my passport is my true age. People just assume that I'm lucky."

Geraldine

"Are you coming in?" Geraldine asked as Cassandra stopped in front of their house.

Cassandra glanced at Shai's car that was parked in the driveway. "I'd better go home."

It still hurt a little to hear her daughter refer to Onegus's place as her home. Cassy still had a closet full of clothes in the house, and she hadn't taken the quilt hanging in her bedroom to her and Onegus's place yet, but it was quite obvious that it was only a matter of time before she loaded all her belongings into her car and made the move final.

Geraldine offered Cassandra a tentative smile. "Help me at least get the shopping bags inside?"

Letting out an exasperated breath, her daughter turned the engine off. "You don't need my help to carry four bags, but fine. If it's that important to you, I can stay for a cup of coffee."

Geraldine gave her a bright smile. "Wonderful. You hardly ever come by the house anymore. I feel like you no longer live here." She stepped out of the car and closed the passenger door behind her.

"Because I don't." Cassandra opened the trunk and pulled out Geraldine's purchases.

Ouch.

Cassy never beat around the bush, which on the one hand was a blessing because Geraldine never had to wonder what she was really feeling, but on the other hand, her bluntness was a little abrasive, alienating some people.

But her directness didn't mean that she shared everything with her mother, and today had been a perfect example of that. Her angry power had been simmering during the entire afternoon and evening, but she'd refused to tell Geraldine what or who had gotten under her skin.

"Your stuff is still here," Geraldine murmured as they headed toward the front door.

"I know." Cassandra followed her inside. "We still share the house with Onegus's roommate, and I don't want to have to move everything twice. I'll do that once we get our own place." She put the bags by the door.

"When is that?" Geraldine headed to the kitchen.

Shai was probably upstairs, taking a shower.

Cassandra pulled out a chair next to the breakfast table and sat down. "As soon as I give it the green light. I should have done it already."

"Why haven't you?" Geraldine loaded the coffeemaker.

"I didn't know how you'd take it."

She rolled her eyes. "I don't need to be coddled, Cassandra. I'm not as fragile as I seem."

A door opened on the second floor, and a moment later Shai's light footfalls sounded on the stairs.

"Hi." He walked into the kitchen and pulled her into his arms and kissed her cheek. "Did you two have fun today?"

"I did." She glanced at her daughter. "But Cassandra was moody the entire time and refused to say why."

Shai threw her a glance. "Is it because of what Andrew found out?"

She arched a brow. "You heard?"

"Of course." He let go of Geraldine. "Being Kian's assistant there isn't much I don't hear." He pulled out a chair and sat down.

Geraldine had had enough. "What are you two talking about?"

"You didn't tell her?" Shai asked Cassandra.

"I didn't want to upset her."

Geraldine pulled out a chair next to Shai. "You'd better start talking and don't leave out any details."

Shai took her hand and gave it a light squeeze. "Leo was the one who told the agents about Roni. That was why they were snooping around Nathalie's café. Turns out, there is a hefty reward for anyone supplying information leading to Roni's capture."

"What a jerk." Geraldine pinned Cassandra with a hard look. "Why didn't you say anything about it to Darlene?"

"Because telling her about it would have meant revealing how I knew, and that would have cast suspicion on Andrew. Besides, I wasn't sure that she didn't know about it, and frankly, I was too much of a chicken to find out. If she knew and didn't warn Roni, I want nothing more to do with her. And if she knew and encouraged Leo to go for the prize money, I shouldn't be around her at all, or I might do something I'll regret."

"Fair enough." Geraldine rose to her feet. "But you should have told me."

"I was afraid to do that before we met her and then have you blurt something out."

Geraldine hated when Cassy treated her like a child, but it wasn't entirely unwarranted. With her memory issues, it was sometimes better not to tell her things that needed to remain a secret.

"We need to arrange another meeting with Darlene." Geraldine poured coffee into three cups. "But this time it will be just Shai and me." She brought them to the table.

"I'll thrall the truth out of her." Shai got up and brought the cream and sugar. "Did she act guilty today?"

"Not at all." Geraldine dropped a sugar cube into her coffee. "In fact, she was in an exceptionally good mood, and that was even before we told her about Orion."

Shai froze. "You did what?"

"Relax." Cassandra chuckled. "We told her the same story we told Rudolf. She was excited about having an uncle who might still be alive."

Shai let out a breath and then eyed Geraldine from under lowered lashes. "Did you do that on purpose?"

She cast him a grin. "It was payback for the two of you keeping me out of the loop as if I was a child."

"It wasn't my fault." Shai lifted his coffee cup. "I thought that Cassandra told you."

"I bet Roni is furious," Geraldine said. "What does he want to do?"

"I don't know." Shai put his cup down. "But whatever it is, Roni has Kian's full support and Andrew's standing offer to exact revenge on his behalf."

Shai

It started raining when Geraldine walked Cassandra to the front door. "Drive carefully."

"I will." Cassandra kissed her cheek and then leaned over to peck Shai on his. "Goodnight, you two."

"Goodnight, sweetheart."

As Geraldine closed the door, Shai lifted the shopping bags Cassandra had left on the floor. "Ready for bed?"

She gave him a seductive smile. "It has been a long day."

It was only ten at night, but he wanted her, and with the cameras watching them from nearly every corner, the bedroom was the only place they felt free to play.

It was strange to live in a house that was monitored twenty-four-seven. Shai felt like he was on one of those reality shows, and given Geraldine's reserved behavior throughout the evening, she felt the same. They were both aware that they were being watched and acted accordingly—their vocabulary a little too formal, their laughter a little subdued, and their usual sexual banter reduced to what was accepted in polite company.

When he closed the bedroom door behind them, Geraldine let out a breath and walked over to the balcony doors. "I love the smell of rain." She opened them and walked outside.

"You'll get wet." Shai dropped her shopping bags on the floor and walked up behind her. Wrapping his arms around her middle, he dipped his head to kiss the spot where her neck met her shoulder.

"It's only drizzle." Leaning against his chest, she let her head drop back.

As if to prove her wrong, a faraway lighting streak was followed by a loud boom. It elicited a soft gasp from her. "That was scary."

"It seems that the drizzle is about to become a deluge." Shai brushed a finger over her soft cheek. "Let's get inside."

Turning in his arms, she lifted on her toes and kissed one corner of his mouth, then the other, her lips soft and teasing.

He tightened his arms around her, carried her inside, and closed the balcony door with his foot. "We haven't made love in the rain yet."

She laughed. "We can go back out and make love on the balcony. With the rain, the neighbors won't be outside to see us."

"Did you forget about the camera? William's guys installed one out there as well." He sat on the bed with her in his lap. "This is our only safe space. Well, this and the bathroom, the closet, and Cassandra's old room."

She pouted. "I can put a Band-Aid over the camera."

"You're creative, I'll give you that, but I'm not giving anyone a show, not even the night owls."

Loosening a disappointed sigh, she cuddled closer and lifted her lips to his. "Kiss me."

He slanted his mouth over hers, and with lazy strokes teased her until her hand closed over the nape of his neck, and she deepened the kiss.

When long minutes later she came up for air, Geraldine regarded him with a seductive smirk and hooded eyes. "Since you are such a dork, we can make love in the shower and pretend that we are standing in the rain."

"A dork, eh?" He laid her down on the bed and straddled her hips. "Let's see what name you will call me once I get you naked." He started on the row of annoyingly small buttons holding her blouse together.

In response, she gave him a lazy smile, her hands roaming over the sides of his arms as he unbuttoned her blouse and pushed the two halves aside, exposing a sexy, red bra. "Is this new?" He flicked the front clasp open.

"Do you like it?" she purred.

"I love it." He parted the cups and dipped his head to kiss one stiff nipple. "But I love naked skin more." He kissed the other.

Her fingers threading into his hair, she moaned softly. "Wait until you see the panties."

The woman was such a tease, but she'd gotten his attention and then some. His imagination going wild with possibilities, he lowered the zipper on her tight skirt and gently pulled it down her hips, exposing the aforementioned matching panties.

"You're killing me." He ran his finger down the center where the lace gave way to a sheer panel that covered nothing.

Finding the fabric soaked through, he debated whether to eat her with the hot panties on or without.

She lifted a hand to his chest, her fingers tugging on his T-shirt. "Take it off first."

He was naked in two seconds flat, flinging away his clothes along with the last of hers, including that scrap of red lace.

When he prowled on top of her, she palmed his erection, running her soft palm up and down in lazy strokes that were more of a hello than a tease.

Shai kissed her again, letting her stroke him for as long as he could stand it without taking over.

"I love you," she murmured against his lips, her hand abandoning his shaft so she could wrap her arms around his torso.

He lifted on his forearms and looked down at her beautiful face. "Always and forever."

Bond or no bond, she was his mate, and he was going to love her to the end of their days, whenever that might be.

Smiling, she arched in a silent demand, her soft petals perfectly aligned with his hardness.

It would have been so easy to slam home into that welcoming heat, but the unique sweet scent of her made his mouth water.

"I need to taste you."

"Okay," she breathed. "I will never say no to such an offer."

"Good." He pulled away and ran a hand down her belly to that throbbing heat between her thighs. "This is mine." He cupped her center.

She didn't argue as he slid down her body and spread her legs, baring her for him.

His woman wasn't bashful, and as he flicked his tongue over that most sensitive spot on her body, she groaned and arched up. "Prove it."

Stifling a laugh, he thrust his tongue into her once, twice, and then looked at her from between her spread thighs. "You're on, love."

Geraldine

As Shai tasted and teased, his strokes featherlight, his kisses soft and sweet, Geraldine's hips churned until he clamped his hands on her bottom and kept her anchored to the bed.

When she mewled and pleaded for more, the evil male laughed against her petals.

Leaning up, she looked at his blond head between her spread thighs, his wicked tongue darting in and out of her.

Oh, goodness. It was too much.

"Please, Shai, please…"

He lifted his glowing eyes to her, lust and mischief dancing in their depths. "Please what?"

"I need you inside me."

"Patience, my love." He slid a finger into her, pulling a ragged groan from her throat.

It was so lewd to see that digit disappear between her folds, making a wet sound as it pumped in and out of her, but it only made her hungrier, needier. When he flicked his talented tongue over her sensitive nubbin, she cried out his name, but the edge still eluded her.

He added another finger, but even that wasn't enough.

Tonight, Geraldine needed the real thing.

She needed his magnificent erection filling her, the weight of his slim body pressing her into the mattress, and his glowing eyes gazing at her with a mixture of hunger and love.

"Shai," she whimpered. "I need you."

Pressing one last soft kiss to her petals, he rose over her and looked into her eyes. "I need you too." He braced a hand on the pillow beside her head, dipped his head, and kissed her.

Tasting herself on his tongue was so wickedly erotic, bringing her closer to the cliff's edge she'd been hovering over. And then he was nudging her entrance, the heat of him amplifying her own.

Geraldine arched up, getting the tip inside of her, but even though Shai was trembling with restraint, he pushed inside of her slowly, gently.

By now they had made love countless times, and yet, even when he was wild for her and more male animal than man, he was always careful, always considerate, showing his love for her with every action, every move.

They both groaned when he completed their joining. She lifted her hands to his face and cupped his cheeks, pulling him down for another kiss and pouring all of her feelings for him into it—the love, the gratitude.

The tenderness was precious, but the gnawing need for more had her end the kiss, dig her fingers into his back, and push her heels into his muscular backside.

Shai went wild, his thrusts going deeper, faster, his back and arm muscles bunching, his forehead beading with sweat. And as his shafting became frenzied, she turned her head, exposing her neck to him.

Growling, he licked the spot in the crook of her neck, and as he hissed, she climaxed even before his razor-sharp fangs pierced her skin.

She knew the venom would soon send her soaring to the clouds, but she forced herself to hang on long enough to feel Shai's own release barrel through him, savoring the feeling of him filling her with his essence.

Fates willing, one day, perhaps even tonight, their lovemaking would result in conception, gifting Cassandra, Darlene, and Rhett with a little brother or sister.

Kian

Shai closed his laptop and pushed to his feet. "Anything else, boss?"

Kian nodded. "Call Eleanor and ask her to come to my office."

"What time?"

"At her earliest convenience. I want to discuss Safe Haven with her."

Shai raised a brow. "Did you make up your mind about buying the place?"

"I want to inspect it first and go over the financials. I want to see how much it's bringing in before making an offer. I have no experience with that sort of business, and it would be foolish of me to buy a cat in a bag just because it seems like a good idea." Kian leaned back. "Perhaps we should lease it instead of buying it outright."

"Right." Shai nodded. "I will never argue with your business instincts. When do you want to go?"

"The sooner the better. We can fly over on Monday two weeks from now and come back the following day. I want to stay the night and experience the place as a guest. Besides, you and I probably will need more than one day to go over the financials."

Normally, Kian didn't need Shai to accompany him on business trips, but this time he wanted the guy's help with sorting through the financial information in a speedy manner. Besides, Shai's incredible eidetic memory would come in handy, noting details that Kian might gloss over or forget.

His assistant looked surprised. "I assume that you want to take Syssi and Allegra with you."

"Of course."

"Did you discuss it with Syssi?"

"Not yet, but I'm sure she'll want to come."

Syssi loved being a mother, but being cooped up at the house for so long was getting to her. She'd even mentioned going back to work and arranging for a babysitter at the university to watch over Allegra. He wasn't enthusiastic about the idea of his daughter leaving the village, where she was the safest, especially before transitioning into immortality, but if that was what Syssi wanted, he wasn't going to say no.

"Can I bring Geraldine along?" Shai asked.

"Of course. The big jet is back from China, so we have plenty of seats, and Syssi would love Geraldine's company." Kian rapped his fingers on the top of his desk. "Naturally, I need Emmett to come with me, which means that Eleanor might be joining us provided that Roberts doesn't die by then. If he does, she will be in West Virginia. That still leaves plenty of seats in the jet. Perhaps I should ask Amanda and Dalhu if they want to come along. We can treat it as a mini-vacation."

Shai shook his head. "I don't think Safe Haven provides the kind of accommodations Amanda will find suitable. From what I've heard, the guest rooms are quite spartan."

Kian hadn't considered that. "Are there any fine hotels in the area?"

Shai shook his head again. "It's in the middle of nowhere, which is why Safe Haven is suitable for our needs."

"Right. I don't mind roughing it out for one night, but Syssi might not be comfortable there with the baby. I'll check with her."

"And I'll check with Geraldine. I'll also call Safe Haven to make sure that they have rooms for us. They might be full."

"What about Emmett's place? Peter said that the bunker under the cottage had several bedrooms."

Shai winced. "They might not be appropriate. From the way Eleanor and Peter described the bunker, it sounded like a shag pad. Perhaps you should ask

Emmett if the rooms are suitable for Syssi's sensibilities."

"I'll do that."

As his assistant walked out of the office and closed the door behind him, Kian turned his swivel chair around to face the window and put his feet up on its low sill.

He'd delayed making a decision about Safe Haven until the Kra-ell investigative team reported their findings. Now that he had their report and also Vrog's testimony, it was time to get off the fence and make a decision.

The problem was that he still wasn't a hundred percent sure that the Kra-ell's leader hadn't gotten Emmett's email, informing her of the existence of immortals other than the Kra-ell, and offering her Peter as an inducer for their Dormants.

Emmett hadn't told her about Safe Haven, so as long as she and the other Kra-ell didn't know about the clan, it should be fine.

Kian was no longer wary about working with Emmett, but despite what the team had reported, he was still worried about the Kra-ell.

All they had was circumstantial evidence, mostly supplied by Vrog but given credence by what Mey had heard in the echoes.

Vrog believed that the males were dead because he'd found their rings, and he believed that the females had been taken because he hadn't found theirs.

That was not conclusive evidence.

The males might have been forced to remove the rings by the attacking force. Or they might have been punished by Jade and told to discard them as a form of humiliation. They could have also done so as a protest. The two pieces of evidence supporting Vrog's conclusions were the contents of the safes that had been left behind, and what Mey had heard from the echoes left in the walls.

Then there were the emptied bank accounts and the abandoned tribe's businesses that could also support Vrog's conclusions but in a more circumstantial way.

Kian needed to get his hands on those files Vrog had mentioned and have them translated. A lot could be gleaned about a society from examining their financial ledgers—everything from what they'd spent their money on to how much they'd invested in those businesses that they'd left behind, and how much they'd kept in liquid assets.

Perhaps it had made sense for the Kra-ell to just walk away from those businesses. They might have been losing money, and abandoning them had been done to avoid paying their debts.

Hopefully, he would find some clues in those files, and the rest was up to Mey. She would need to go in again, perhaps with Vrog this time, so she would have free access to the entire school.

Kian had no real reason to keep holding the guy in the dungeon. It seemed that Vrog hadn't been doing anything unsavory with his thralling powers, however weak or strong they were, and he'd laid low for the past couple of decades, pretending to be human.

If the guy wanted to wait around for his mistress to return, it was his prerogative. Naturally, Kian would keep an eye on him in some fashion, probably with advanced surveillance gadgets rather than boots on the ground.

There was no reason to waste resources on the guy either, or so he hoped. Kian was a good judge of character, but no one was infallible, and Vrog might be a superb actor, feigning his strong sense of honor and unwavering loyalty.

It would be interesting to see how things went between him and Vlad. Vrog seemed excited about meeting his son, and if he extended the same feelings of loyalty and devotion to the kid, maybe that would be enough to ensure his cooperation.

After all, unless Vrog abandoned his post at the compound, joined the clan, and mated an immortal female, he would never have any other long-lived children. Vlad would be the only one who would carry on his legacy.

That must mean something to Vrog even if he was as emotionally distant as the other Kra-ell.

Still, only time would tell if Kian's gut feelings about the guy had been right.

The one thing Kian had no more doubts about was that Emmett had told him the truth about his people. So far, there wasn't even one piece of information he'd provided that Vrog hadn't confirmed.

Vrog had added a few details from his own experience, and his view of his people was somewhat less critical than Emmett's. Perhaps Vrog was more of a follower, while Emmett was more of a leader, and that's why Vrog had been more accepting of the totalitarian rule of his mistress.

Other than safety considerations, which Kian was confident were not an issue, the Kra-ell business had little to do with his decision regarding Safe Haven. His instincts were telling him that he should go for it and buy the place, but he needed more information for his mind to agree with his gut.

Eleanor

Shai hadn't told Eleanor what Kian wanted to see her about, but she assumed it had something to do with the Kra-ell investigative team returning from China and bringing with them Vlad's father.

She'd heard about it from Kri, and when she'd told Emmett, his reaction was part excitement and part worry. She just hoped the worry wasn't about the male disputing what Emmett had told Kian.

If Emmett lost credibility, all her plans would go to the crapper.

Hopefully, that wasn't the case. If it was, no doubt Kian would have summoned Emmett to his office, either alone or with her, but not just her.

Maybe Roberts had died?

That would be a good reason for the summons.

So far, the old bastard had refused to die, but he hadn't woken up either. The males stationed there hadn't heard anything about a new director being nominated, but then their only access to information was gone.

She knocked on Kian's door, waited for his gruff *come in*, and entered.

"You wanted to see me?"

"Yes." He waved at the chair in front of his desk. "Take a seat."

She lowered herself to the chair, leaned back, and crossed her legs in a show of confidence that she actually felt. Kian still intimidated her, but not as much as he had at the beginning.

"How is Roberts doing? Do you have any news on him?"

"Still clinging to life, but it's a matter of days before he gives up the fight."

"What if he doesn't? If he doesn't die, I can't go to his funeral. I will need another way in." She uncrossed her legs. "We could do him a favor and help end him. Even if he regains consciousness, he will be severely disabled. If it were left up to me, I would prefer to end it."

His eyes shot daggers at her. "We are not in the business of ending lives."

She grimaced. "Yeah, I didn't think you had the stomach for it. I just don't like it that we have no access to information. They could have shipped everyone in the paranormal program to another state, and we wouldn't even know."

He regarded her with his intense gaze, but his anger had subsided. "If I didn't know you better, I would think that you really cared about these people."

Ouch. That was uncalled for. She was assertive and ambitious, but she wasn't an evil, cold bitch, especially when there was nothing for her to gain by it.

Then again, she'd implied that he was a softy, which was true despite all his bluster, but he didn't like being called soft, so he'd paid her back with an insult of his own.

"I care."

He arched a brow.

"Fine. I don't care for all of them, but I care about some. I also care about the safety of this village, and I want us to have access to the Echelon system."

She half expected him to refute her claim or accuse her of lying to make herself look good, but he didn't do that.

"Same here," Kian said. "That's what I wanted to discuss with you. I like your idea about Safe Haven, and now that I've gotten verification for the information Emmett provided me, that's still on the table for you both. But I want you to go to West Virginia first, find a couple of people who work in the Echelon system, and compel them to cooperate with us. The more senior the better. Only after that is done, can you start working on moving the paranormal program to Safe Haven."

That would take time, but the prize was worth it. Running the paranormal program and helping Emmett manage Safe Haven would be a huge step up in status for her. She would be the boss, the head honcho—a role she was born for.

"Are you going to buy it from Emmett?"

"I need to see the place first and go over its financials. If the numbers don't justify a purchase, I might lease it from him."

She snorted. "The place is a goldmine."

"It was. We don't know how well it's doing now. I plan on taking Emmett with me when I go to inspect Safe Haven. If you are not in West Virginia by then, I don't mind if you tag along."

"When are you planning on going?"

"In two weeks."

Roberts would be dead by then for sure, which meant that she wouldn't be joining them. She'd seen the place, so it wasn't a big deal, and with Kian keeping an eye on Emmett, she didn't need to worry about her mate straying.

"In two weeks, I will probably be in West Virginia. But even without seeing Safe Haven again or knowing how well it's doing now, I'm sure that with Emmett back at the helm, it will get back on track."

"I'm not so sure." Kian leaned his elbows on the desk. "I will not allow Emmett to empty the accounts of new community members, and I will demand that he return what he took from the current ones. I will also disallow free labor. I don't know how profitable the place will be when people are paid fair wages for their work, and no one is being swindled out of their money."

"Emmett is not going to like giving the money back."

Kian's lips lifted in a smirk. "If he wants his flock of devoted admirers back, he will have to part with some of the money. On the upside, he will get to make more by running the new paranormal retreats. That might double his revenue."

"I think that you should talk it over with him."

"You're absolutely right. I just wanted to clear things up with you first. Do you have any objections or suggestions?"

"I didn't hear your offer yet, but I'm sure it's going to be fair. You're an honest businessman."

Eleanor actually believed that, but she said it to prime Kian to offer Emmett a good deal.

"There is one more thing that I forgot to mention. When it's time for you and Emmett to take over management of Safe Haven, Peter is going with you." He smiled. "I need someone to keep an eye on you two."

Eleanor leaned back in her chair. "Emmett is not going to like that."

"What about you? I was under the impression that you liked Peter."

"I do. But unless Peter finds a mate between now and then, Emmett's jealousy is going to be a problem."

Kian chuckled. "The guru of free love has become overly possessive?"

"You might say so."

"I'm sure you'll put him in his place." Kian rose to his feet, indicating that the meeting was over. "After you talk it over with him, I want to have a meeting with both of you."

"When?"

"Preferably today." His smile vanished. "I have bad news for Emmett, but hopefully my offer will cheer him up."

"What bad news?"

"Didn't you hear? I'm sure that by now everyone knows about Vrog."

"I heard that the team brought back Vlad's half Kra-ell father."

"Then I guess you didn't hear what happened to the rest of them."

Kri hadn't told her, maybe because she didn't know or maybe because it was classified information. "What happened to them?"

"It seems that Vrog is the only one left. He returned home from Singapore twenty-two years ago to find that most of the compound had burned and everything was gone. He dug through the ashes and found what he believes is evidence pointing to the demise of the Kra-ell males and capture of the females. He built the international school on the old compound grounds, and he's been waiting for the females to return ever since."

"Why does he think they'll come back?"

"Hope springs eternal, I guess. But after over two decades of them being gone, there is no reason to think that they will return."

Eleanor pushed a strand of her unruly hair behind her ear. "Emmett didn't like living under Jade's thumb. But it's going to be difficult for him to hear that they are all gone. Who do you think did that?"

"The two leading hypotheses are that they were either attacked by another Kra-ell tribe or that their own hybrids rebelled. Mey will go back to listen to the walls, and Vrog will give me the files that survived the fire. We might learn more."

She nodded. "I'll deliver the news as gently as I can."

Kian gifted her with another one of his rare smiles. "I'm sure that the prospect of seeing his beloved Safe Haven in two weeks and possibly staying on to manage it will cheer Emmett up."

He hadn't mentioned leaving Emmett there before, but he sure as hell didn't mean to leave him there without proper supervision, which meant that Peter was going to join him.

That wasn't good.

"With Peter, I assume?"

"Obviously, and if Roberts doesn't die by then, you as well."

"When did you decide that?"

"Right now. I originally planned on taking Emmett with me to show me around the place and introduce me to his community, but since we will need to come up with a good story for why he left and why he returned, having him leave again would complicate things."

Vlad

Wendy wrapped her arms around Vlad's middle. "Do you want me to come with you? I can take the afternoon off."

"If you want."

She winced. "Can you sound any less enthusiastic?"

He cupped her cheeks and kissed her. "I'm not eager to meet Vrog. If not for my mother, I probably wouldn't even go. But she insists that I have to."

Wendy looked up at him with her warm, brown eyes. "What are you afraid of?"

He let out a breath. "I'm afraid to find out who contributed half of my genes. What if he's a terrible person?"

She grimaced. "There's no chance that he's worse than my father. You were the one who told me that I decide who I want to be, not my genetics."

Vlad arched a brow. "Did I? It's true of course. But I don't remember saying that."

"You did, among other things. Or maybe it was Bowen? I don't remember." She shook her head. "It's not important who said it, just that it's absolutely true despite what they say about nature being half of the equation. Before I met you, I thought that I was part monster, and that I should never get married and have children because of my rotten genetics. Look at me now. I'm in love, I'm happy, I'm about to get married, and if by some miracle I get pregnant, I will be overjoyed. Bottom line, even if Vrog is terrible, which I'm sure he's not because Stella speaks fondly of him, you shouldn't think that you will turn out just like him. You decide the kind of man you want to be, not your genes."

"You are so smart." He kissed the tip of her nose. "Come with me."

Her smile was radiant. "Give me fifteen minutes to get ready. I want to look nice for my first meeting with your dad."

"He's not my dad." Sighing, Vlad pushed his bangs back. "I need to talk to Richard."

"Why?"

"You saw him yesterday. He's been in a shitty mood. I think he needs a pep talk."

"Yeah, I noticed. It must be difficult for him. Having Vrog suddenly appear is bad enough. Then he attacks your mother and Richard fights him off, and then they bring Vrog back here. I would be upset too if it were me. Is Richard home, resting?"

"He's in the office building, going over the plans of Kian's new building project. Kian hired him to do the same thing he did for Kalugal."

"Awesome. Congratulate him for me." Wendy lifted on her toes and kissed his lips. "I'll meet you back here in twenty minutes."

"Take your time. I'm not in a hurry."

If it were up to Vlad, he would have waited a few more days to meet the sperm donor, but his mother wouldn't hear of it.

Apparently, Vrog had conditioned his cooperation with the clan on meeting his son.

As if he suddenly was so concerned.

He'd known that he'd gotten Stella pregnant, and he'd known that she wanted to keep the baby. It wasn't hard to reach the inescapable conclusion that he had a son somewhere out there, and yet Vrog had never attempted to find him.

But what if he had?

The guy wouldn't have known where to start. Stella had been just as cryptic with what she'd told Vrog about herself as he had been with her. Had she even given Vrog her fake last name?

Not that it would have helped him find her or her son. Since then, she'd changed it at least twice.

With a sigh, Vlad walked over to the office building, pulled the door open, and took the stairs to the second floor. He found Richard in Gavin's office, poring over construction blueprints.

"Vlad." Richard straightened and walked over to pull him into a bro embrace. "What are you doing here?"

"I came to see how you were doing. Wendy says congratulations on the new job."

"Thank you. And thank her for me."

"I will." Vlad glanced at the building plans. "She's coming with me to see Vrog."

"Oh, yeah?" Richard tried to feign nonchalance. "Meet the future father-in-law and all that?"

"You are the one who holds that title, Richard. You've been a rock for both of us." Vlad chuckled. "I don't want to say father figure because it's ridiculous given how young you are. But you were there for me and for Wendy when we needed help."

Richard waved a dismissive hand. "Bowen was there for her much more than I was, and now he's her stepdad."

"True, and you are her father-in-law. After all, you are mated to my mother, so the job is yours whether you want it or not."

"I want it. But Vrog is your biological father. Nothing can change that." Richard patted his still healing cheek. "Not that it's bad. The guy is as strong as two immortals, he's not ugly, and since he founded an international school that is fairly successful, he's also not stupid. There is nothing wrong with the genes you inherited from him."

That was a very grudging approval, and it had probably cost Richard to say nice things about Vrog, which made Vlad appreciate it even more.

"How is he as a person, though? Is he like Emmett?"

Richard snorted. "Not at all. Emmett is a born leader, a charmer and a snake oil salesman. Vrog is a much simpler guy, but he's honorable in his own way, which Emmett is not so much."

"Do you want to come with us?" Vlad asked hesitantly. "I'm sure Kian wouldn't mind if you took the rest of the day off for that."

"I'd rather not." Richard rubbed the back of his neck. "I can't help the rage that bubbles inside of me every time I look at him. All I can see is him holding a knife to your mother's neck, and it doesn't help that he apologized for it twice and that Stella forgave him. I can't. Not yet."

"I get it." Vlad patted Richard on the back. "If not for you, I would have torn Wendy's father's throat out with my fangs. I still feel rage every time the images of what I saw in his head flash before my eyes."

Vrog

Vrog couldn't sit still if his life depended on it. Well, that was an exaggeration, but anything less than death couldn't stop him from his nervous pacing.

Stella was coming with Vlad and Wendy—the pretty young woman Vlad was engaged to.

Vrog had bribed Alec to get him refreshments for his guests with one of the five gold coins he carried around with him in his pocket for good luck.

They had been part of the stash he'd found in one of the safes that had been buried under the rubble. Jade had been smart to buy gold and hide it while it had still been possible. With the advances in technology, smuggling valuables into China was difficult even for someone with mind control abilities.

Perhaps nowadays, the ability to control artificial intelligence was more valuable than the ability to control human minds. He wondered if any of Stella's clan members had that. It would explain how they were thriving despite having to hide.

When the door started to open, he held his breath, but it was only Alec with the takeout bags.

"Are you still pacing?"

Vrog nodded.

"You'll make a track in the carpet."

He glanced down at the floor. "I'm walking on the stone tiles, not on the area rug."

"Just kidding, man." Alec put down the bags on the dining table. "For the gold coin you gave me, I will also set it up nicely." He winked.

"Thank you. I'm too nervous to do it myself."

"Relax." Alec started taking the boxes out of the bags. "Vlad is a good kid. He has a heart of gold and the patience of a saint."

Something warm and fuzzy unfurled in Vrog's chest. "I bet he got that from his mother."

Alec looked at him over his shoulder. "He didn't get it from Stella. She's a hellion with mood swings galore. She's much better now that she's mated to Richard. But before that Vlad had to manage her if you know what I mean."

Vrog didn't, but he knew all about demanding females.

"It must have been difficult for her to raise a son on her own."

"No more or less difficult than it was for the other clan females. Up until very recently, there were no fathers in the clan. We had mothers, uncles, and cousins."

Vrog stopped his pacing. "Why is that?"

Alec hesitated for a moment but then waved a dismissive hand. "I don't know why they're keeping you in the dark about us. The immortal gene is passed only through the mothers, but because we are all the descendants of one goddess, we are all related and can only hook up with humans or immortals that are not her descendants. A child born to a female immortal with a human male is a dormant carrier of the immortal gene and can be activated. A child born to an immortal male and a human female is fully human and cannot be activated. That about sums it all up."

Vrog shook his head. "So you are in the same boat as the hybrid males of my tribe. You can't have long-lived children."

"If I find a dormant female who is not Annani's descendant, I can. Up until recently, we didn't find any, but lately the Fates have blessed us with several. I hope they will send one my way as well."

"Wait a second." Vrog lifted a hand. "How do you activate those dormant genes?"

Alec winced. "Sorry, dude, I can't tell you unless Kian approves it. I've already told you too much." He finished setting up the plates. "Ask him the next time he comes to talk to you."

"I will."

Vrog wasn't going to wait until Kian deigned to pay him another visit. Alec and Vernon were Guardians, so getting them to talk was difficult, but Stella, Vlad, and Wendy were civilians, and he might have better luck with them.

Except they were his family, so maybe The Mother of all Life would frown upon tricking them into revealing clan secrets to him?

Worse, what if Kian punished them for it?

There would be no tricking them into anything, then. He would just ask straight up, tell them that Kian hadn't authorized releasing that information to him, and leave it up to them whether they wanted to answer his questions or not.

When a few minutes later the door opened again, Vrog squared his shoulders, plastered an amiable smile on his face, and got ready to meet his son for the very first time.

Vernon entered first. "Your guests are here."

"Let them in, please."

"Hi." Stella walked in next, and right behind her the young couple walked in hand in hand.

Vlad was an impressive, good-looking young man, but he didn't smile. His fiancée smiled for the both of them.

"Oh, my gosh. You look so much like Vlad. Stella told us that you did, but seeing you in person. Oh, wow." She turned to Vlad. "It must be like looking in the mirror."

"That's an exaggeration." Vlad cast her a loving smile before walking up to Vrog and offering him his hand. "We meet at last."

"Yes." Vrog found his voice and shook the hand he was offered. "I want to hear all about you. What do you do? Are you in college? What are you studying?"

"Slow down." Stella put a hand on his shoulder. "We will get there. Say hello to Wendy first."

"Yes, my apologies." He dipped his head and offered the girl his hand. "You must excuse me. I'm a little overwhelmed."

"That's okay." She took his hand in both of hers. "I understand."

"Thank you." He dipped his head again. "I ordered some refreshments." He pointed to the table. "Let's sit down and have a bite while we get acquainted."

Vlad

Vrog was nothing like Vlad had expected.

He seemed so human, in the way he looked and in the way he acted. In fact, he looked more human than Vlad.

The guy was nervous, excited, polite, and respectful.

If Vlad had met the guy in a coffee shop, he would have never suspected that he was an alien. Perhaps living alone among humans for so many years with no influence from his savage tribe had softened Vrog, humanized him.

"That's so thoughtful of you to order snacks for us." Wendy sat down on the chair Vrog had pulled out for her. "Thank you."

Perfect manners. Was that the Kra-ell way? Or was it just Vrog?

Wendy was overdoing it, though, trying to infect everyone with her cheerful attitude and defuse the anxious energy in the cramped living room.

Vlad had forgotten how small the dungeon apartment was, or perhaps he hadn't noticed it before. Now the walls seemed to press in on him, and there wasn't enough air for him to get in a full breath.

"So, Vlad. Tell me about yourself."

At least Vrog was just as nervous about their meeting as he was.

"I'm studying graphic design, and I work in a bakery to cover my expenses."

"He doesn't need to work," Stella said. "The clan gives every one of its members who are over twenty-five or enrolled full time in college a share of the clan's profits. Vlad started baking when he was a senior in high school, and he has continued throughout his studies."

Vrog nodded his approval. "That's admirable. We have many spoiled kids from rich families in our school. And even though the tuition is more than enough to pay for a staff of cleaners, I insist on students cleaning their own rooms and performing other chores around the campus. Work builds character."

"What made you open a school for international students?" Wendy asked.

"Originally, I thought that it would provide me with a great excuse for traveling extensively all over the world.

But I discovered that I enjoyed shaping young lives, and I found it very satisfying to see my students reach success."

That was also such a human thing to say. Then again, Emmett had chosen a similar path once he got away from his tribe, so maybe it wasn't their human half that had motivated them to become teachers. Maybe once they were free of their leader and their people's traditions, they sought to learn more about themselves.

Vlad leaned back in the chair. "Did my mother tell you about Emmett?"

Vrog nodded. "The other Kra-ell hybrid that joined your clan."

"Do you know that he did something similar to you?"

Vrog frowned. "I heard that he founded a cult. That's not the same thing as running a school. We don't brainwash our students."

"Some might call it a cult, and it has cultish attributes, but Emmett really wanted to improve the lives of those who didn't fit in." Vlad glanced at Wendy. "Wendy's mother was one of his followers for many years. Isn't that a strange coincidence?"

"Indeed." Vrog smiled at Wendy. "I hope your mother was treated well by my tribesman."

Wendy grimaced. "It was a mixed bag. He's done some things he shouldn't have, but he took her in when she had nothing and nowhere to go, so I can't be mad about the things he did. Besides, even though his methods were questionable, he probably saved her life by keeping her from leaving Safe Haven."

"Forgive me, but I'm confused." Vrog glanced between the three of them. "Did Emmett keep your mother imprisoned against her will?"

"It wasn't like that." Wendy dove into a summary of what had happened to her mother, surprisingly omitting nothing from the story of abuse and healing.

When she was done, Vrog's fangs were on display, and his dark eyes flashed red. He no longer looked even remotely human or civilized.

"My apologies." He covered his mouth with his hand. "I don't let my Kra-ell side emerge often, but that story just pushed all of my buttons. I was raised to respect females, to revere them as the goddess's earthly embodiments."

Vlad shook his head. "I don't get it. Emmett claimed the same, and yet he told us that the Kra-ell females were vicious, and that they enjoyed hurting their partners during sex. I find it hard to reconcile these conflicting statements."

Vrog nodded. "Our culture is very different. But when you understand that it's all about the survival and continuation of our kind, these strange practices start to make sense. With four males to one female, human-style marriages would have resulted in many males who never got access to a female. So instead of a family of two adults and their offspring, our family is more of a tribe. Two or three females with eight to twelve males. But our tribe grew much larger than that."

"What happens when a tribe gets too large?" Stella asked.

"It's supposed to split. Jade was grooming the young generation of purebloaded females to one day become independent and take the young purebloaded males with them."

"But why the brutality?" Stella asked.

Vrog winced. "I guess that for the purebloods it's a big turn-on. Because of their scarcity, the females are in charge of reproduction, and they need to ensure that the next generation is fathered by the best males. The Kra-ell rituals and customs are all about regulating that." He smiled apologetically. "Only the most worthy get to father the next generation, and since the Kra-ell are a warrior race, worthiness is determined by brute strength."

Vlad wondered if Vrog believed in his own words. There were so many holes in his theory, and he could think of several possible methods of solving the gender disparity issue that didn't involve brutal sex. Hell, even Emmett's free love community style could work just as well if not better.

Then again, the brutality might not be a cultural construct. Maybe it was part of their physiology, and it was necessary for conception.

"Fascinating," Wendy said. "What seems strange to us might seem perfectly normal to others and vice versa."

"Indeed." Vrog folded his napkin over his knee. "I find the clan's predicament fascinating as well. With so many of its members being the descendants of one goddess, they have to breed with humans because they can't breed with each other. And then the whole thing about dormant immortal genes and their activation. I wonder when Kian will finally allow me to learn how the process works."

Vlad cast Stella a glance. "Why doesn't he?"

She shrugged. "He's paranoid. I respect the hell out of him, and I appreciate everything he has done for our clan, but sometimes he can be a pain in the rear."

Visibly tensing, Vrog leaned closer to her. "You shouldn't say things like that about your leader."

She patted his arm. "Don't worry. Kian is nothing like your old vicious mistress. I could say it to his face and there would be no repercussions."

Emmett

The news Eleanor had delivered had been a hard pill to swallow. According to Vrog, Emmett's tribe was gone—the males slaughtered, and the females captured. But until they had solid evidence to indicate that they had indeed been killed, he would cling to the hope that there was another explanation.

He needed to talk with Vrog. Perhaps there were other clues that indicated an alternative explanation.

Right now, he opted to focus on the second half of Eleanor's news.

Emmett hadn't been this excited or anxious since he'd fled his tribe nearly four decades ago.

Kian must have lost his mind, but in the best possible way because he was seriously considering reinstating him as the head of Safe Haven.

Eleanor had mentioned that there were some caveats, but Emmett had been too buzzed to hear them. Hell, he would part with one of his testicles for what Kian was offering him.

Well, perhaps not a testicle, but maybe some other, less important body part he could live without.

"Calm down." Eleanor patted his arm as they entered the office building. "You need to play the game with a clear head. If Kian sees how excited you are, he will take advantage of your eagerness and offer you a crappy deal."

"Kian is a sanctimonious prick, which in this case benefits me. It will not sit well with him to take unfair advantage of me."

She huffed out a breath. "He's a businessman. And you're much less important to him than his clan. I want to say that it's human nature to look for weaknesses and exploit them, but he is not human and neither are you. Just don't let him think that you will take any deal he offers you. Play it cool."

"Yes, ma'am." Emmett leaned closer to her and took her lips in a quick kiss. "Thank you for looking out for me."

Her pinched expression softened. "I'm looking out for both of us. If we play this right, we can have a very sweet arrangement in Safe Haven. We will be in charge of our future." She winced. "Well, almost."

He frowned. "What aren't you telling me?"

"Kian wants to send Peter with you. He still doesn't trust you enough to let you fly solo, not even when I'm there with you."

Emmett stifled the growl that started down low in his belly. "Kian has a sick sense of humor."

Peter was pretending to be Eleanor's buddy, but he was an attractive male, and she was an attractive female, and Peter had a score to settle with Emmett. He might seduce Eleanor just to get back at him. On the other hand, if Peter was assigned to guard him, he wouldn't be going with Eleanor to West Virginia, and Kian would send her with another Guardian.

Except, Emmett didn't like that she would be going without him no matter who accompanied her. But that was a concern he would address later. Right now, he needed to focus on striking a good deal with Kian.

"We can make it work." Eleanor took his hand. "Come on. We don't want to keep Kian waiting."

"Is Peter going to be there?"

"I don't know. Kian didn't mention that."

They took the stairs to the second floor of the office building, and as they walked up to Kian's door, Eleanor knocked.

"Come in," Kian said.

Forcing a nonchalant smile on his face, Emmett opened the door and motioned for Eleanor to go ahead. "Ladies first."

"Good afternoon," Kian greeted them. "Please, take a seat." He motioned to the chairs in front of his desk.

"Good afternoon to you too." Emmett sat down and leaned back in a show of bored indifference. "I have to admit that I admire your decisiveness. When you decide to do something, you don't wait, you don't procrastinate, you get a move on."

"Thank you." Kian cast him a perfunctory smile. "I liked Eleanor's idea for Safe Haven, but I needed to make sure that you are trustworthy. Vrog confirming your story helped your case."

"I'm glad. So how exactly are we going to play this? After disappearing without a word for months, I can't just show up with you and your entourage and pick up from where I left off."

"I don't see why not." Kian leaned back and crossed his arms over his chest. "Given the role you played, you could make up a number of stories to explain your absence."

Emmett had thought of a couple of possibilities, one involving compulsion, and the other a good story, but he was curious to hear what Kian had come up with. "Like what?"

The guy unfolded his arms and lifted them in the air like a prophet, imitating one of Emmett's favorite poses. "You suffered a spiritual breakdown and needed to go back to your roots in the Himalayas to meditate in complete silence."

Emmett chuckled. "That's actually not bad. How would I explain you and what you want to do to the place?"

"You met me in the Himalayan mountains, where I too had retreated to meditate upon the state of the world. Our encounter was guided by The Mother of all Life, who wished us to merge our dreams for a better world and make Safe Haven a beacon of light for humanity."

Lifting his hands, Emmett clapped. "I didn't know that you were so creative."

Kian laughed. "I'm not. This was all Shai's idea. Personally, I think that The Mother of all Life is too much. Shai also suggested the spirit of Gaia as an alternative. That's what the Greeks called the goddess of Earth, or The Mother of all Life."

Kian seemed in a surprisingly good mood.

"I'm well versed in Greek mythology and many others," Emmett said. "It would seem that different cultures on different worlds all revere The Mother of all Life. It might be a coincidence, or it might not."

Kian narrowed his eyes at him. "What are you implying?"

"Nothing overly profound. It's not surprising that many cultures revere the power of nature. Still, I have often wondered whether the Kra-ell who comprised my group were the first to arrive on earth, or if there had been prior expeditions that brought their mythology with them, influencing human religions. It is also possible that your ancestors, the gods, influenced both the Kra-ell and the humans."

"The gods didn't have a formal religion, and they didn't revere The Mother of all Life. Although given their matrilineal tradition, they might have in the distant past."

Emmett nodded. "Perhaps they transferred their ancient belief in The Mother to the Fates. I'm told that many of your clan members strongly believe that the Fates guide their lives, especially in everything that has to do with finding true-love mates."

Kian winced. "With good reason, but we digress. The cover story for your absence solves only part of the problem." He waved a hand at Emmett's face. "Without the beard and the long hair, you look too young. You're supposed to be in your sixties. You need to let it grow back to how it was before."

"My hair grows fast, but not that fast. I can't regrow it in two weeks."

"Naturally. Eva can help you with that. I sent her your picture from the Safe Haven brochure so she would know what kind of wigs to order, and I told her that you will call to make an appointment."

"I'll also need to purchase a couple of gowns." Emmett looked down at his trim body. "I have to hide my fantastic physique."

Eleanor shook her head. "Or you can have Eva put you in a fat suit."

"I prefer a gown." He looked Kian in the eyes. "What exactly are you planning to do with Safe Haven?"

"Several things. I want you to start running retreats for people with paranormal abilities. It will mesh perfectly with your other self-help programs and not raise suspicion. If we get lucky, we might even find Dormants among the attendees."

"That might be more difficult to do than you think. I don't know how well the place did in my absence, but the lodge might be booked for months in advance. Also, we will need to create courses and workshops geared toward the paranormal, and that will take time."

Kian nodded. "I'm well aware of that, and I don't expect you to start doing that right away. First, we need to see if we can attract people with paranormal talents or who are interested in the subject. We might discover that there is no demand. If there is, we will then need to create a new program for them, and either alternate bookings between the paranormal and the self-actualization retreats or add another building to house the paranormal. I understand that you own a large chunk of land over there."

"I do, but most of it is not developed. It requires a lot of grading work."

Kian shrugged. "That's not a problem, and if need be, we can acquire more land. If Eleanor manages to convince the people in charge of the government paranormal program to transfer it to Safe Haven, I will probably have to build another structure to house them. I'm also thinking of building a couple of guest cabins for testing the potential Dormants."

Kian was talking as if he already owned the place, but so far, he hadn't said anything about buying it. Did he think that Emmett would just hand it over in exchange for getting to head a place that he'd founded and owned?

"You have so many exciting plans. Are you going to make me an offer to buy the place?"

Leaning back, Kian crossed his arms over his chest. "Only after I inspect it and take a look at the financials. I want to see if Safe Haven is profitable when it doesn't exploit its members."

"I assure you that it is, and I'm not interested in selling it."

As Eleanor sucked in a breath, Kian frowned. "Why not?"

"Because it's my baby. But I'm willing to share. How about we form a partnership? We can negotiate the terms after your inspection."

Kian shook his head. "I don't do partnerships unless I'm in a controlling position, especially when I invest a lot of money to expand the operations. If you don't want to sell, I can lease the place from you, but I'm not leaving you in charge."

It was Emmett's turn to frown. "I thought that was the plan."

"You will run the place as the director or chief executive officer. Naturally, you will also be its spiritual leader, but you will have to answer to me."

"What about the money?"

"You'll be given a salary, a share in the profits, and the lease payments." Kian leaned forward. "Right now, you are making nothing from the place, and all the profits are going to the Safe Haven community. So, I would say it's a good deal."

That was true, and unless Emmett reached an agreement with Kian, the guy was going to drop the plan and keep him under watch in the village. He hadn't even mentioned removing the damn cuffs from his wrists.

"How long of a lease?"

"At least fifteen years with an option to buy."

"What about the cuffs?"

"They stay on. I can't let a powerful compeller roam free."

"I'm bound by the Clan Mother's compulsion to do no harm to her clan. I have no problem with her adding another do-no-harm clause that includes humans."

Kian pinned him with a hard stare. "We both know that there are ways to circumvent compulsion. That's the deal I'm offering, Emmett. You can take it or leave it. I can find another remote location and build a retreat for paranormals there. It will just take me a little longer to get it off the ground."

Kian was bluffing, and Emmett was going to call him out on that. "Much longer. You don't have the personnel to run a place like that, and you need people who are experienced, motivated, and who keep their mouths shut." He chuckled. "You use human volunteers to run the sanctuary for the trafficking victims because you can't get clan members to work there. They are busy doing their own things or nothing at all. Giving them a share of the clan profits without demanding any work in return is demoralizing."

The wince Kian tried to stifle was most satisfying. Emmett had touched on a sore spot.

"All of that is true." Kian unfolded his arms and leaned forward. "But there is no way I'm releasing you into the world without proper precautions. I'm not going to take advantage of you financially, Emmett, if that's what you are worried about. The deal we will negotiate will include fair compensation for the property you own and for your services."

"How do I know that? You've got me by the throat. I don't have any leverage to negotiate with."

Emmett didn't really believe that, but he knew how Kian's mind worked. Wanting to prove the opposite, he might offer him an even better deal than he'd planned to.

"Of course you have leverage. I need you to do a good job running the place and covering up for the paranormal operation. You won't do that as well if you are not motivated by profit, station, and the level of autonomy I'll allow you. It's a give and take, Emmett, and it's fluid. The more I can trust you not to take unfair advantage of people, the more autonomy I will grant you."

Letting out a breath, Emmett closed his eyes. Eleanor had been right. Kian was a much tougher negotiator than he'd expected, but even though the guy was a businessman, he wasn't motivated by profits alone.

Kian really feared releasing him into the world without safeguards.

That was the price Emmett had to pay for having the ability to compel. Even a powerful immortal like Kian feared him. The only people who weren't wary of him were the immunes and those who didn't know what he could do.

That didn't mean he wasn't grateful for the gift The Mother of all Life had given him. Without it, he would probably be dead, slaughtered along with the other males of his tribe.

Besides, no gift from The Mother came without giving up something else. Emmett didn't possess even a fraction of the innate aggression of the Kra-ell males, which was one of the main reasons his father had barely deigned to acknowledge him. He was a shame to his people's warrior race—a male who preferred to read and engage in intellectually stimulating conversations than to fight.

His people were savages, and Emmett had never felt as if he belonged with them. Sometimes, he wondered if his escape hadn't actually been sanctioned, and if Jade had let him go knowingly. No one had come looking for him. No one had chased him.

"Well?" Kian asked.

Emmett opened his eyes. "We will work out a deal, but don't expect me to lease the property to you for one dollar a year."

Kian smiled. "I wouldn't dream of it."

As Shai pulled into the driveway in a huge motorhome, Geraldine opened the front door and stepped out. "What is that?"

Grinning out the open driver side window, he waved her over. "Come and take a look." He opened the door for her. "I figured that if we are taking a road trip, we can do it in style."

"It's gorgeous." It was like a small apartment, complete with a kitchen that had a full-sized fridge and a small stove, and a sitting area. There was a door in the back that she assumed led to a bedroom. "Where did you get it?"

"It belongs to the clan. Kian approved the purchase a while ago for clan members to borrow whenever they want. I was lucky that it was available."

Geraldine walked to the back and opened the pocket door. As she'd suspected, it was a bedroom suite, with a nice bathroom and a small closet.

"I love it." She sat on the bed to test the mattress. "What a great idea."

"If you are all packed, we can leave now. I already stocked it with supplies for the road."

"I made dinner." She rose to her feet and went back to check out the kitchen, "But I can pack it up, and we can stop on the way to eat it."

"I'll help you." He followed her out of the vehicle.

"How much does a thing like this cost?"

"A lot. This one was over four hundred thousand dollars."

"Oh, wow." She looked at it over her shoulder. "I would never have guessed. Why is it so expensive?"

"The interior is custom made. We bought this motorhome as is from someone who'd ordered it and then decided to sell it, which made it a little cheaper and a lot more expeditious. Usually, it takes over a year to have one of these built."

In the kitchen, she pulled the fish out of the oven and put it in a glass container. The spaghetti went into another, and the salad into a third. "Does the kitchen in the motorhome come fully equipped?"

"It does. And I filled the fridge and the cupboards." He smiled apologetically. "I probably overdid it. We are going to eat at restaurants."

"It could be fun to cook in the motorhome." She put the containers inside a carrying bag and handed it to him. "I'll get my overnight bag."

It was on the entry table by the door, and as Geraldine slung the strap over her shoulder, she took a quick look in the mirror. "I thought about using the wig."

"Why?" Shai opened the door.

"You are going to introduce me to Rhett as your girlfriend, and since you are pretending to be in your early forties, I should too." She locked the door behind him.

"You don't need to." He took the bag from her and carried both to the motorhome. "I could have a much younger girlfriend."

She followed him inside. "I thought about saying that I was forty, but if I want to mention Cassandra, which I want to, that's a problem. She's semi-famous and it's easy to find out that she's thirty-four."

As Geraldine turned to look at the house, a wave of anxiety swept through her. "What if Orion shows up when I'm gone?"

"Don't worry about it." Shai put the bag with the containers inside the fridge. "The surveillance cameras are on, and the guys watching the feed have had two days to learn who your neighbors are." He put her overnight bag in the bedroom. "If anyone comes snooping around the house, they will get him."

Geraldine sat down in the passenger captain chair and put the seatbelt on. "The village is half an hour drive from my house. How are they going to get here in time?"

"There are always Guardians on rotation in the keep. They can be here in fifteen minutes."

"He won't stay around that long if I'm not here."

"That's fine. The Guardians watching the house will activate the drone and it will follow him."

"What drone?"

"William's guys put a mini drone on your roof. It's controlled remotely through an internet satellite connection. Its battery should last until the Guardians from the keep reach Orion." He gave her an apologetic smile. "It would have been better to have a Guardian assigned to your house, but we are short on trained people. Besides, it would have been an even greater intrusion on our privacy."

"That's okay. I prefer the drone. I just wish I had known about it." She let out a long sigh. "I feel so bad about the whole surveillance thing and entrapping Orion. It's a shitty way to repay his kindness."

"I wouldn't call it kindness. At best, it was the assuaging of guilt. But what prompted the sudden change in feelings? You were fine with the idea. Did you remember more things?"

She nodded. "He always brought Cassandra and me fancy chocolates and marzipans from all over the world. I guess he couldn't bring gifts that would remind us of him, so he brought sweets that we consumed right away."

"Did he travel a lot?"

"Yeah. Being old and having a good eye for style lent itself to making a lot of money on trading in antiques. He collected them from all over."

"That's interesting." Shai turned the engine on. "I wonder if Orion had anything to do with Leo getting a job in an antiques gallery."

"Do you think that Orion got him the job?"

"If he was helping you, he might have been helping your daughter and her son, and by extension, her husband."

Shai

Orion must have felt guilty as hell to help a creep like Leo, but then arranging a good job for him was a circumventive way to ensure Darlene's well-being.

Why hadn't she pursued a career? She had a degree from a prestigious university, and she had only one child who had left home a long time ago. What did she do with herself? Watch soap operas all day?

"Leo got the new job several months after Roni's escape," Geraldine said. "Orion wouldn't have been helping Roni by getting a job for Leo, only Darlene."

He was surprised that she remembered that. Even after the Clan Mother had restored her memories, Geraldine still had trouble remembering details. But apparently, some things registered in her mind better than others.

"Orion might have been helping them before that as well." Shai stopped and waited for the gate to open. "Leo lost his job shortly after Roni's capture. Maybe Orion couldn't help while the Feds were around." He carefully eased the large vehicle through the two arms of the open gate.

Geraldine shrugged. "All we can do is guess. I hope that once Orion shows up, we can get some answers. I just hate thinking about being the bait for his entrapment. He deserves better from me after everything he's done for me."

"Don't forget that he might have been doing it to atone for the wrong he had done you. We don't know what his story is."

"The more memories that resurface, the more fondly I think of him. He really was like a brother to me." She chuckled. "Or rather a really nice uncle who took care of me. It wasn't only treats that he gave me. He helped me financially, and he got me the fake documents that helped me stay undetected. I would have been lost without him, or worse, I would have been found." Geraldine shivered. "Imagine what would have happened if I had gotten caught, what they would have done to me. To Cassy."

He reached over and took her hand. "If he helped prevent that, then I'm grateful to him."

She smiled. "Remember that when he comes back. Be nice to him."

"I'll try."

"You'd better."

"I just hope that he shows up before next Monday."

She turned to him. "Why? What's special about that Monday?"

"Kian wants to visit Safe Haven. Do you remember what I told you about it?"

She nodded. "It's a cult in Oregon that a guy named Emmett Haderech founded. He was its guru before the clan caught him."

He arched a brow. "I'm surprised that you remember his name."

"It's unique. After you told me what it meant, it stuck in my mind." She sighed. "The true way. I wish I'd thought of something that clever for my own fake name. I often wonder why I chose Geraldine."

"It suits you." He squeezed her hand. "Anyway, Kian wants me to accompany him, and I want you to come with me. He's taking everyone on the clan's jet, and we are going to spend the night in Emmett's fancy underground bunker. It will be like a mini vacation."

"Who is everyone?"

"Syssi, the baby, Kian's butler, Emmett and Eleanor, and Kian's two Guardians."

"Why does he need you there?"

Shai shrugged. "He needs to go over the financials, and I can do that much faster than him. He's also trying to get me more involved in decision-making." He chuckled.

"Kian believes that I have what it takes to become much more than just his assistant. He wants to promote me to a managerial position."

Geraldine beamed at him. "That's amazing. I'm so proud of you."

"I'm not really interested. You know what my real passion is."

"I do." She squeezed his hand. "But when was the last time you wrote anything creative?"

He grinned. "I came up with a story to explain Emmett's absence, his return, and how he met Kian. It was very creative."

She rolled her eyes. "You know what I mean. When was the last time you worked on a screenplay?"

"It has been a while."

"Then maybe you should take Kian's offer and become a manager of something. You're immortal, there will always be time for writing scripts."

"Not necessarily. What if by the time I get around to it, AI can make novelists and screenwriters obsolete?"

"Don't be silly. A computer doesn't have the creativity and never will. Just look at the Odus. They are the most advanced AI on earth, and they can only imitate, not create."

Shai lifted a brow. "I wouldn't be so sure about that. Up until Okidu and Onidu's reboots, their capabilities were limited by design. Now that they are experimenting and learning, they might evolve the same way humans did, but much faster."

For a moment, Geraldine chewed on her lower lip. "It's scary and exciting at the same time."

"I agree, but I like the way Syssi sees it. She believes that the Odus are learning like children do, and since they are surrounded by good people who treat them and each other with kindness and respect, that's what they will learn."

"I like that. She's a smart woman, and I would love to get to know her better. Maybe once I move to the village, I'll start a book club and invite her to join."

It was music to his ears that Geraldine no longer regarded the move as potential but as impending.

"If you come with me to Safe Haven, you won't have to wait. You'll have a chance to spend time with Syssi and Allegra."

Knowing how much Geraldine loved babies, he dangled Allegra as bait on purpose. She would have a hard time saying no to that.

"I would really love to come with you, and if Orion is captured before the trip, then I definitely will. But if he isn't, I can't." She smiled sadly. "I feel anxious about leaving on this less than twenty-four-hour trip to Berkeley, let alone a two-day trip to Oregon."

Geraldine

Geraldine yawned and stretched her arms over her head. "You have no idea how glad I am that Rhett sleeps late on the weekends. I'm so well rested."

They'd arrived at Berkeley at three o'clock in the morning, continued driving another half an hour north of it to a Walmart, and parked there overnight. She hadn't even known that the national chain allowed that.

Shai chuckled. "A breakfast at ten in the morning on a weekend is considered very early for a college student. To wake up before noon, Rhett must be anxious to meet you."

"What's more likely is that he's excited to see the motorhome. Once you told him about it, he right away offered to come to us instead of us going to him." Geraldine got out of bed and straightened the comforter.

"He wanted to save us from Ubering to Berkeley." Shai fluffed the pillows.

"I think it was just an excuse to see this." She waved a hand around the surprisingly luxurious bedroom. "But I don't mind. Making breakfast in this tiny kitchen is part of the adventure."

The motorhome was too big to park just anywhere, so Ubering to Berkeley had seemed like a good solution. But Rhett wouldn't hear of it. They were having breakfast in the motorhome with him, and later, he would take them for a tour of the college. They would have lunch together in town, and then he'd drive them back to the Walmart's parking lot.

"Right. Do you have everything you need? If not I can get it by the time you finish getting dressed." He opened the screen and waved at the big store at the other side of the parking lot.

"No need. I'm just making omelets, and I checked last night that I have all the ingredients. But if you want to be a dear, make us some coffee while I get ready."

"I'm on it." Smiling, he kissed her cheek.

After a quick visit to the small bathroom, Geraldine pulled out the outfit she brought with her for the occasion. A pair of dark blue slacks, a red silk blouse, and a pair of red kitten mules. She looked good in it, but not young, which was precisely what she was aiming for.

When she was done, she rearranged the bed pillows the way she liked them and walked into the living area of the motorhome.

"How do I look?"

Shai's eyes blazed. "Good enough to eat."

She laughed. "You did that last night. What I want to know is whether I look like a forty-something woman."

He shook his head. "Not even close. If Rhett asks, which I hope he doesn't, you are thirty-four years old."

"That's Cassandra's age. Do I have children?"

"If you want to tell him about Cassandra, you can say that she's your sister."

Geraldine opened the fridge and pulled out a carton of eggs and a stick of butter. "It's not easy to be an immortal." She put them on the counter and pulled out an onion and a box of mushrooms. "I don't like lying, but out of necessity, I've become very good at it."

As a memory of a nearly identical conversation surfaced, she put the two items on the counter and rubbed her temple. "Orion said the same thing."

"In what context?"

"He kept saying that we were a family, and when I asked him in what way we were related, his expression turned pained, and he said that it was better I didn't know so I wouldn't have to lie about it. I remember thinking that it was an odd thing to say since he made me forget him every time he left. It didn't matter what he told me because I would forget it along with everything else. Why did he need to keep that information from me?"

"Perhaps he feared exactly what happened. That you would somehow meet another powerful immortal who would unlock those memories."

Geraldine pulled out the cutting board and peeled the onion. "That would imply that he knew about Annani, but I don't think he did. He never mentioned the clan or the Doomers. His only concern for me was being discovered by humans."

Shai smoothed his hand over his short beard. "Maybe he knew of other immortals that were not connected to the clan or to the Brotherhood, and those immortals were just as powerful as he was. He wanted to hide you from them as well."

"I don't think so." She started chopping the onion. "The impression I got was that he was very lonely, and that other than Cassandra and me, he had no one." She turned to look at Shai. "But then Darlene and Roni were his family as well, and I wonder if in addition to helping Leo find a well-paying job he also visited them."

Shai leaned against the fridge and folded his arms over his chest. "We've already decided that the next time you meet her I'm going to thrall her to reveal the truth about Leo. I might as well look a little deeper and scan her memories for Orion."

Shai

As Rhett pulled his car up into the spot next to the motorhome, Shai opened the door and stepped down.

"She's a beauty." His son got out of the Honda Shai had gotten him as a high school graduation present. "Is she yours?"

"It's borrowed." Shai pulled Rhett into a tight embrace and clapped him on the back. "How is school?"

Rhett grimaced. "Tough. In high school, I was at the top of my class. Here, everyone is as good as me or better."

"Hi," Geraldine said from behind them.

Shai let go of his son and stepped aside. "Rhett, this is Geraldine, my partner. Geraldine, this is my son, Rhett."

"A pleasure to meet you." Rhett offered her his hand.

"Likewise." She treated him to one of her charming smiles, lifted on her toes, and kissed his cheek. "You look so much like your father." She turned her smiling face to Shai. "The girls must be going wild for your boy."

Rhett cleared his throat. "I wish."

"And you're just as modest and unaware of your masculine charms as your father. But let's continue this inside. Breakfast is getting cold."

"I thought we were going out." Rhett followed her up the stairs into the motorhome.

She looked at him over her shoulder. "What would be the fun in that?"

"Right." As he got inside, Rhett whistled. "This is bigger than my dorm room." He turned to Shai. "Is there any chance I can borrow it for the next four years?"

"Sorry." Shai clapped him on the back. "But I have to return it tomorrow."

"Who does it belong to?" Rhett sat on one of the benches flanking the small dining table that Shai had already set up for breakfast. The only thing missing were the omelets that Geraldine left in the pan to keep warm.

"My reclusive boss." Shai sat across from him.

The cover story he'd used to explain why Rhett couldn't visit him in his home was that he worked for an eccentric billionaire who lived on a secret mountain compound and didn't allow any visitors.

Rhett's lips twisted in a familiar way. "I get it that he pays you well, but you live like a recluse because of him. How did you even meet Geraldine?" He looked up at her. "Do you work for Mr. X as well?"

Putting a steaming omelet on his plate, she glanced at Shai. "Why don't you tell Rhett how we met, dear?"

They hadn't prepared a story, which they should have.

She put the remaining omelets on the other two plates, sat down, and unfurled a cloth napkin.

Shai slid next to her. "Geraldine's sister introduced us. She's dating a guy who also works for my boss."

That was close enough to the truth.

"How did that guy meet your sister?" Rhett cut a piece of the omelet and put it in his mouth.

"At a charity gala." Geraldine cast Shai a sidelong glance.

It was time to change the subject. "So, Rhett, how are your grades so far this semester?" Shai lifted the carafe and poured coffee into their cups.

Rhett finished chewing before answering. "Average, which is as good as it gets in computer science." He smiled at Geraldine. "My father studied English literature and took a few classes in business administration. It's not hard to get good grades in those."

Shai snorted. "You should have met some of my professors. At least computer science is not open to interpretation. Your program either works or doesn't. You are not graded on style, or creativity, or any other subjective criteria."

"You'd think that." Rhett reached for a piece of toast. "A program can work but still be clumsy and not elegant enough." He turned to Geraldine. "What did you study in college?"

A blush colored her cheek as she stammered, "I didn't go to college."

He nodded. "With your beauty, I bet you were a teenage model who made enough money without having to bother with that."

His son was smooth—by complimenting Geraldine on her looks, he made her feel less awkward about her lack of education.

"I was never a model, but my sister Cassandra was. She's much taller than me, and her beauty is striking and exotic. She wanted to study graphic design, but one semester of art school convinced her that it was a waste of time and money and that she could learn everything she needed online for a fraction of the cost."

"Smart woman." Rhett shoved the rest of the omelet into his mouth.

"College is not just about learning a craft," Shai said. "It's also about meeting new people and making social and business connections." He lifted his coffee cup and took a sip. "And it's never too late."

"I don't even know what subjects interest me," Geraldine said. "I like to read, so maybe I should study literature."

Shai laughed. "If you want a sure way to lose your love of reading, that's the way to go. The sheer number of books you'll be forced to read will make you not want to pick a book up for years."

Eleanor

Eleanor got off the phone with Kian and put it down on the coffee table. "You heard him." She looked up at Emmett who'd stopped his pacing and faced her. "He's okay with you visiting Vrog, but I have to come with you, and the Guardians in charge of him need to be in the room with us."

He nodded. "I don't mind you being there. In fact, I need you with me. And frankly, I don't mind the Guardians either. I don't know Vrog, and I have no secrets to exchange with him."

Emmett had taken the news about his people's fate too calmly. He didn't have fond memories of the compound, but still, for better or for worse, they were his family. His mother was long gone, but now he'd lost his father as well.

Pushing to her feet, she walked up to him and pulled him into her arms. "I know that you don't know Vrog, but I thought that with just you in the room, he would open up. The two of you are all that's left from your tribe."

"Vrog knows that there are surveillance cameras all over the place. He wouldn't have talked anyway."

"I'm glad that you want me with you." She pressed a light kiss to his lips. "We are a team, you and I. We've got each other's backs."

The smile he gave her was heartwarming. "Yes, we are, and I couldn't have asked for a better partner in crime and in love. You are the perfect female for me."

Lowering her arms to his waist, she leaned back and regarded him with a wry smile. "You're full of compliments today. Is that because I made it possible for you to return to Safe Haven?"

He cupped her behind and rubbed himself against her. "I don't know what I find more sexy, your knockout body or your devious mind. You played Kian better than I ever could."

She chuckled. "I wish I could take credit for planning it. The idea just formed in my head as I was trying to avoid us being sent to West Virginia. You would have hated the underground city."

"Indeed. But West Virginia is still on the table."

"Regrettably, that's true." She pushed out of his arms. "I'm just waiting for Roberts to die so I can go to his funeral and use my powers on his superiors."

"I'm coming with you."

"About that." She took out the pin holding her hair up. "I might be able to convince Kian to let you come with me to the funeral, but even that will be a difficult sell. When he suggested that I take over as director of the paranormal program, I told him that I would do it if he allowed you to come with me. He refused, saying that he couldn't monitor you inside the underground facility. That's how the idea of moving the program to Safe Haven was born. He can have you monitored there, which is the only reason he's letting you do it."

"That's not the only reason. Without me, the entire plan to move the paranormal program there falls apart. Kian needs me as the face of Safe Haven."

"I can compel everyone to make it happen."

He shook his head. "That's not how the government works. The proposal to move the program to Safe Haven will be sent over to the pencil pushers for security and financial evaluation. Since you don't have direct access to those departments, you won't be able to influence their decisions. They will check the history of Safe Haven, and if they find that I've been running the place pretty much the same way from the very beginning, they will most likely approve the move provided that it makes sense financially, and we will make sure that it does. But if they find that the place has changed management recently, they might become suspicious and less inclined to recommend the move."

"Everything you said is true, but that doesn't change the fact that Kian will not allow you to come with me to

West Virginia. I hate the idea of being apart from you, but to make Safe Haven happen, I have no choice. I would probably have to stay there for a couple of months while I negotiate the move and find people in the Echelon system who I can compel to cooperate with the clan."

His eyes blazed red. "A couple of months? I can't be apart from you for so long."

"Oh, baby." She wrapped her arms around his neck. "I can't either, but it's for our future."

He shook his head. "We need to find a way to convince Kian to let me come with you. Roberts didn't live in the underground facility, right? You can insist on living outside of it and then I can come with you. He can send a Guardian to monitor me twenty-four-seven. I don't care as long as it makes it possible for me to be with you."

She smiled. "Even if that Guardian is Peter?"

"Even if it's damn Peter. I'll tolerate the bastard to be with you."

"That's sweet, but it's not going to work. You need to be in Safe Haven, and we can't let the government officials know that we are a couple. Otherwise, your pencil pushers will think that I want to relocate the paranormal program to Safe Haven to line my boyfriend's pockets."

As the light dimmed in his eyes, he sighed. "I hate to admit it, but you're right. How are we going to survive months away from each other?"

"Twice a day of video calls?"

"That's not going to cut it."

"We will figure it out somehow." She kissed his cheek. "For the sake of our future, we can suffer through a couple of miserable months."

Emmett

As Emmett stood in front of his old cell's door, he wasn't looking forward to crossing that threshold again. It had taken a miracle and Eleanor's wits and courage to get him out of that luxurious coffin, and he never wanted to go back.

Why was he even there?

Did he really want to meet the hybrid male? He must have been a young boy when Emmett had left.

The uncomfortable feeling churning in his gut was about more than facing Vrog, though. He hadn't expected Eleanor to agree to a two-month or more separation from him, and he'd expected even less how much the prospect of that separation would affect him.

He loved Eleanor, but he wasn't in love with her. The mystical bond the immortals talked about hadn't formed between them. Theirs was a marriage of convenience, so to speak. A comfortable pairing of two like-minded people who enjoyed each other in bed and outside of it.

What more could he possibly ask for?

Emmett wasn't a believer in the fated-mates nonsense even the skeptical Kian had accepted as real. He was perfectly fine spending his life with Eleanor by his side as his lover, his partner, and his friend. It was more than he had ever imagined he would have with a female.

Her leaving on a mission shouldn't make him feel a visceral sense of abandonment, a sharp pain scrambling his insides. It should not bother him as much, and yet it did.

What did it mean?

Perhaps the bond had formed without either of them realizing it?

As the Guardian named Vernon, a fellow who Emmett hadn't met before, activated the door mechanism, Eleanor squeezed Emmett's hand. "Excited?"

"Not really," he drawled as he walked into his former cell.

A friendly smile stretching on his handsome face, Vrog pushed to his feet. "Good afternoon." He offered Eleanor his hand first. "I'm Vrog, but you can also call me James. That's my human name."

"I like Vrog better." She shook what he offered. "I'm Eleanor, Emmett's partner."

"And I'm Emmett." He shook the guy's hand. "I don't use my Kra-ell given name."

Vrog looked down at the cuffs on Emmett's wrists, identical to the ones he'd been shackled with, but he didn't comment on them. "I haven't used mine for twenty-two years." He motioned for them to take a seat. "Most of the time I even think of myself as James. Although since my capture, I've been using the old name, so it's coming back."

"Why are they keeping you here?" Emmett asked. "Do you pose a threat to the clan?"

Vrog glanced at the two Guardians seated at the dining table. "I don't, but I guess Kian needs more time to make sure that I'm harmless to him and his clan. He told me that he plans to send me back to China with a team of investigators, so my stay here is not going to be long."

"That's good." Emmett sat down on the armchair that used to be his favorite and crossed his legs. "I hated living underground, and they kept me here for months."

"I heard." Vrog cast a sidelong glance at the Guardians. "Alec and Vernon told me what you had done and why you were here for so long. I didn't know any hybrids who could compel anyone other than humans." He looked as if he had another question on the tip of his tongue but was too embarrassed to ask it.

Emmett had a pretty good idea what that question was.

"Don't be bashful, Vrog. Ask me whatever and I'll either answer or choose not to, but I won't get offended."

"How did you get free of your vow to Jade? Is it connected to your ability to compel?" Vrog shook his head. "She's been gone for over two decades, and I still can't do it."

Emmett smiled. "It is connected to my compulsion talent, but not directly. It just provided me with a loophole. I told myself that I was serving her by leaving. If I had stayed, and she discovered what I could do, she probably would have had me killed. Not an execution because I had done nothing wrong, but she would have perceived me as a threat and ordered one of the purebloaded males to challenge me to a duel. The Mother of All Life would not have approved, and Jade would have suffered the consequences."

"Clever," Vrog admitted. "What about your parents? Your friends? Weren't you afraid that she would retaliate against them?"

Emmett shrugged. "I had no friends, my human mother was gone, and my purebloaded father could go to hell as far as I was concerned."

"Who was your father, if I may ask?"

"Tuvor."

Vrog winced. "Yeah. I don't blame you. I didn't know he had a son who left. No one ever mentioned anything about you. It was as if you'd never existed."

"Obviously." Emmett folded his arms over his chest. "That would have made Jade look bad. She must have ordered my excommunication and ordered everyone to forget me. Who was your father?"

"Sybor." Given the sadness in Vrog's eyes, he hadn't hated his sire.

"I remember Sybor as one of the two semi-decent pure-blooded males. The other one was Voril."

Vrog chuckled. "Jade didn't like either of them. She considered them weaklings because they weren't as cruel as the others."

"Indeed." Emmett grimaced. "That's why she loved my sire, not that she loved anyone other than herself. A better way to describe her feelings for him is that she found him adequate enough to invite him to her bed more often than any of the others. He failed to impregnate her, though, and it was one more reason for her to detest me."

Vrog

Emmett's father had been a favorite of Jade, which had probably made Emmett's life even more miserable than those of the other hybrids.

No wonder he'd left.

Jade had accepted the necessity of her males fathering more children with the humans, but she hadn't liked it. She'd regarded humans as inferior, and the males she'd favored knew better than to take human females into their beds for anything other than breeding when they were fertile.

"What makes you think that the males were killed?" Eleanor asked.

Vrog sighed. He'd repeated the story several times already, and it pained him every time anew. But Emmett was a former tribesman, and even though he'd deserted, he deserved to know.

When he was done, Emmett nodded. "They wouldn't have taken those damn rings off even if their lives depended on it. I agree with your assessment that they are dead."

"What if Jade commanded them to do that?" Eleanor asked.

"They would have obeyed." Emmett twisted one of his own rings, made from gold, not from polished precious stone like the ones the purebloods had worn. "But she wouldn't have demanded it unless they were accused of treason."

Eleanor arched a brow. "And that's not possible?"

"It's unlikely," Vrog said.

"Could she and the other females have killed the males?" Eleanor asked.

"Why would they do that? They sneered at human males, and they needed the purebloods to father long-lived children."

"If the Kra-ell are related to the immortals, then the females don't need purebloded males to produce long-lived children. If they weren't such snobs, they might have discovered that their children with humans could have been activated."

Alec cleared his throat. "That's information Kian is not ready to share with Vrog."

"Why not?" she asked.

The Guardian shrugged. "He has his reasons. I'm just following orders."

Letting out a long-suffering sigh, Eleanor leaned forward. "So, what are your plans, Vrog? Are you going to join our clan? Or are you going to keep waiting for your bitchy mistress to return?"

He'd given it a lot of thought, and the decision was difficult—on the one hand, he had a son that he wanted to get to know, and a wedding that he wanted to attend. On the other hand, the international school he'd founded was his life project, and even though it had started as a cover, it had become much more than that.

"I have a life in China."

Eleanor waved a dismissive hand. "You have a job, and you are waiting for someone who is not coming back and who is not even worth waiting for. Here you have a son, and because of Vlad, Kian can't refuse you membership in the clan if you ask for it." She pinned him with a hard stare. "Ask for it, Vrog. You can have a life with the clan."

He looked around the small but lavish apartment. "This is very nice and comfortable, but I don't want to spend my life in here."

She laughed. "Of course not. You will come to live in the village, and you might even find a nice female to have a good life with—as her equal, not her slave." She smirked. "If you want to play kinky games in bed, you can be a slave all you like, but you don't need to play that role outside of the bedroom."

He didn't like playing kinky games, and having an immortal partner who would treat him as her equal sounded too good to be true.

The question was whether he was willing to give up the school for that. He already had a long-lived son, and although he wouldn't mind having another, that yearning had been satisfied.

"I need to think about it." He turned to Emmett, who hadn't commented on anything Eleanor had said so far. "What's your advice?"

"Same as Eleanor's." Emmett unfolded his arms and got up. "I thought I was happy as can be in my Safe Haven." He opened the bar cabinet and pulled out a bottle of wine. "I had all the women I wanted, people who worshiped me like a god, and I was making a fortune." He took out five glasses and filled them with wine. "But even though I was surrounded by people, I was lonely. I didn't have a partner. The life I built for myself was exactly the kind of life I dreamt about having before I left the compound."

He handed Eleanor a glass of wine, another to Vrog, and two to the Guardians sitting at the small dining table.

"When Eleanor and Peter showed up, and things happened the way they did, I thought that being captured and imprisoned was the worst thing that had ever happened to me." He took a sip from his wine. "Turned out that I was wrong." He stopped behind Eleanor's armchair and put his hand on her shoulder. "It was the best thing that had ever happened to me. I met a female who's my perfect counterpart, my friend, my lover, my partner. And that's worth more than the cushy life I made for myself in Safe Haven."

Smiling, Eleanor put her hand on top of Emmett's and winked at Vrog. "As you can see, my partner has a penchant for drama."

"I meant every word." Emmett took Eleanor's hand and lifted it to his lips for a kiss. "I guess my human half yearned for an exclusive relationship that would have been abhorrent to a pureblooded Kra-ell." He turned to Vrog. "Which half is more dominant in you?"

"I suppose that it's the human half. I was a young male when I was sent to Singapore, and I've spent my life among humans ever since. I don't think I could easily adapt to the Kra-ell lifestyle and its rigid hierarchy after all these years." Vrog thought of his school, and how much he enjoyed being in charge. "I won't accept being treated as an inferior again."

"Then you have your answer." Emmett finished the last of the wine in his glass. "Sell your school, and come live in the immortals' village."

"We need a school," Eleanor said. "Not right now, but in the future. Your experience might be useful to the clan."

One of the Guardians cleared his throat, probably meaning to warn Emmett and Eleanor not to say more about their village and where it was located. Or maybe the warning was about the future need for a school?

"Thank you." Vrog dipped his head. "Your warm invitation means a lot to me, but I need more time to decide, and I also need to ask Vlad what he prefers. Perhaps he doesn't want me to join the clan."

Eleanor frowned. "Why wouldn't he?"

"Stella is in a relationship with a male who hates me, and who Vlad is fond of. That might be a problem."

Geraldine

As Shai stopped at the gate to her community, Geraldine opened her eyes and waved at the guard. "Good evening, Karl."

"Good evening, Ms. Beaumont." He waved back and opened the gate.

They had spent a lovely morning and part of the afternoon with Rhett, touring the university and later the town. Regrettably, they hadn't had time to visit the museums or the botanical gardens, but Shai had promised her that after the Orion thing was done with, he would take her on another, longer vacation to Northern California.

Hopefully it would be soon because it was wrecking her nerves and keeping her from fully enjoying her new life with Shai. It was a shame that Rhett couldn't become a greater part of it, though, and her heart ached for Shai and the future he would have to face.

If the Fates were kind they would give them a child, and perhaps that would make things a little easier for him, but one child couldn't substitute for another, and it would always be difficult for Shai.

Geraldine knew that pain. Now that she had found out about Darlene, the guilt over missing so many years with her was a constant ache in her heart. Perhaps if Darlene were happily married with a gaggle of kids, Geraldine would have felt a little less guilty. But knowing that her daughter had a miserable life was adding another layer to the guilt.

Hopefully, Darlene could transition, and they would have eternity to make up for lost time.

When Rhett got married and had a family of his own, knowing that his son was happy and settled down would help Shai. But Rhett could never become immortal, so there was that.

Shai didn't even have the sliver of hope Geraldine had.

Shai had to make the most of the time he had with Rhett, using clever disguises and prosthetics when he visited him.

As he parked in her driveway, she covered up the wave of sadness and the tears stinging her eyes with a yawn and a forced smile. "What time is it?"

"Almost eight. Did you have a nice nap?"

There was an edge to his tone, and Geraldine wondered whether she talked in her sleep. She'd dreamt about Orion, but it hadn't been a memory.

"I did. I'm so sorry for not keeping you company. It's the engine noise. It always lulls me to sleep."

He smiled and reached to cup her cheek. "I enjoyed watching you napping peacefully until you started to frown and whimper. What did you dream about?"

Had she made those noises while thinking of Rhett?

Her eyes had been closed, so she might have drifted off into that state between sleep and wakefulness. But telling Shai her depressing thoughts would just make him sad as well. Telling him about her dream was better.

"I dreamt about Orion, but it wasn't real. I saw him walking down the street and I called after him. He looked at me over his shoulder, but there was no recognition in his eyes, and he kept walking. I started running to catch up to him, but even though he was just walking, the distance between us kept widening. When I called out his name again, he didn't even turn around, and then he just disappeared. One moment he was there and then next he was gone. I stopped and started crying, which was probably when you heard me whimpering."

"Oh, sweetheart." He unbuckled her seatbelt and pulled her onto his lap. "I'm not a psychologist, but I think that you feel abandoned by him."

"How can I feel that when I can barely remember Orion?"

"Your subconscious remembers him well enough, and that's where dreams are made."

She rested her head on his chest. "Maybe it's more about guilt than abandonment. Or perhaps it's a combination of both. When he's caught, he will blame me for setting a trap for him, and he might never forgive me."

"Makes sense." He stroked her back. "I still think that you should talk to Vanessa. "

Thankfully, the therapist had told Shai that the earliest she could see Geraldine was in three weeks. The truth was that she didn't believe a shrink could do anything for her, especially after the goddess herself had unlocked her memories. The Clan Mother was smart enough to prevent a flood of them from overwhelming her mind, and Geraldine didn't trust the psychologist to do better. In fact, she feared Vanessa would do worse.

"It's not my fault that Vanessa is so busy. I was okay with going to see her on Wednesday."

"I know. It's frustrating that she doesn't deem your case as an emergency."

"Because it's not." She lifted her head to kiss the side of his mouth. "You're just impatient. My memories are coming back slowly, just as the Clan Mother intended. At first, I was also disappointed that it didn't happen right then and there, but now I understand how smart she was not to allow that."

"You're right." He hooked a finger under her chin and kissed her.

Wrapping her arms around his neck, she kissed him back, and as he deepened the kiss and fire started low in her belly, she pushed out of his arms. "I need to shower, and so do you." She rose to her feet and stretched her arms over her head. "We can continue this conversation inside."

Amusement dancing in his eyes, he opened the motorhome's door. "A conversation, eh?"

"Or whatever else you have on your mind." Geraldine went back for her bag. "Can we wait to clean this up until tomorrow? I'm really not in the mood to do it now."

"Neither am I." He followed her to the motorhome's bedroom and lifted his own overnight bag. "Anyway, I plan to return it on Monday. I left my car in the village."

"Which means that if we want to go anywhere tomorrow, we have to take the motorhome."

Shai's grin was wolfish. "Then I guess we are not going anywhere."

Shai

Shai hated that Geraldine's memories of Orion were percolating to the surface, not because they were slow to emerge, but because they were there.

On the one hand, he wanted her to remember more so he would know what the bastard had been up to, and what his motives were for being in her life. On the other hand, though, he resented the immortal's very existence and hated himself for feeling possessive and jealous like some damn caveman.

The guy had helped Geraldine over the years, and Shai was well aware that without Orion's assistance, her life would have been either much more difficult, or worse, she might have been discovered by greedy humans who would have experimented on her to find out the secret of her immortality.

But it wasn't just about that.

Even if jealousy and possessiveness were not clouding his attitude, Shai couldn't get rid of the nagging suspicion that Orion had something to do with Geraldine's so-called accident, and until he was convinced that hadn't been the case, he couldn't feel gratitude toward the guy.

As Geraldine headed to the bathroom, she cast him a look that had invitation written all over it, but he needed time to cool off and pretended not to get her meaning. "I'll whip us up something to eat while you are showering."

"Okay." She looked disappointed. "I'm not hungry, but I would love some coffee."

"I'll get the coffeemaker going." He turned around and walked out the door.

In the kitchen, he pulled out his phone and called the security office in the village.

"Shai," Morgard answered. "How was your trip?"

He'd told Kian that he was taking Geraldine on a short one-day romantic vacation, which hadn't been a total lie. They had made love in the motorhome twice, and they'd had a good time with Rhett and also by themselves.

"It was great. Was there any suspicious activity around Geraldine's house while we were gone?"

"I would have let you know if there was. Though to tell you the truth, with all the deliveries her neighbors receive, it's difficult to tell, especially with Uber Eats and

Grubhub and even Amazon using private operators. Anyone can pretend to be a delivery driver. And then there are the gardeners, cleaners, pest controllers, satellite dish installers, carpet cleaners, and so on."

Shai ran a hand over the back of his head. "So what good are those cameras? Unless the guy knocks on the door and gets his face in front of the camera attached to it, we won't know that he was snooping around."

"Since he has no reason to suspect anything, we are counting on him not being overly careful. He's been visiting her for years, so he's probably grown complacent."

"I hope you're right. Thanks for the update."

"No problem." Morgard ended the call.

With a sigh, Shai put the phone on the counter and got busy with the coffeemaker.

Geraldine came down just as it finished brewing, wearing a knee-length silk robe. With the fabric draping ever so lovingly over her body, it was obvious that she wore nothing underneath.

The problem was that they were being watched, and he didn't want the guys in security to ogle her.

"Aren't you cold?"

"That's not the question I was expecting." Looking disappointed, she pulled out a chair and sat down. "What's bugging you, Shai?"

"Orion. The wait is grating on my nerves. I want this to be over already."

"You and me both. But that's no reason to brood. I come down here half naked, and you ask me if I'm cold? I'm lucky that I don't have confidence issues, at least as far as my attractiveness goes, or I would have thought that I no longer excite you."

"Don't be silly." He prowled up to her and lifted her out of the chair. Cupping her naked bottom under the robe, he commanded, "Wrap your legs around me."

When she did, he swiveled his hips, grinding himself into her and letting her feel what seeing her in that skimpy thing was doing to him. "Is that proof enough of how much you excite me?"

Her smile was pure feminine satisfaction. "Carry me to bed, big boy," she whispered throatily.

"What about the coffee?"

"It can wait." She nipped his ear, then blew into it, the tease turning his erection into a hard rod that strained his zipper.

"Feisty kitten." Kneading her bottom, he headed up the stairs.

"Don't forget the cameras," she whispered in his ear. "We are giving them a show."

"Now you're suddenly concerned with privacy? You didn't seem to care when you came down wearing cobwebs."

"Why do you think I didn't do it naked?"

Geraldine

Geraldine clung to Shai as he carried her up the stairs, worried about the short robe revealing too much to those watching eyes in the village. Despite what he thought, she was keenly aware of them and kept her sexual innuendoes to a minimum.

It was a struggle not to run her tongue all over the strong column of his neck, to nibble at his ear and make him forget all about Orion.

The road trip and the day they'd spent with Rhett had been wonderful, and then she'd opened her big mouth and told Shai about the dream. Except, she hadn't expected him to get upset by it.

Usually, he got jealous when she said nice things about Orion, or when she expressed regret about the trap they had set for him with her as bait. But the dream hadn't been pleasant.

The truth was that she didn't know how to handle Shai's mood swings, or why he was having them. Their relationship used to be so easy, so natural, it was like winning the mate lottery. Shai should be over the moon with happiness, and so should she, but the thing with Orion hung over them like a dark cloud.

So Geraldine turned to the best tool in her arsenal, which was seduction, hoping to get Shai's mind off Orion. But with those damn surveillance cameras all over the house, she had been limited with what she could do outside their bedroom.

It was a relief to reach that sanctuary, and as Shai kicked the door closed behind them, Geraldine let loose, attacking that strong neck column with her lips and her tongue and her teeth, licking, sucking, nipping, and kissing.

When he lowered her to the long ottoman at the foot at the bed instead of the bed itself, she wondered what he had in mind, hoping it was something naughty.

Rising on her knees, Geraldine reached for Shai's zipper, but he shook his head and turned her around to face the headboard.

Well, that was a big fat clue as to his intentions.

"Don't move," he whispered against her ear.

Stifling a smile, she put her hands on the footboard and listened to him ditch his clothes.

She was still wearing the robe, but that barrier was easy to remove.

Wrapping his arms around her waist, his fingers splayed over her belly, he kissed the column of her neck, small teasing kisses that soon turned into little nips that sent shivers of desire straight to her burning core.

When one of his hands left her belly, dipping between her thighs and cupping her there, while the other slithered under her robe, closing over her breast, Geraldine bit down on her lower lip to stifle the moan rising up in her throat.

"Don't hold it in," he murmured against her neck. "I want to hear you moan, and beg, and shout my name when you come."

"What about the cameras?" she managed to ask.

"Forget them. The guys probably already muted the sound."

His fingers plucked at her nipple while his finger dipped between her folds.

Closing her eyes, she let her head drop against his shoulder and surrendered to the sensations.

"Bend down." He pushed gently on her back.

She did, pressing her chest against the footboard and sticking her bum out.

He lifted the robe, exposing her bottom, the cold air cooling the heat he'd stoked.

For a moment, he did nothing, making her wonder what he was up to, but then the tip of his shaft nudged her entrance, teasing her as he moved it up and down her folds, coating it with her wetness.

Geraldine held her breath, waiting for him to join them.

She didn't have to wait long.

Clamping one hand on her hip and the other on her shoulder, he surged inside her until he was all the way in, his chest on her back, his groin pressed against her bottom.

Then he started moving.

Slamming against the soft cushions of her butt cheeks, he pumped into her with abandon and roughness that got her fire reaching the level of inferno. When he circled his arm around her and pressed his finger to her throbbing nub, she bucked, her muscles clamping on his shaft.

As his movements became frenzied, and as he rubbed that most sensitive spot, she exploded, shouting his name and not caring who heard her, be it the neighbors or the Guardians in the security room miles away from there.

The loud hiss was her only warning before his fangs closed on the crook of her neck, the twin incision points a delicious burn that had her climaxing again.

She felt his seed erupt into her sheath at the same time the venom slid into her vein. A moment later the familiar bliss obliterated the last remnants of reason, sending her soaring on the now familiar cloud.

Kian

"Good morning, Peter." Kian opened the door to his office. "You're early."

"I know." The Guardian glanced at his watch. "It's five minutes to seven. I thought you started your day at six."

"Normally I do."

Allegra had been a little fussy this morning, and he didn't want to leave before she calmed down. Syssi claimed that the baby was already aware of their routine, and that his daughter didn't want him to leave.

He didn't know enough about babies and what they should be aware of at such a young age, but in his layman's opinion, Allegra was still too young to be so observant. Then again, he had no doubt that his daughter was brilliant and developing faster than other children. Besides, he trusted Syssi's assessment.

Kian put his coffee cup down on the desk and motioned for Peter to take a seat. "How are things going for you?"

"Fine, I guess. It took some time to get used to field work again."

Kian smiled. "If you prefer, I can put you back in charge of the dungeon."

"No, thank you. I've had enough of the underground. I enjoy fresh air."

"Then you are going to enjoy your next assignment." Kian leaned back in his chair. "I have plans for Safe Haven, and since you know the place and some of the people currently running it, I want you to head that project."

Given Peter's surprised expression, Eleanor hadn't shared her ideas with him.

"What do you want to do there?"

"You know that Roberts is no longer in the picture."

Peter nodded.

"That means several things. First, someone else will be appointed as the director of the paranormal program, and second, we lost our access to the Echelon system. I came up with an idea for how to remedy the situation, and Eleanor improved on it. I want her to be the new director, which can be achieved with the help of her compulsion power and our assistance in providing her with the proper credentials. She likes the idea of heading the program, but she doesn't want to leave Emmett behind, and I can't allow him to accompany her to West Virginia. Her solution was to move the program to Safe Haven, where we can keep an eye on Emmett and also have free access to the paranormal talents in the program."

"If she can make it work, that's actually brilliant." Peter smoothed his fingers over his goatee. "But it's a big if."

"She's a compeller. She can make it happen. But first, she needs to spend a couple of months in West Virginia until things start moving. I also want her to find people working for the Echelon system and compel them to provide us the information we need."

Peter seemed doubtful, but he decided to keep his doubts to himself. "What's my part in this?"

Kian smiled. "There is a lot to be done, and I need a capable person to be the clan's representative in Safe Haven. The job requires leadership skills."

"I might not be the best person for the job. Watching over Emmett was my first command, and it was not very demanding."

"This is your chance to prove that you can be in charge of a bigger operation. Emmett knows how to run the place, and you can rely on him, but you also need to ensure that he doesn't exploit the community."

Peter grimaced. "I get it. It's the same job of being Emmett's keeper just with expanded responsibilities. Are you sure about letting him run the place?"

"This entire thing is hinged on him resuming his guru persona. He's been running the place as a spiritual retreat for nearly four decades. When Eleanor suggests moving the paranormal program to Safe Haven, it will look much better with him there than under new management. Also, no one would think it strange if the place started retreats for people with paranormal abilities. It's right up there with the other New Age stuff Safe Haven promotes."

"I see. So, Eleanor would suggest both to the decision-makers in the government to whet their appetites. A retreat for paranormals could be the perfect recruiting ground."

"You are a smart guy, Peter." Kian tapped his temple. "Neither I nor Eleanor have thought of that. The idea was for us to screen the attendees of those retreats for potential Dormants. But you are right about it being a big selling point that Eleanor can use to dangle in front of the government higher-ups."

His eyes glowing with excitement, Peter straightened in his chair. "When do you want to get a move on that?"

"I'm organizing a visit to Safe Haven on Monday two weeks from now, and I'm taking Syssi and Allegra with me, along with Eleanor, Emmett, and Shai. I thought you would go ahead of us and get it ready for our visit."

Looking unsure, Peter rubbed his hand over the back of his neck. "To be frank, I don't know how to go about it. What do I do? Do I just show up and demand cooperation?"

"More or less. I will have a document drafted that spells out an agreement between Emmett and one of our business entities. First, though, I'll have Emmett email the person in charge of the place and tell her that he's coming back and expects his place to be ready for him."

"How is he going to explain his absence?"

Kian grinned. "Shai came up with a plausible story. Emmett answered a spiritual calling to meditate in the Himalayas and revisit the limitations he had imposed on his flock—mainly the prohibition on forming exclusive relationships and having children. While meditating, he met a kindred spirit, i.e. me, and we decided to form a partnership. In exchange for my investment in Safe Haven, he will grant us the use of the land for the next twenty-five years and access to all of its facilities."

"What if after the visit you decide not to go through with it?"

Kian shrugged. "Deals fall apart all the time."

"I see that you've got it all figured out."

"I hope so."

"I have a suggestion if you don't mind."

"Go ahead." Kian waved a hand. "The more minds working on this plan, the better."

"It might be a good idea to have Bowen and Margaret come along. She spent decades in that place. She knows everyone there."

Kian nodded. "I'll discuss it with them, but I don't think Margaret will be interested. She wants to be near Wendy."

"It doesn't hurt to ask. I think Margaret will be offended if you don't."

"Right. I hadn't considered that."

It wasn't a big surprise that he hadn't taken into account Margaret's feelings, but Syssi would have mentioned it if she thought that it was an issue.

Before talking to Margaret, he needed to talk it over with her. In matters such as this, he trusted Syssi's opinion the most. Heck, he trusted her opinion on any and all topics. His mate was smart, but she wasn't opinionated, and she wasn't a know-it-all. When she decided to voice her opinion, it was only when she was a hundred percent sure about it and decided that it was worth mentioning.

Emmett

Emmett had had two weeks to prepare, and he'd expected a smooth slide into his old role. He relished the return to his flock, but the guru costume felt strange, and instead of transforming him into the spiritual leader of Safe Haven, it made him feel like an actor.

An imposter.

Perhaps quality was the problem. The wig on his head was made from real hair, but it was heavy, and everything about it was off—the dull color, the rough texture, the lack of luster. The robe draping awkwardly over his body was made from synthetic fabric—a cheap imitation of the ones he'd had custom tailored for him before.

Or maybe he was just a different person than the one who'd fled Safe Haven three months ago, with Peter in his sports car and a renewed hope for the future of his people.

Damn, Emmett missed that car. He missed driving down the Oregon coast, he missed putting on a show, he missed the admiration bordering on worship of his followers, the high he'd gotten from that.

What he didn't miss, though, was the mindless debauchery he'd taken part in, or watched others engage in.

Sitting next to him in the rented limousine heading for Safe Haven was the person that had changed him from the inside out, forcing him to reevaluate his life and what he wanted to do with it.

He'd once heard a proverb about how lucky was the man who found a woman of valor. At the time, he'd sneered at it because in his mind it referenced the Kra-ell pure-blooded females, and Emmett didn't consider the Kra-ell males lucky at all. He'd preferred the softness of human women, not realizing that there could be a happy medium.

Eleanor was a fighter through and through—ambitious, demanding, and assertive, sometimes even abrasive. And yet, she was soft when she wanted to be, and she wasn't cruel—never inflicting pain on him unless it was to spice things up for his pleasure.

Hell, he'd had to beg her to bite him.

Now that she knew that it drove him wild, she did it often, and he loved her even more for stepping out of her comfort zone for him.

"What are you smiling about?" Eleanor whispered.

"You." He tucked her closer against his side. "You've changed my life for the better, and you're still doing it."

Kian chuckled. "Save it for later, Emmett," he said softly, not because of any tender feelings for Emmett or Eleanor but because he didn't want to disturb the peaceful sleep of his infant daughter, who was curled in the car seat between him and his wife.

Fatherhood made the big boss much less intimidating. No man looked scary while pushing a stroller or carrying his child in a baby pouch strapped to his chest.

Still, Emmett wondered what Kian had meant by saving it for later. Had he meant it as in 'get a room,' or as in 'save the theatrical performance for the Safe Haven community'?

"Are you nervous?" Syssi asked. "You haven't given a sermon in a long time."

It had been the second one then. Syssi knew her husband better than anyone, so the meaning had been clear to her. They both thought that his expression of love and appreciation for Eleanor was nothing more than a performance.

Emmett kissed the top of Eleanor's head and smiled. "As long as I have this incredible woman by my side, I have nothing to be nervous about."

Let them chew on that.

Kian narrowed his eyes at him, but Syssi smiled. "Since Eleanor can't deliver the speech for you, I hope you have it memorized."

"Not at all. I always make them up on the spot. They sound better when they are not rehearsed, and I take cues from my audience. There is no substitute for spontaneity."

"I would have never had the guts to improvise like that," Syssi admitted. "Public speaking terrifies me, but I can handle it if I'm well prepared, and by well, I mean memorizing every word, practicing in front of the mirror, and recording myself to hear how I sound and to see how I look delivering it."

"That's a lot of prep," Eleanor said. "I also like to be prepared, but I don't bother with how I sound or look. I only care about the script." With a sigh, she leaned her head on Emmett's arm. "I need to rehearse what I'm going to say to the higher-ups to get myself reinstated. As Emmett can attest, compulsion requires very precise phrasing to work as intended."

Out of habit, Emmett glanced at Kian's left ear. His long hair covered the right, but he'd tucked it behind the other one and there was no visible earpiece in it.

He either wasn't wearing one, or William had invented a device so tiny that it was invisible. Except, a small device was no good as a physical barrier. It had to be large enough to block the compulsion sound waves from reaching the ear canal.

Emmett grinned. "I see that you finally trust me. You no longer bother with the cumbersome earpieces."

"I trust you a little more than I did before, but that doesn't mean that I'm careless." Kian motioned with his head toward the partition. "I brought Okidu along, and since he's a machine, you can't compel him. He holds the remote to your cuffs."

The guy thought that he was so smart, and even though it wasn't in Emmett's best interest to annoy the boss, he just couldn't help bringing Kian down a notch.

He smirked. "Since Okidu is programmed to obey your commands, theoretically, I can compel you to command him to relinquish the remote to me."

Kian returned with a smirk of his own. "That's not going to work. I told Okidu not to do that even if I commanded him to. He's to hold on to the remote until we are back in the village. Besides, Anandur and Brundar are both wearing earpieces, and they would stop you before you could finish the sentence."

Emmett racked his brain to find a loophole in that, but anything he came up with sounded like the retorts of a petulant teen. Instead, he decided to use the opportunity to butter Kian up. "I concede defeat." He dipped his head. "You've outsmarted me."

Kian had never seen Emmett in action, not like that, and not live. Through his office window, he'd watched the guy proselytizing to a group of smitten clan females, and he'd heard recordings of Emmett's inspirational teachings, but he had never seen and heard Emmett while the guy was in his full costume regalia and pumped on the attention and admiration of his flock.

The result was impressive and quite entertaining. In fact, if Kian hadn't known that the essence of the story Emmett was telling with such dramatic flair had been fabricated by Shai, he might have been moved.

"The Mother of all Life called me to her." Emmett raised his arms. "She was angry at me, angry for denying her most precious gift to humanity, the gift of rebirth. I had to atone for my sin, the sin of convincing you all to go against nature and deny you the gift of children. I've spent weeks in silence, fasting, crying, praying, begging the goddess for forgiveness, until she answered me."

Emmett turned toward Eleanor, gazing at her lovingly. "The goddess sent her earthly embodiment to teach me the value of love. Eleanor taught me that there are many ways to love. For some, freedom is the only way—the freedom to choose a different partner each night, the freedom to experiment, the freedom to share their heart and body with as many as would have them. For others, this is a burden, for them, there is just one person they want to share their life with, and that's okay. There is no right or wrong in love."

As he paused, Eleanor started clapping, and soon the rest of Safe Haven's community joined her.

Riley, the one who had taken over for Emmett, had tears in her eyes, but Kian wasn't sure whether they were about the emotional impact of Emmett's 'New Way' or the realization that he would no longer share her bed.

When they'd arrived, the woman fawned over Emmett, finding every excuse to touch him until Eleanor snarled at her.

The speech continued for another hour, with Emmett gushing over the bright future of the community, the new buildings his new partner was going to erect, the new retreat for people with paranormal abilities, and so on.

At some point, Allegra woke up and began fussing, giving Syssi an excuse to leave the dining hall where the speech was delivered.

Brundar followed her outside.

Emmett smiled indulgently. "Soon, we will have many more fussy babies on our hands, and The Mother of all Life will rejoice."

Next to Kian, Anandur shifted his weight on the chair and stretched his long legs in front of him. "He's good," he whispered so low that only immortal ears could hear him. "But he needs to wrap it up. I'm hungry."

Emmett must have heard him because he smiled and lifted his arms again. "The coming months will be full of excitement. They will also be difficult. It's never easy to adjust to a new way, and the building project will disturb the community's tranquility. But no progress can be made without disrupting the status quo, and children cannot be raised in silence. Embrace these sounds. They herald a better future for us all."

In a flurry of robes, Emmett walked toward their table, leaned down, and kissed Eleanor on the lips. "You are my future," he said loud enough for everyone to hear.

As the room exploded in applause, Emmett straightened up and lifted his hand to silence his people.

"Let me introduce to you my dear new friend, Kian—the man who opened my eyes and helped me shape Emmett's New Way. Give him a round of applause."

Kian was thankful for the lack of smartphones in Safe Haven. No one snapped pictures of him as he took the spot Emmett had vacated.

"Everyone is hungry, so I'll make it short. Thank you for the heartwarming welcome your community has extended to me, my wife and daughter, and my friends. It is my pleasure to be your guest tonight, and I hope that together we will create a better future for the Safe Haven community. *Bon appétit*, everyone."

As a new round of applause erupted, several people rushed out of the dining hall, and a few moments later came back rolling buffet tables and lining them against the wall.

"I'm going to check on Syssi," he told Anandur.

The guy fell in step with him. "You're not going anywhere alone, boss."

People smiled and clapped as they passed them by, a few whispering thank you, but some didn't look happy.

Kian couldn't blame them.

They came to Safe Haven to escape the world, and here he was, a stranger who was bringing the world to them, upending their way of life, and forcing the change down their throats.

Shai

As they exited the main lodge, Shai zipped up his windbreaker. It was still mostly sunny in Southern California, but the Oregon coast was cold and breezy.

It wasn't bad, but it wouldn't have been Shai's first choice for a paranormal retreat. First of all, it was far away from their village, and secondly, the nearly permanent overcast was too glum for year-round living.

The proximity to the ocean was the place's biggest selling point.

The community building was shabby, bordering on shameful, and the lodge needed work, but the grounds were meticulously maintained.

"This place is perfect," Syssi said as Emmett opened the side gate with a card key.

His old one had been removed from the database, and when he'd asked Riley to issue him a new one, she'd done so gladly, but she had been disappointed that he hadn't invited her to join their tour of the property.

A big smile stretching across Syssi's pretty face, she turned in a circle and sucked in a long breath. "The fresh ocean breeze, the quiet, the sprawling grounds, I love it here."

Shai glanced at Kian, who didn't seem to share his wife's favorable opinion.

"It needs a lot of work," he said quietly.

Carrying Allegra in a baby pouch that was attached with straps to his chest, Kian kept his growling to a minimum and his facial expressions in neutral.

It was a bit disconcerting.

Normally, Kian was one of the easiest people to read because he never felt the need to pretend. Now that he was making accommodations for Allegra, Shai had to work harder to guess what Kian wanted.

Nevertheless, fatherhood was good for the guy, smoothing out his rough edges and making him less intimidating.

"Do you mean the new buildings?" Emmett asked.

Kian shook his head. "Everything needs to be remodeled. The decor is outdated, the community quarters are inadequate, and that's putting it mildly. The guest rooms are spartan, and on top of that, the workmanship is crap. The paint, the flooring, the tile in the bathrooms, everything needs to be replaced. I think it would be best to just demolish these buildings and build new ones."

"You're not going to recoup the expense," Shai said. "You're thinking about Safe Haven in terms of the hotels you build, but this is not a hotel. People don't expect luxury when they come to a spiritual retreat."

Kian cut him a sidelong glance. "Is suffering part of the experience? Because for what they are charged, the guests should receive better accommodations."

Shai wondered whether Kian was really that disillusioned with the place, or if it was just a negotiation tactic to get Emmett to lower his price.

"I didn't notice any major issues," Emmett said, sounding defensive. "You should listen to your assistant."

Kian pinned him with a hard stare. "You want to tell me that no one ever complained about the living conditions in the community building? Or that no guests demanded their money back after seeing their rooms?"

Emmett squared his shoulders. "There are always people who find fault with everything, and who are a pain in the butt no matter how well they are treated. Thankfully, we had only a handful of cases over the years, and I gladly refunded their money and sent them on their way."

Kian's eyes shifted to Peter. "You were a guest. What did you think about the accommodations?"

The Guardian shrugged. "The room was clean, the mattress was comfortable, and I had everything I needed.

Between the classes, the workshops, and our side activities, we didn't get to spend much time in the rooms."

As they reached the beach, Syssi spread her arms. "Who cares about the rooms when they have this as their backyard?"

Kian grimaced. "I bet it's not as lovely in the winter."

Eleanor turned her back to the ocean and gazed at the main lodge. "It looks nice from here, and I like the rustic vibe. I bet Ingrid can wield her magic and transform the guest rooms into cozy havens. If she managed to do that with the dungeon cells, she would have no problem doing even better with the lodge guest rooms."

"There are cracked tiles in the bathrooms," Kian grumbled as softly as he could. "Some of the faucets are rusted, and I smelled mold. No amount of decorative magic can solve those problems."

As their group continued their discussion about what was necessary to fix and what could be improved with furniture and decor, Shai thought about the night he was going to spend away from Geraldine.

They had been inseparable from nearly the first day, sleeping in each other's arms every night, waking up together, having breakfast together.

He kept telling himself that it was only one night, but the vise on his heart refused to loosen. The tether connecting him to Geraldine pulled and tightened the further away from her he got, and the more time had passed since he'd last been with her.

It was ridiculous.

He'd seen her earlier that morning, and if he were back in California, Shai would still be in the office. But knowing that he wasn't going home to Geraldine tonight was enough to make him miss her as if he hadn't seen her in days.

How were Anandur and Brundar tolerating being away from their mates?

Was it easier for them because they'd been mated for a while, so the bond could be stretched a little further?

The bond.

Had he and Geraldine bonded without realizing it?

"What do you think, Shai?" Kian asked.

"I'm sorry. I wasn't listening."

His boss shook his head. "We were discussing splitting Safe Haven into two separate sections. The old one will continue doing business as usual, and we will build a new one that will meet our needs."

"Sounds good to me. Who is going to maintain the new section, though? The only workforce to be had out here is the community." He looked at Emmett. "Is there enough of them to run both places?"

Emmett shook his head. "We will need to get more people. Perhaps some of those paranormally talented guests would like to stay and join a community of like-minded people, and by that I don't mean Safe Haven's old community because these people are like-minded in different ways."

"A community of paranormally talented people," Syssi said. "I love it."

"You're forgetting one thing." Eleanor lifted a finger. "Someone needs to come up with a program for paranormals that will have enough classes and workshops to fill two whole weeks. Who's going to do that?"

"Margaret," Emmett said. "She's very good at creating new workshops, and she is one of us now."

"Excellent idea." Kian clapped him on his back. "She declined my invitation to join us because she has no interest in coming back to live here. But I'm sure she'd love to work on a new program for paranormals."

Eleanor pursed her lips. "Margaret has no paranormal talent and no training. How would she know what to include in those classes?"

"That's true." Kian cut a glance to Syssi. "Is it something you would be interested in?"

"I'm not qualified either. You need Amanda, but now that I'm on maternity leave, she has her hands full at the university, and soon she will become a mother herself."

He nodded. "Perhaps it's something you two can put together while on leave from the university, and Margaret can help with the final touches."

Eleanor

"Being back here gives me the creeps." Eleanor sat on the bed and pulled one of her boots off. "It's not the same room you were in before." Emmett joined her on the bed. "Besides, this is where our relationship started." He kissed her neck. "I was a goner from the first taste."

Eleanor rolled her eyes. "How romantic." She lifted her leg and pulled off the other boot. "You thought that I was tasty?"

"And sexy." He kissed her neck again. "Strong." He kissed the soft spot behind her ear. "Alluring." He nibbled on her earlobe. "Intriguing."

She couldn't think with him electrifying her skin and sending sparks of desire right down to her center.

"You're such a smooth operator." She pushed on his chest. "If you want to play, you need to take off the damn wig. I'm surprised no one noticed that it wasn't your natural hair."

He'd managed to grow a short beard over the last two weeks, the nearly black hair so soft and lush compared to the dead feel of the wig.

He smirked. "I had them all under my thrall."

"I hope you're joking."

"Of course. I don't need to use compulsion to have an audience eat out of my hand."

He was such an arrogant peacock, but he wasn't wrong. He knew how to enchant a crowd with nothing more than the power of his personality and his innate charm.

And yet, he looked at her with an expression of a boy waiting for a girl's approval.

"Are you fishing for compliments?" she purred.

"Naturally."

"You were awesome." She whipped her blouse over her head, which was the best method to render Emmett speechless.

His dark eyes blazing, he palmed her breast through her bra, but as a muffled baby wail percolated through the walls, Emmett dropped his hand and glanced at the door. "It's weird having Kian and Syssi in the room across the hallway, and Peter's room is right next to ours. The soundproofing in here is not as good as it is in the village."

She folded a leg under her bottom and regarded him from under lowered lashes. "You haven't said more than two words to Peter since we got here. You should make an effort to befriend him."

"I don't want him here."

"I know." She sighed. "But when I leave for West Virginia, it's going to be just you and him. You need to get along."

"I don't want you to go." He put his hands on her waist and lifted her into his lap. "I need to find a way to convince Kian to let me come with you. I don't even care if he sends Peter with us. It's a price I'm willing to pay to be with you."

"What about Safe Haven? You just got back. You can't leave."

He shrugged. "I can do whatever I want. Riley did a good job running the place in my absence, and she can keep doing that for a couple more months. I can tell her that you and I are working on the new paranormal retreat plan, which is true."

"About that." She grimaced. "Now everyone knows that I'm your girlfriend."

"And that's a problem?"

"Of course it is. When I campaign for moving the paranormal program here, they might accuse me of nepotism. It will look as if I want to do that here to help my boyfriend make more money."

"First of all, you are not going to campaign, you are going to compel, so it doesn't matter what they think. They will approve the transfer. And as to the ones in charge of approving the budget, they will not come here to check out the place or investigate its background for such a small project. Besides, politicians do that all the time, with complete impunity, I might add, and in amounts that make the cost of your paranormal program seem utterly insignificant."

"Yeah, I know." She pouted. "I just like being cautious and not leaving any holes in my plan if I can help it."

She also didn't like the reminder that heading the paranormal division wasn't as big of a deal as she'd made it up to be in her mind. It was a small, insignificant program that would probably get canceled if she didn't save it by compelling the higher-ups to let her run it.

Emmett caressed her back, his hands warm on her chilled skin. "Do you want me to compel the community to forget about you being my girlfriend?"

She shook her head. "Kian told you not to use compulsion on them."

"Then you can compel them. He didn't forbid you to use your power."

Casting Emmett a mock glare, Eleanor straightened in his arms. "I don't want them to forget because I don't want Riley to put her greedy little hands on you. When I'm gone, I want her to know that you're taken."

"You're not going anywhere without me."

"And you're being greedy." She wrapped her arms around his neck. "You're getting everything you wished for and more, and you are still complaining."

He sighed. "I'm not as enthusiastic about being here as I thought I would be. If you are not with me, I'd rather wait for you in the village."

"Really? How come?"

"I don't need to pretend in the village. Everyone knows my story, the good and the bad, and people still accept me. Here, I have to keep up the show twenty-four-seven. The only reprieve I get is when I'm alone with you."

Geraldine

Geraldine clicked the TV on and started flipping through channels. When that didn't yield anything interesting, she switched to Netflix.

Surely, she could find a nice movie or show to take her mind off Shai and how much she missed him.

Usually at this time, he would come through the door, take her into his arms, and kiss the living daylights out of her. Then they would have dinner together, tell each other about their day, they would read a little before bed, and finally they would make love, usually at least twice.

Would she be able to fall asleep without him in the bed with her?

Probably not.

She couldn't even concentrate on reading, the words swimming in front of her eyes, her mind wandering this way and that.

Ugh, why hadn't Orion shown up yet?

More than three weeks had passed since the Clan Mother had released her memories, and as more of them percolated through the barrier between her subconscious and conscious mind, the more of Orion she remembered.

Sometimes, many months would pass between his visits, and other times, he would come every month, but that had been a long time ago. In recent years, after Cassandra had gotten the promotion and their finances had improved, his visits had become much less frequent.

He also hadn't engaged with Cassandra for at least eighteen years. He'd always come when Cassy was at school or at work and leave before she came home.

Orion had explained that Cassandra didn't need him, only Geraldine.

Oddly, he'd never mentioned Cassy's potential to transition. It was as if he didn't know it existed. Perhaps he and his group were like the Kra-ell, and they didn't know that Dormants could be activated.

What if he was a Kra-ell?

Geraldine shivered.

From the little she'd heard about the Kra-ell females, they were vicious and cruel, and she didn't want any of that in her genetic makeup.

No. She and Cassy were descended from the gods, not from the Kra-ell.

Ugh, she needed Orion to show up and give her the answers she needed.

Who had induced her?

Had her inducer or her immortality had anything to do with her accident?

What if her becoming immortal had been a mistake, and her inducer had tried to kill her?

What if Orion was his people's Guardian and had come to punish her inducer and help her survive?

Why hadn't he been interested in her romantically?

In all the restored memories, their encounters had been purely platonic. He'd treated her like a sister or a cousin or a good friend. Their physical contact had been limited to a quick embrace and a kiss on the cheek.

Heck, what if Orion wasn't into females?

Onegus's roommate preferred the company of other males, so it wasn't as if immortals were all heterosexual.

It might be vain of her, but Geraldine was relieved to have stumbled upon a possible explanation of Orion's lack of romantic interest in her. She hadn't met a single man yet who'd been immune to her charms, not unless he was in love with someone else or not interested in women.

Geraldine had so many questions and so few answers, and in the meantime, she was putting her life on hold.

She needed Orion to come already so she could start living her life.

His last visit had been nearly six months ago, so it shouldn't be long before he showed up again. But what if something had happened to him?

"Stop it." Geraldine clicked the TV off and rose to her feet.

In the kitchen, she put the electric kettle on and leaned against the counter as she waited for the water to boil.

As her phone rang, the one that was clan issue, her heart skipped a beat and she rushed back to the living room to get it.

"Shai," she breathed into the receiver. "I've been waiting for you to call."

"I was waiting to call you too, love. Kian dragged us all around the Safe Haven compound, inspecting every corner and grumbling about how everything needed to be remodeled. Then after dinner, he commandeered one of the offices and we worked for a couple of hours going over Safe Haven's financials. When I got back to the room, I remembered that there was no reception in Emmett's bunker, so I went back outside. I'm freezing my butt off, sitting on a rock in his backyard."

"My poor baby. Does that mean no phone sex?"

He chuckled. "Not on my side, but I don't mind watching if you want to give me a show."

"I'll save it for when you come home. It's tomorrow, right? Because I don't think I can survive one more night without you. I've been a total wreck since you left."

"Same here," he admitted. "I feel like there is a vise clamped over my heart, with a coiled string attached to it that has you on the other side. The coil can stretch, but it pulls on the vise, tightening it."

Geraldine's eyes misted with tears. "I feel the same. Do all people in love experience so much pain when they are separated?"

"Not as much, no." He was silent for a brief moment. "Those who are bonded report that it's practically impossible to be apart. It gets easier after they've been together for a while."

It took her a moment to internalize what he'd said, then it hit her, and her hand flew to her chest. "What are you saying, Shai?"

"I think that we've bonded. It must have happened gradually, that was why we didn't feel it snap into place. I talked to Brundar, Anandur, and Kian, not together of course, and each one of them described it differently. Apparently, it's not the same for every couple."

Something eased inside of her, a level of worry and uncertainty that she hadn't been aware of carrying around with her. "I love you."

"Always and forever, my heart."

Shai

Shai had done everything in his power to get things moving as fast as immortally possible, hoping Kian would wrap up their visit before lunch, but his boss wasn't cooperating.

"I know you're in a hurry." Kian clapped Shai's back as they walked out of the dining hall. "But before we leave, I need to have a meeting with Emmett and Riley to discuss the declining revenues."

Last night they'd gone over the books, and provided that the information hadn't been doctored, Safe Haven was self-sufficient in that it wasn't losing money, but it wasn't making much either. What's more, revenues had been steadily declining for a while now, even when Emmett had still been in charge of the place. The sharpest drop, though, was a month after he'd left.

Hopefully Emmett's return would stop the downward trend, but unless Safe Haven got a booster shot of new blood, meaning Uncle Sam paying handsomely for the housing of its paranormal program, it wasn't likely to return to its glory days. Not that they needed it to. The objective wasn't to make money, it was to provide a safe space for the paranormally talented. If they managed not to lose too much, that would be good enough.

Shai arched a brow. "What's there to discuss? You've seen the books. The big drop was after Emmett left. Without their star showman, they had no hook. Now that he's back, things should get better."

Kian cast him an indulgent smile. "It's a management issue, Shai. The advertising continued as usual, showcasing Emmett as the main attraction even though he wasn't there, so the guests didn't know that he would be a no-show. And yet, bookings for the retreats were almost a quarter less than before. That quarter is the cream. The remaining seventy-five percent only covers the expenses."

"So what was the problem? Emmett didn't deal with any of the mundane management issues anyway. It was all done by Riley and her team."

"Riley and the others did their best because Emmett demanded it from them, and they wanted to please him. With him absent, the motivation to go the extra mile was gone. I need to talk to them about customer service and how they respond to inquiries, but I promise to make it short."

He shouldn't have promised what he couldn't deliver.

The meeting dragged on, with Riley coming up with excuses for the poor performance, Emmett suggesting new advertising campaigns, and Kian moderating the discussion while Eleanor was punching away on her phone's calculator and throwing numbers at them.

After an hour of that, Shai tuned them out, his mind going back to last night's conversation with Geraldine.

He felt like an ass. He shouldn't have told her over the phone about the pull of the bond he felt while away from her. He should have done it over a romantic dinner, or perhaps while she was taking a bubble bath, preferably with a bottle of champagne chilling in a bucket of ice on its lip.

Perhaps he could make it up to her?

He should stop somewhere on his way home and get her an outrageous present, like a four-carat engagement ring. What woman wouldn't love a marriage proposal with a fancy ring to sweeten the deal?

Was it crazy?

Maybe. But the idea of surprising Geraldine with a ring and a proposal filled him with excitement and happiness, so why not?

He was still figuring out the details when Kian wrapped up the meeting. They said goodbye to Eleanor, Emmett, and Peter, who were staying in Safe Haven, and headed to the private airport where Charlie was waiting for them with the jet.

"What's been bugging you, Shai?" Kian asked when they boarded the plane and took their seats. "You seem distracted."

Shai wasn't about to share his romantic musings with his boss. The guy could have guessed what was troubling him from the questions he'd asked him the day before about the bond, but apparently Kian still needed to work on his emotional intelligence.

Instead of lying, Shai chose a half truth. "Frankly, I don't like the place." He glanced at Syssi. "I know that you do, but it reminds me too much of Alcatraz."

Syssi gasped. "How can you say that?"

"Just think about it. It's completely isolated, overcast most of the year, and cold. All that's missing is it being on an island surrounded by shark-infested waters."

Kian didn't dispute his observation right off the bat. Instead, he turned to look at the brothers. "What do you think?"

Anandur shrugged. "I wouldn't want to live in Safe Haven all year long, but I wouldn't mind spending a couple of months there, preferably in the summer."

"What about you?" Kian asked Brundar.

"I like it."

Of course, he did.

The Guardian would have probably turned the place into a kink club, which was actually perfectly fitting. Everything that Shai didn't like about Safe Haven was the perfect backdrop to an adult playground for those with kinky tastes.

"What's so amusing?" Syssi asked him. "You're smirking like a Cheshire Cat."

Shai folded his arms over his chest and cast a sidelong glance at Kian. "If you really want to make money on the place, let Brundar manage it."

The Guardian arched a brow. "What do I know about managing a spiritual retreat?"

"That depends on what spiritual experience you're after. I bet some of your club members reach a spiritual level of revelations while engaging in certain activities."

Covering her mouth and blushing profusely, Syssi laughed. "You have a wild imagination, Shai. You should write stories."

"He was an English major," Anandur said. "Go for it, man. A secluded retreat for the sexually adventurous. It could become a bestseller." The Guardian winked. "I even have a name for it—Kinkyland."

Kian snorted. "Knowing Emmett, he would demand part of the royalties. After all, he was the one who came up with the original idea, creating a place for those seeking free love and sexual diversity. Kinkyland is just a variation on the theme."

Anandur grinned like a fiend. "I knew it would catch on. Tell me that I'm not a genius."

"You're not," Brundar grumbled under his breath. "You're a clown."

Anandur shrugged. "I'll take it."

Geraldine

Shai was coming home soon.

Geraldine could feel him getting closer—the tether pulling on her heart slackening a little, allowing her to breathe.

Like so many things, it was probably all in her head. She wanted to feel the bond, so she was imagining that she did.

He'd called a couple of hours ago, telling her that the plane was about to land, and also that he needed to run a quick errand on the way home. It wasn't difficult to estimate that he should walk through the door any minute now.

Ever since their conversation last night, she'd been thrumming with excitement.

They'd bonded.

It hadn't happened overnight like what Cassandra had described happened for her and Onegus, but rather gradually, sneaking up on them while they had been preoccupied worrying about other things.

Shai's trip to Safe Haven had made the power of the bond evident, with both of them suffering because of the separation.

Sleeping had been nearly impossible, in part because the bed was empty and Geraldine missed Shai so much that it hurt, and in part because she'd been thinking about the bond and what it meant for their relationship.

It meant forever, for real, and she thanked the Fates for their wisdom in arranging her and Shai's pairing. The only thing still casting a shadow on their happiness was Orion, but hopefully that too would be over soon.

In the kitchen, Geraldine checked on the prime rib roast. It had been cooking for nearly three hours, and it was about ready. The dish was a bit fancy for a weekday dinner, but she felt like celebrating. Hopefully, Shai would like the roasted Brussels sprouts and glazed carrots she'd made to complement the rib roast. They weren't everyone's favorite, but they were hers and Cassy's.

When the door opened, her heart skipped a beat, and then she was running, her short-heeled mules clicking on the tiled floor.

She flung herself into Shai's outstretched arms. "I missed you so much." She clung to him.

"I missed you too." His lips found hers in a ravenous kiss that lasted long minutes.

Out of breath, she finally pushed away from his chest. "Look at us. We're acting as if we haven't seen each other in months."

"It surely felt like that." Shai picked up the overnight bag he'd dropped on the floor to catch her and took her hand. "Let's go upstairs."

Evidently, he hadn't noticed the table that was set with a white tablecloth, the candles, the wine, the crystal goblets she only used for special occasions.

Still, it was tempting, oh so tempting. But her prime rib roast had to be served as soon as it was out of the oven. Geraldine had spent hours preparing the special meal, and Shai wasn't going anywhere, not if she could help it.

She tugged on his hand. "I made a special dinner for us. It would be a shame to let it cool down and then reheat it."

He finally turned to look at the dining table. "Oh, sweetheart. Is that all for me?"

"Who else?" She pulled him toward the chair. "If you'd come a little earlier, you would have had time to freshen up, but my prime rib roast is ready right about now."

"Then we shall dine, my love." He pulled out a chair for her. "Do you have a moment to share a glass of wine with me before you need to get that delicious-smelling roast out of the oven?"

"A moment." She sat down.

Shai uncorked the bottle and poured the red wine into the two glasses, handed her one, and lifted the other. "To the love of my life."

Tears stung the back of her eyes, but she kept them at bay and smiled. "To my perfect, fated mate."

After they'd clinked glasses and sipped on the wine, Shai took her hand and brought it to his lips for a kiss. "I picked up a little something for you on the way." His other hand went into his pocket.

"What did you get?"

Geraldine's excitement ratcheted up a notch. She loved presents. It didn't even matter what it was as long as Shai spent time choosing it for her.

She hadn't expected a small velvet box, though, a box that was just big enough for a ring or a pair of earrings.

When Shai dropped on one knee, she knew for sure that the box didn't contain earrings.

"Will you marry me, Geraldine?"

As happy tears slid down her cheeks, she cupped Shai's cheek. "We are already mated, but I would love to marry you in front of our family and friends."

A grin splitting his handsome face, he lifted the small box and opened it. "I think I was supposed to do this first and ask you to marry me second, but I'm glad I didn't have to bribe you to say yes."

Geraldine gaped at the enormous solitaire diamond. "I don't know what to say."

He took the ring out of the box. "You already said yes." He slid it over her finger. "Now it's final and you can't take it back."

She wanted to tell him that he was insane, that he shouldn't have emptied his bank account to buy her this outrageous ring, but how could she?

He looked so happy, so proud to be able to give her this unbelievable engagement ring, that all she could say was thank you.

"It's beautiful, Shai. I will cherish it forever."

Kian

It was ten o'clock Thursday morning when Onegus walked into Kian's office and pulled out a chair. "Roberts died last night. Two doctors certified that he was brain-dead, and he was disconnected from life support this morning."

"When is the funeral?" Shai asked.

"Next Tuesday." Onegus pulled out his phone. "I'll text you the details. We need to get Eleanor to West Virginia."

Shai turned to Kian. "Did you decide who you want her to take to the funeral? I need to know who to order the tickets for."

"Peter is the best choice." Kian crossed his arms over his chest. "I spoke with Leon. He and Anastasia are willing to take Peter's place in Safe Haven until he and Eleanor return."

Onegus arched a brow. "Does she need Peter for anything other than accompanying her to the funeral?"

Kian shrugged. "You are the one who always insists on sending Guardians in teams. It's better that she has someone with her to watch her back."

"Eleanor is not a Guardian, and this is not a regular mission. She's a solo operator on this. If she needs Peter at all, it's for moral support."

"I want someone to keep an eye on her," Kian finally admitted. "I know that she's proven herself time and again as reliable, but having access to so much information might go to her head. Besides, she might need Peter for her other mission, which is finding people who work in the Echelon system and compelling them to give us information."

Onegus's lips twisted in a grimace. "I always feel like I don't have enough Guardians, especially now that we might be close to capturing Orion and discovering a new group of immortals." He leaned back in his chair. "Two Guardians are wasting their time babysitting Vrog, and I have people watching the surveillance feed from Geraldine's house twenty-four-seven. By now, they know all her neighbors, the license plates of their cars, where their kids go to school, and who are their gardeners and housekeepers. The problem is the damn deliveries. So many are done by Uber drivers, and if Orion is smart, he would pose as one."

"Why would he do that?" Shai asked. "He doesn't know that we are waiting for him."

"Right." Onegus cast him a smile. "But if he's old and experienced, which I suspect he is, given his powers, he's most likely very cautious."

Shai waved a dismissive hand. "He wasn't careful thirty-some years ago when he showed up with a fancy car to his weekly meetings with Geraldine." He shook his head. "I'd rather think of it as him meeting Sabina, not Geraldine. But I digress. Even I would have known not to call too much attention to myself with a flashy car, and I'm neither old nor experienced."

"But you're smart," Kian said. "Perhaps Orion is not the sharpest tool in the shed. Being a powerful immortal doesn't mean that he's also intelligent."

Shai let out a breath. "I just hope that he shows up soon, so Geraldine and I can finally move in together and have a life."

Onegus chuckled. "You're practically living together already, so I don't know what's the big deal. Is it so difficult for you to drive to and from work every day?"

Shai glared at the chief in a way none of the Guardians would have dared. "I want her in the village where I know she's safe. I'm sure you can understand that."

Theoretically, Shai was soon to become Onegus's father-in-law, so he was allowed some leeway, but he shouldn't push it. Onegus only seemed mellow and accommodating, but he was the chief for a reason.

"Is Geraldine ready to leave her house?" Kian asked. "I thought she was quite attached to it and to her human friends."

"She is." Shai walked toward the door. "Is it final about Peter joining Eleanor? I need to make the travel arrangements."

Shai seemed on edge, and Kian wondered if it was only because of the uncertainty regarding Orion, or if there was trouble in paradise.

"Unless she wants someone else, it is Peter," Kian said. "I'll call her and let you know in a few minutes." He pulled out his phone and scrolled for Eleanor's number.

"What do you want to do with Vrog?" Onegus asked as the door closed behind Shai.

"I want to send him back to China with Mey and Yamanu and perhaps one additional Guardian. I want to take a look at those files Vrog found at the site. Also, now that Mey can have free access to the entire facility, she might learn something more useful from the echoes." He checked the time on his phone. "Stella asked to speak with me about Vrog. I told her to come at nine, which is twenty minutes from now. You're welcome to stay and join our discussion."

Onegus didn't look happy. "When do you want to send them back to China?"

"That's what I'm going to discuss with Stella and later today with Vrog. He might want to stay a little longer to spend more time with Vlad."

"I hope Orion will show up before that, so my Guardians are not spread so thin. Although that might open a whole new can of worms that I'm not looking forward to catching."

Eleanor

"Kian called." Eleanor entered Emmett's office and sat down on his brown, worn out couch. "Roberts died last night, and the funeral is next Tuesday."

Emmett tensed. "I suppose that you're going."

She nodded. "That was the plan all along." Except for the part that Emmett was not going to like, and there was no way she could sugarcoat it so it would become more palatable for him. "He's sending Leon and Anastasia to take over for Peter."

Emmett narrowed his eyes at her. "Why?"

"He wants Peter to accompany me to West Virginia to attend the funeral as my pretend boyfriend, and stay around to watch my back."

Emmett's eyes blazed red, making him look more demonic than ever. "I don't want you going alone with him." He pushed out of his chair and strode toward her.

"Convince Kian that I have to come with you. Tell him that you're not going without me."

"He's not going to agree."

"Try." Emmett sat next to her. "I can stay in the hotel during the funeral, but we will spend the night together. He has Guardians over there, right?"

She nodded.

"If he's concerned about me running off, he can have them watch me."

She shook her head. "Perhaps you should talk to him. He might be more sympathetic toward your macho male possessiveness."

Emmett arched a brow. "You want to talk about possessiveness? It wasn't me who came up with the idea for Safe Haven. You didn't want to leave me alone in the village with all those immortal females hanging on every word I say, so you convinced Kian that Safe Haven was the perfect place for the paranormal program."

So he'd figured it out. She'd thought she'd been so clever, masking her intentions with all those excellent reasons for going to Safe Haven. But whatever, Eleanor had no problem fessing up to it. Rising to her feet, she put her hands on her hips and glared down at him. "I did that because I wanted to be with you, and I knew that Kian wouldn't let you move in with me into the government facility. And even if he did, you would have been miserable living in the underground city."

Letting out a breath, Emmett took her hand and tugged her onto his lap. "Why are we fighting when we both want the same thing?"

Her anger dissipating, Eleanor pouted. "Because from a free-love guru, you turned into a jealous alpha-hole."

"You're not any better, love." He kissed her on the lips. "Call Kian and we will speak to him together." He smiled. "I'll put on the charm."

Her suggestion that he call Kian had been sarcastic, but maybe it was actually not a bad idea. Unlike her, Emmett was a diplomat, who had a great way with people. Maybe he would be able to charm Kian into letting him accompany her.

"I'll text him." She pulled out her phone and typed up a short message. "That's less unnerving than hearing him bark at me."

A few minutes later, her phone rang.

"What's up, Eleanor? Do you have a problem with what we discussed?"

Damn, the man was intimidating, but she knew that underneath that rough exterior he had a soft heart. "Thanks for calling back, Kian. I have Emmett here with me, and he would like to talk to you. I'm putting you on speakerphone."

"What is it about? I have a meeting in a few minutes."

"Hello, Kian," Emmett said. "I'll make it short. As one mated male to another, I ask that you permit me to accompany Eleanor to West Virginia. I can't stand the thought of being away from her, and even more so, I can't tolerate the thought of her being alone with Peter. I know that you have Guardians stationed there, so you can have them keep an eye on me while Eleanor and Peter are in the field."

"The two guys stationed there are not my Guardians. They are Kalugal's men, and they have better things to do than babysit you."

"Then send one more Guardian with us."

"The Guardians also have better things to do."

Emmett closed his eyes and sighed. "I'll make it worthwhile for you."

"What are you suggesting?"

"I won't charge you anything for using half of Safe Haven to build your section of it. I'll lease it to the clan for one dollar a year for the next one hundred years, with an option to renew for another century."

Eleanor gaped at him. "You can't be serious. I will be gone two months at the most, and I will come to visit you on the weekends. You are giving up millions for nothing."

"Not millions," Kian said. "But it is a significant amount of money. I'm surprised that you didn't begin with a lesser offer to give yourself room to negotiate."

Emmett smiled. "Anything less than that would not have impressed you, and I needed to make it clear how strongly I feel about being separated from Eleanor. It's unbearable to me."

If Eleanor hadn't consciously forced her jaw to close, it would have still been hanging.

Emmett couldn't be serious. What kind of game was he playing? Why was it so important to him to come with her to West Virginia? The short separation couldn't be that insufferable because they were not bonded.

But maybe they were?

She hadn't felt any snapping into place, and although she didn't like the thought of leaving Emmett behind in Safe Haven, she didn't find it as intolerable as he did. She could survive five days without seeing him.

Could she, though?

"Fine, you can go." Kian's answer made her knees buckle. "I'll speak with Kalugal about his men watching you."

"Thank you." Emmett dipped his head even though they weren't on video call.

"And since I'm a fair man, I'm not going to take advantage of your mated bond. Our original deal stands."

If Eleanor's knees had gone soft before, now they turned into a pair of useless noodles.

Kian had said it so casually, as if it was obvious that they were mated.

Emmett smiled. "You are very gracious. Thank you."

When the call ended, she narrowed her eyes at him, "You played Kian."

"Naturally." The smile turned into a satisfied grin. "I needed to make him realize how important being with you was to me, but I knew that he was too honorable to take my offer."

On the one hand, she was disappointed that Emmett hadn't been really willing to part with a huge chunk of money just to be with her. But on the other hand, she was proud of him for being so clever and manipulative.

"What would you have done if Kian had taken the offer?"

He shrugged. "It would have still been worth it."

She slapped his arm. "You're such a liar."

"I'm not. I'm a gambler. And as the saying goes, never gamble what you are not comfortable losing. I could afford to lose the money, but I can't afford to lose you."

"You had nothing to worry about. Despite what you think of Peter, he's not interested in me, and I'm not interested in him." She cupped his bearded cheek. "Frankly, I'm starting to think that we are bonded. It didn't happen overnight like it did for some of the other couples. Instead, it grew slowly. That's why we didn't realize it was there."

"I agree." He closed the distance between their mouths and took her lips. "You are mine, Eleanor Takala."

"And you are mine, Emmett Haderech." She put her finger on his lips. "Are you ever going to tell me your Kraell name?"

He grimaced. "No. My father gave me that name, and it wasn't a good one. It was an insult. I created Emmett Haderech, and I like the male he became."

She hadn't known that—hadn't suspected that the proud male before her had grown up ashamed of his own name. No wonder that he'd escaped the first opportunity he got.

It also explained why they fit together so well.

Eleanor had been ashamed too—still was. She'd loved a man who hadn't loved her back and had used compulsion to keep him from leaving her. She cringed whenever she thought about that time in her life.

Except, her shame was her own doing, while Emmett had done nothing to deserve it other than being born to a human mother.

"I need to ask you something." She took his hand in hers. "If your people treated you so badly, why did you want to go back and bring Peter to them?"

He sighed. "Because if Peter could have activated their Dormants, I would have been a hero, I could have proven that I was worthy, and that my asshole of a father was wrong about me."

Kian

Stella pulled out one of the two chairs facing Kian's desk. "I wanted to talk to you about Vrog." She hung her satchel over the back of it and sat down. "Is he a prisoner?"

"No."

"Then there is no reason to hold him locked up in a cell."

"What do you want me to do with him?"

She looked him straight in the eyes. "Let him come live in the village."

"Does he want to?"

She hesitated for a moment. "He doesn't know it's on the table. Vrog is smart enough to realize that an invitation from Emmett doesn't count because he has no authority to issue it."

Kian arched a brow. "Emmett invited him to live in the village?"

"In so many words."

"Then Emmett must not view Vrog as a threat. That's good to know." Kian leaned forward. "How is Vrog getting along with Vlad?"

Stella sighed. "They've met only twice so far. Between Vlad's part-time job in the bakery and the final project he's working on for school, he has a busy schedule."

It sounded to Kian like Vlad wasn't too eager to spend time with his biological father. He wondered if things were different for Stella.

"What about you? Have you visited him more often?"

"I was there yesterday. Vrog is lonely and worried. Despite your assurances that we are not going to keep him here for long, he wonders what your real plans are for him." She pushed a strand of hair behind her ear. "Richard threw a jealous tantrum when I went to see Vrog without Vlad. I don't want to fight with him over this, but I also can't leave Vrog all alone in that cell with no visitors and no one to talk to other than Alec and Vernon."

"I thought the three of them were getting along just fine. Alfie and Jay were supposed to take over from Alec and Vernon, but Vrog asked them to stay, and they agreed."

She rolled her eyes at him. "Of course, he asked them to stay. They are the only two immortals he's gotten to know and who treat him well. I wouldn't be surprised if he has a mild case of Stockholm syndrome, becoming dependent on the two people who are taking care of him.

You need to either let him go back to his school or invite him to join the village."

Kian's temper flared at her issuing orders instead of making requests, but Stella looked upset, and he decided to let it go.

"Did you ask Vrog what he would prefer?"

Stella shook her head. "I wanted to talk to you first, so I would know whether the village was an option."

Leaning back in his chair, Kian crossed his legs. "If Vlad asks me to invite his father to live in the village, I will grant his request. But I can't allow Vrog to roam free. I don't think that he will betray us to humans, but he seemed bound by vows of loyalty to his former leader. If she somehow makes an appearance, I have a feeling he will do anything she asks of him, including betraying his own son."

Stella winced. "What if he bonds with a clan female?"

"I don't think a Kra-ell immortal couple can bond. Emmett and Eleanor seem perfectly suited for each other, but they haven't bonded yet, and they've been together long enough for that to happen."

In truth, Kian was no longer sure of that after the phone conversation with Emmett, but he suspected that the guy had put on a performance, knowing that Kian would refuse to take advantage of his desperate need to be with his mate. Emmett could have lost that bet, though, and if he was willing to put his most precious asset on the line, then perhaps he was really in love with Eleanor. Love could exist and be a powerful motivator even without the bond.

Stella pursed her lips. "You can't generalize based on one couple. It might be that they are not each other's fated mates."

"True. If Vrog decides to join the clan, we can wait and see what happens, but in the meantime, I need to exercise caution. That being said, even if he wants to join and I agree, I still need him to return to China with Mey and Yamanu first."

"And after that?"

"It depends on what I find out in those files he talked about, and what Mey hears from the echoes. If it's a dead end, I will give Vrog the option to join the clan provided that Vlad wants that. If it's not a dead end, I might need Vrog to assist in the investigation."

Kian hoped that he wasn't making a mistake. Compared to Emmett, Vrog seemed harmless, but what if it was just a very convincing act?

"Who are you sending in addition to Mey and Yamanu?"

"I don't need Jin to go, but I want them to have Guardian backup. If Alfie and Jay are not up for another trip, I'll assign two other Guardians."

"What about me? Do I get to go?"

"Do you want to?"

She grimaced. "I want to be part of this investigation, but Richard can't stand Vrog, and I'm not going without him. But if you need me to go, I will, and I'll deal with Richard's attitude."

Kian hadn't planned on sending Stella with the team, but having Richard there was not a bad idea. The guy didn't trust Vrog, which meant that he would watch him carefully and notice any signs of subterfuge no matter how insignificant.

"Your fluency in the language would be helpful to the team, but you need to talk it over with Richard. "

"I will. But you can count me in. Richard might grumble, but there isn't much he can do." Shifting on the chair, Stella adjusted her skirt. "Are you going to remove the cuffs before sending Vrog home?"

"I have no right to keep them on him when he's out of my jurisdiction and also helping us."

"But you still don't trust him."

"Obviously," Kian confirmed.

"So maybe it would be a good idea for Jin to tether him. If Vrog has been lying to us all along, he will try to contact his people as soon as he's set free."

"Do you suspect him?"

Stella sighed. "Not really, but I don't know him well enough to be sure. He might be putting on a great act."

"The same has occurred to me. I'll speak to Jin."

"What do you want me to tell Vrog?"

"Nothing." Kian straightened in his chair and pulled it up closer to the desk. "I'm seeing Vrog later this afternoon, and I can discuss the options with him." He gave Stella a slight smile. "Andrew is accompanying me. I just hope that his lie detecting abilities work on a hybrid Kraell as well as they work on humans."

Vrog

As Stella's clan leader explained his proposal, Vrog listened without interrupting, not out of respect and not because he didn't have questions, but because he needed time to think.

He'd spent two weeks locked up in the cell, and during that time, Vlad had visited him only twice, both times with his lovely fiancée who had done most of the talking.

Vrog had a feeling that Vlad resented him, and that he wasn't interested in getting to know him better. Not that he could blame him.

His son had probably heard from his mother about Vrog's request to abort him. If not for Stella's courage and resilience, Vlad wouldn't have been born.

"Do you have any questions for me?" Kian asked.

"How soon do you want me to go back to China?"

"Whenever you are ready."

That wasn't the answer Vrog had hoped for. "Does it have to happen soon?"

Kian let out an exasperated breath. "What are you really trying to ask me?"

The guy seemed like a straight shooter who wasn't much of a diplomat. Perhaps it was in Vrog's best interest to just say what was on his mind. "I want to get closer to my son, but he doesn't seem interested. Down here, there isn't much I can do about it, but if I stay in your village, I might be able to see more of Vlad and get to know him better."

"So you don't want to go back home?"

"I do, just not right away if it's possible." Looking at the cuffs, Vrog rotated his wrists. "Are these really necessary? I have no ax to grind with your clan. I thought I had, but I know now that I was wrong. Where would I run? And why would I?"

Kian cast a quick sidelong glance at the guy who'd accompanied him to the meeting instead of the two bodyguards he'd had with him before. Unlike the other two, though, this one wore a suit and tie and looked like he was someone important.

Kian had introduced him, but Vrog had been too anxious for the name to register. Was it Andy? Edward?

When the guy nodded, Kian crossed his arms over his chest. "You tell me."

The name suddenly popped into his head. It was Andrew.

"I have a son who is part of your clan, and who is the only long-lived offspring I will ever have. I would never endanger him."

Andrew nodded again.

What was the deal with that?

"If I let you into the village, the cuffs stay on, and you can't leave, not even to go out to dinner with Vlad. If you choose to go home, I'll have the cuffs removed when you land in Beijing."

Vrog nodded. "So that's the price of staying in your village?"

"There are other complications. We don't have guest rooms, so either Vlad or Stella would have to host you in their homes."

"Richard will never allow me in his house."

Kian didn't look surprised. "That leaves Vlad. He'll have to invite you."

Vrog groaned. "Perhaps I should just stay down here."

"That's no longer an option either. I have better use for these two Guardians than babysitting you."

Vrog felt as if the walls were closing in on him. "So my options are an invitation from Vlad to stay with him and Wendy or going home?"

"Correct."

"Can I call him?"

"Sure." Kian pulled out his phone. "I can dial his number for you."

Vrog swallowed. "I'm not ready to do this now. I don't know what to say."

"Would you prefer to ask Stella?" Andrew asked. "She could talk to Vlad for you."

Vrog shook his head. "That would be a cowardly thing to do. I'll call him a little later." He looked at the two Guardians sitting at the dining table. "Can either one of them let me use their phone?"

"Yes." Kian rose to his feet. "You have until tomorrow morning. If you don't get an invite from Vlad, I'll start organizing the team going with you to China."

That was good enough. Vrog just didn't want to have that talk with his son while Kian listened in. Getting a no, which was probably the answer Vlad would give him, would be humiliating enough without Kian witnessing it.

"Thank you. I'll call him later this evening."

"Very well." The clan's leader motioned to Alec to open the door.

Once it closed behind Kian and Andrew, Vernon got up and walked over to the bar. "Care for some whiskey?"

"I would love some, thank you."

The Guardian poured him a tall glass. "Vlad is a good kid. He will not say no."

"I don't know about that." Vrog emptied half the glass down his throat. "I have no doubt that he's a great person, but he just doesn't like me well enough to invite me to stay with him and his fiancée."

Vernon pulled out his phone. "Should I place the call for you?"

Apparently, the Guardian had figured out why Vrog hadn't wanted to call Vlad while Kian listened in.

"Give me a moment to gather my thoughts."

Vernon put the phone on the table. "Let me know when you're ready."

How was he going to phrase it? Perhaps he should just repeat what Kian had said, so Vlad would know that it hadn't been his idea? Or maybe the opposite was true, and he should claim that he wanted to stay with his son and his fiancée so he could get a taste of what having a family felt like?

Usually, Vrog was an eloquent guy, or rather James Wu was. As the head of the school, he had to be. But now he found himself lost for words.

Pacing around the small room, he rehearsed what he was going to say to his son, changing a word here, a word there, then discarding the entire thing and starting from scratch.

"You're overthinking it," Vernon said. "Just call him." The Guardian placed the call without waiting for Vrog's answer.

"Hello?" Vlad answered.

Vernon thrust the phone into Vrog's hand.

"Hi, it's Vrog."

"They gave you a phone?"

"The phone belongs to one of the Guardians. He placed the call for me. I need your advice."

"Sure." Vlad sounded surprised.

"Kian came to visit me earlier, and he gave me two options. One was to go back to China with the investigative team and help them search for more clues about my people, and the other one was to come to your village and stay for a little bit, spend some time with you and Wendy, and then go to China."

"What do you want to do?" Vlad asked.

"I would like to stay for a couple of weeks, but the problem is that the village doesn't have guest accommodations. My only options would be to stay either with you and Wendy or Stella and Richard." Vrog held his breath as he waited for Vlad's answer.

"Can't you stay with the Guardians? I'm sure some of them have a spare room in their house."

Vrog's heart sank. "Kian didn't offer me that option, so I guess it's not on the table."

Vlad sighed. "You can come stay with Wendy and me."

Vrog's relief made him lightheaded. "Are you sure? I'm a very easy guest, but you and Wendy are a new couple. I wouldn't want to intrude on your privacy."

"That's okay. Wendy says that she would love to host you."

So it was the girl's doing. He'd take it. "Tell Wendy that I'm grateful. I'll do everything I can to repay the kindness."

"Wendy says that inviting us to China and giving us a tour would be an acceptable repayment."

Vrog smiled. "Any time. I would be overjoyed to be your tour guide."

"When are you coming?"

"I suppose sometime tomorrow. Kian doesn't want to waste Guardian time on me."

Vlad chuckled. "That sounds like Kian. Wendy says that she'll have the room ready for you."

"Thank you. I really appreciate it."

"No problem. Have a good night, Vrog."

As Vlad ended the call, Vrog slumped on the couch, the phone still clutched in his hand.

"Told you that the kid was a sweetheart." Vernon took the device from him.

"Wendy is too. I don't think he would have invited me if she wasn't there to pressure him into it."

"Whatever works, man." Vernon walked over to the bar. "The important thing is that you'll get to spend time with your son."

"Yes. It is, and I plan to make the most of it."

Orion

Orion stopped at the gate into Geraldine's neighborhood, opened the window of the nondescript Honda Civic, and smiled at the guard. "Delivery for the Beaumonts. They called ahead to let me in."

Just a little pulse of compulsion was enough. The guy nodded, and a moment later the gate opened.

Nowadays there were cameras everywhere, which was why his long hair was gathered under a baseball cap, and his eyes were shielded by speciality eyeglasses that didn't correct vision but prevented facial recognition.

Orion missed the days when he could have roamed free with no disguise needed, when he could drive fancy cars and pay cash and not worry about being found out. Life was becoming more and more difficult for an immortal who needed to hide who he was and frequently change identities.

There was a car parked in Geraldine's driveway, but he knew that it didn't belong to her or to Cassandra. Geraldine didn't own one, and Cassandra always parked hers inside the garage.

Perhaps it was a new boyfriend?

Not Geraldine's, because she never brought them home, but maybe Cassandra's. It was about time that she found someone. The girl was thirty-four years old, gorgeous, successful, and nearly six feet tall, which apparently human males found intimidating. That made finding a worthy partner challenging even though she had none of her mother's limitations. Being human made things much less complicated.

Perhaps he should come later when the guy was gone. If Cassandra was dating someone seriously, Orion didn't want to interrupt their romantic interlude.

But what if the guy had moved in? What if he wasn't worthy of Cassandra?

He needed to find out who the boyfriend was, what he did for a living, and what his intentions were for Geraldine's daughter.

Parking on the other side of the street, Orion pulled a paper bag from the back seat, stepped out of the car, walked up to the front door, and rang the bell.

He knew the elderly woman who opened the door—he'd used her for the same purpose before. "Hello, Mrs. Gilbert. I have a delivery for you." A very light compulsion usually did the trick.

"Come in." Smiling, she smoothed her hand over her house dress and stepped aside.

Sometimes he wondered whether she let him in because he compelled her or because she fancied him.

He could peer into her mind, but his curiosity didn't justify the intrusion. It was enough that he was using her house to spy on her neighbors across the street.

Since neither Geraldine nor Cassandra ever bothered closing the curtains in the living room, he could see clearly nearly the entire interior of their ground floor from Mrs. Gilbert's front room window.

After instructing the woman to go back to her television show, Orion walked over to the window and looked at the house across the street from behind the sheer curtains.

Surprisingly, it wasn't Cassandra who was cuddling on the couch with a young man, but Geraldine, and the two seemed on very friendly terms.

Orion groaned. One more boyfriend that he would have to make her forget, and since she'd brought this one into her home, he would have to make him forget her as well.

Immortals could not afford to mix with humans, but Geraldine didn't know why she wasn't aging, not since she'd lost every scrap of memory in her near-fatal accident. Regrettably, he couldn't tell her again because her mind no longer worked as well as it should, and she might forget that she needed to keep it a secret.

Orion's gut churned with guilt as he watched her smiling at the young man. Even from across the street, he could see the love in her eyes. The only mercy he could afford her was to make her forget that she'd ever been in love with the man.

Cassandra must have moved out because Geraldine wouldn't have brought a man to her house while her daughter was still living with her. Except, up until his last visit, it hadn't been in the cards. Cassandra wouldn't allow herself to have a life until her mother found someone else to take care of her.

It had been a catch-22 that he was glad Cassandra had finally gotten free from, but regrettably, Geraldine's guy couldn't be allowed to stay.

Geraldine

Geraldine looked herself over in the mirror and smiled. Shai was taking her out on a real date tonight, just the two of them, in that fancy-schmancy restaurant owned by one of Shai's many cousins.

Or was it an uncle?

The clan made things simple. Unless a person was their mother's sibling, which made them an aunt or an uncle, everyone else was a cousin even if they were ancient.

Normally Geraldine didn't like wearing black, but it was the best color to serve as a backdrop for the gorgeous engagement ring sparkling on her finger. The dress was curve-hugging, reached a little below her knees, and had a plunging back.

Sexy as hell was what Shai would probably call it.

With a pair of four-inch black pumps on her feet, she looked slender and tall and beautiful. The rest of her jewelry was fake diamonds, but Geraldine felt like a million bucks nonetheless.

Giving her hair one last fluff, she tucked her small evening purse under her arm and headed downstairs.

Shai rose to his feet and whistled. "I'm glad it's so dark in By Invitation Only. Otherwise, every male in the place will be drooling over you and I'll have to deal with them."

Smiling, she gave him a small peck on the cheek. "I expect you to dance with me, and do your best not to growl at anyone. I won't be the only pretty lady on the dance floor, you know."

"But you'll be the prettiest." He glanced at his watch. "Our reservations are for nine, if we leave now, we will get there too early."

"I know." She took his hand and led him to the couch. "Instead, you can tell me about the story you started writing."

He eyed her from under lowered blond lashes. "How do you know that I did?"

"I heard you clicking away on the keyboard last night, but as soon as I entered the bedroom, you closed your laptop. I know that you don't have any secrets from me, so I figured that you started writing a new script but were embarrassed to show me your work in progress."

"You know me so well that it's scary." He wrapped his arm around her shoulders.

"Why is it scary?"

"Because it means that I'm transparent, and I can't afford to be."

She knew what he meant. "I don't think anyone other than me would have figured that out. Besides, you've been successfully hiding your relationship with Rhett for nineteen years. I don't think you have anything to worry about." She patted his knee. "Now tell me your story."

He chuckled nervously. "It's not a script this time. I'm actually writing a horror story."

She winced. "Ugh, why horror? I want to read it, and I can't stomach horror. Can you turn it into a romance?"

"It has some romance in it, or rather sex. I got the idea on the way back from Safe Haven. Kian asked me why I was brooding, and I didn't want to admit that I had a hard time being away from you, so I told him that Safe Haven reminded me of Alcatraz."

She arched a brow. "You said that it's isolated, overcast, and cold, but you didn't tell me that it reminded you of a prison."

"It was a slight exaggeration. When Brundar said that he liked it, I thought that it suited his tastes. He's part owner in a club that caters to people who are into the spicier side of sex. Then I said that Safe Haven would be the perfect location for a kink club, which got everyone talking and joking about it, and Anandur said that I should write a story about it. That's how the idea was born."

"I think it can be very interesting. But it sounds sexy rather than scary."

"Ah." He lifted a finger. "There are also unexplained murders, dark shadows slithering through the dungeons, and lots of kinky sex." Shai eyed her with a wary expression on his handsome face. "That's why I didn't tell you about it. I was afraid that you'd find it too racy."

Geraldine laughed. "If you expect me to feel scandalized by a kinky story, you don't know me as well as you think you do. I'm a lady, so you'll never hear me talk about those darker kinds of pleasures, but that doesn't mean that I'm not aware they exist. After all, my favorite genre to read is romance, and some of those books are quite spicy." She lifted her head and nuzzled his neck. "Some are about vampires who enjoy those sorts of sex games, which make them doubly spicy."

Shai glanced at the light fixture, the one that had been outfitted with a surveillance camera. "If we weren't being watched," he whispered into her ear. "I would pull this sexy dress up your thighs and have my wicked way with you."

"Oh, dear." She pretended to be shocked, covering her mouth with her hand and whispering, "Do we have time to go upstairs?"

He lifted his hand to check the time. "Regrettably, we will have to save that thought for later. We need to go."

Orion

When Geraldine and her guy rose to their feet and headed for the door, Orion stepped away from the window.

"Goodnight, Mrs. Gilbert." He smiled at the neighbor whose house he'd used as his spying post. "I've never been here, and you've never seen me before in your life." He opened the front door and got into his borrowed Honda.

The owner of the car, an Uber delivery driver, was sitting on the couch in Orion's Airbnb, eating the Chinese delivery Orion had ordered, and watching sitcoms on the television. The guy wouldn't move from that couch until he returned and released him from the compulsion.

Driving out, Orion caught up to Geraldine's boyfriend's car and followed them until they stopped at a valet station of a restaurant that he'd heard about but had never visited.

The guy must be loaded to afford a place like that.

In days past, Orion would have thought that the young man came from a rich family, but nowadays, people in their early twenties were making millions as software developers or as influencers.

Only a decade ago, no one could have imagined that people could make a fortune from posting silly amateur videos on social media. The world was changing, shrinking, and as usual, Orion was adapting, but it seemed like he was always a couple of steps behind the technology, the politics, and the attitudes.

As an antique dealer, he had no need to explore the latest technological innovations, as a drifter with no attachment to any particular country, politics had never interested him, and as a loner, societal changes interested him only as far as they pertained to him.

Lately, though, Orion had been forced to pay more attention to what was going on in the world around him because his very survival and that of a handful of people he cared about depended on it.

He had to be much more careful.

Following Geraldine and her guy into the restaurant was too risky, and other than to satisfy his curiosity, it would serve no purpose. Instead, he snapped a photo of the license plate of the boyfriend's car and kept on driving.

He would return to Geraldine's house early in the morning to check whether the man had spent the night. If they had been living together for a while, it would be much harder to make them forget each other. They would sense the loss even if they couldn't remember what they were missing.

Orion's gut twisted with guilt.

Geraldine deserved so much better from life.

Perhaps he could allow her to enjoy her latest lover for a little longer, provided that the guy was worthy of her love.

Some of the men she'd dated in the past had definitely been unworthy, and that included Cassandra's father. The guy was a liar, a philanderer. When Emanuel had befriended Geraldine, he hadn't told her that he had a family in Ethiopia, a wife and five children. He'd lied to her, claiming that he was single, and seduced her. But it hadn't been a one-night stand like most of her encounters. Emanuel had spent the entire summer with her, and regrettably, Orion had been away the entire time. When he'd visited her again, she was pregnant, and her store of memories of the guy had been difficult to erase.

Nevertheless, it had to be done.

By erasing the bulk of her memories of Emanuel, Orion had done her a favor, saving her a lot of heartache down the line, but it was a shame that she'd liked the cheating bastard so much.

Out of all the lovers Orion had muddled and suppressed her memories of, Emanuel still remained the one she remembered best, and after several attempts, Orion had given up on trying to get rid of the remnants of memories she clung to.

The guy had been gone for years, back to Ethiopia to his wife and children. Orion hadn't bothered checking up on him, but if he was alive, Emanuel was probably still philandering despite being in his late sixties.

In his experience, humans seldom changed.

Parking a block away from the valet station, Orion considered his options. He could wait until Geraldine and her new guy finished dinner and follow them, or he could return early in the morning to Geraldine's house to check whether the guy had stayed the night.

In the end, what tipped the scales toward leaving now was the Uber driver he'd left in his Airbnb rental.

Before compelling the guy not to move away from the couch, Orion had checked that he lived alone. He also instructed him to clock out from the Uber application so no one would miss him. But if he didn't release the driver from the compulsion soon, he might have to deal with nasty cleanup.

After eating all that Chinese food and sipping on all that beer, the guy would need to answer nature's call, but because of the compulsion not to move from the couch, he wouldn't be able to get up and use the bathroom.

Orion

Six o'clock in the morning was too early for food delivery. Orion had to come up with another service that would not raise the guard's suspicion.

Then again, as long as he had his special glasses and baseball hat on, he didn't need to worry about the surveillance cameras that would record his presence. Besides, there was no real reason for him to be so clandestine. Perhaps he was taking all this new technology too seriously.

After all, someone needed a reason to look at that surveillance feed, and since he wasn't planning on robbing anyone, his only concern should be the guard in the gate recognizing him from the day before, and even that could be handled with a little thrall or compulsion.

Nevertheless, he should try to look at least a little different. Another pair of glasses, a new hat, and his own rental car should suffice. The vehicle wasn't anything fancy, just a simple Chevy Malibu.

And as for the story why he was there? He could say that he was Mrs. Gilbert's nephew, delivering a prescription medicine he'd picked up for her from the pharmacy.

Satisfied with his plan, Orion donned his specialty glasses and a white baseball hat and headed out.

When he arrived at the gate, a different guard greeted him, and just like the day before, he opened the gate for Orion with the help of a little thrall.

The boyfriend's car was still parked in the driveway, confirming his suspicion that he'd moved in with Geraldine.

Like the day before, Orion parked in front of the neighbors' house, but this time he wasn't going to knock on the door.

Mrs. Gilbert was no doubt still sleeping, but he had a key. After the first time he'd used her house to observe what was going on in Geraldine's, he'd asked her for the code to the alarm and for a spare key.

Mostly, he had done so to make sure that Cassandra wasn't in the house when he visited Geraldine. She had a strong personality and a suspicious mind, and as she grew older, she'd become more and more difficult to thrall.

Besides, he wasn't worried about her.

She was a human with nothing to hide, and she didn't need his assistance. All it had taken to put her on the track to success was to give her boss a nudge in the right direction. Cassandra's talent and tenacity had been enough to take it from there.

Standing by Mrs. Gilbert's living room window, Orion couldn't see inside the house across the street because the sunlight reflected from the windows, but that wasn't what he was interested in. Since the boyfriend had stayed the night, Orion wanted to follow him when he left for work to find out more about him.

Hopefully, he wouldn't follow the guy to another house and a family.

When the door opened, the boyfriend didn't walk out right away. Standing in the doorway, he bent down to kiss her goodbye, and as she wrapped her arms around his neck, he caught the glint of the diamond ring on her finger—a big diamond, the kind a man in love gave his future bride after proposing to her.

Orion's gut twisted.

Was there another way? Could he allow her to enjoy this man for a few years?

Maybe he could compel his silence?

First, though, he needed to find out whether the man was at least decent, let alone worthy of Geraldine.

When the guy got into his car, Orion waited another minute before going out the door, locking it behind him, and getting into his Chevy Malibu.

With a heavy heart, he followed the fiancé's car from a safe distance, hoping for Geraldine's sake as much as for his own that he would not discover anything rotten about him.

Shai

When the gate closed behind Shai as he drove out of Geraldine's neighborhood, a prickling sensation at the back of his neck had him glance at the rearview mirror. A car had stopped at the gate, waiting for it to open again.

He'd been leaving the neighborhood through the same gate at the same time most mornings, but he hadn't seen that particular Chevy model before. It was probably nothing. One of Geraldine's nearly three hundred neighbors had gotten a new car.

Out of habit though, he glanced at the license plate, his eidetic memory taking a snapshot of the number.

Nearing an intersection, he purposely turned his right blinker on and moved into the right lane even though he needed to continue straight. There were now three cars between him and the cream-colored Chevy, and when its blinker didn't come on, Shai released a relieved breath.

Just to be sure, though, he turned right at the intersection, but the Chevy continued straight.

He was becoming overly jumpy for no reason.

Why would anyone follow him?

Even if Orion showed up, he would have waited for Shai to leave and then approach Geraldine when she was alone in the house. He wouldn't follow someone who he would assume was an inconsequential boyfriend.

Unless he was jealous.

What if Orion had eliminated all of Geraldine's other boyfriends and then had done his best to erase them from her memory?

He could be in love with her, but for some reason, he couldn't be intimate with her.

Shai had never heard of an immortal male who suffered from erectile dysfunction, but then it wasn't something a male would advertise. The source of it could only be mental, though. Immortal bodies didn't develop circulation or hormonal problems.

Preoccupied with his thought, Shai had forgotten to readjust his route for the detour he'd taken. He could either make a U-turn or have the navigation system reconfigure a route for him. Stopping at the next light, he activated the system, and as he waited for it to reboot, he took a quick look in the rearview mirror.

At first, he didn't see the Chevy that was separated by several vehicles, but as the light changed and the cars started moving, he caught a glimpse of it.

It could have been a different car, but he decided not to take chances and called Onegus.

The chief answered right away as if he had been waiting for the call. "What's up, Shai?"

"I have a feeling that I'm being followed. It's a cream-colored Chevy Malibu. Write down the license plate number." He recited the combination of seven numbers and letters.

"Give me a moment," the chief said.

As he waited, Shai kept glancing at his rearview mirror, hoping to see the Chevy turn at one of the intersections they were passing through, but it kept going, following him from a distance with several cars between them.

Whoever the tail was, they weren't pros. If Shai could spot the car following him without any training, then anyone could.

"Shai." Onegus came on the line. "I think this is our guy. The security feed from Geraldine's front door caught the same car parked in the driveway of the neighbor across the street. The guy went into the house using a key, so my Guardians didn't become suspicious. I just checked, and he'd told the guard that he was Mrs. Gilbert's nephew delivering a prescription medicine she'd asked him to pick up. The guys in security should have gotten suspicious when he left Mrs. Gilbert's house a minute after you drove away, but he locked the door behind him and didn't seem hurried as he got into his car, so they didn't think it was connected to your departure. But he's following you, so there is that."

"What do you want me to do? I can take a few more random turns and check whether he's still behind me."

"If it's indeed Orion, I don't want him to get suspicious. Drive toward the village as you normally would, not too fast and not too slow, and when you get to Malibu, turn onto Red Canyon Road. We will be waiting for him there."

"That's a dead end and he will see that it is on his navigation system. Won't he find that suspicious?"

"He might, but that's the best place to trap him. I'll have two more Guardians stationed down the road in case he doesn't turn after you. One way or another, we are going to catch him."

Onegus

Onegus glanced at his tablet, tracking Shai's progress. It had been one of the modifications Onegus had asked for when Kian had ordered the self-driving cars for every clan member. They were all equipped with trackers, so in case of an emergency they could be activated from the security office, but only when authorized by Onegus or Kian.

It was coming in handy now as he and his Guardians were lying in wait.

Orion had decided to show up at a most opportune hour—when most of the Guardians were still in the village and available to be deployed, but Onegus hadn't had much time to explain what was going on and distribute earpieces to everyone. Thankfully, his force was trained for quick response, and they were all in position and ready with minutes to spare.

Two cars with two Guardians each were waiting at the end of Red Canyon Road, while two others were idling on the side of the main road several hundred feet west of it, waiting for the Chevy to either turn after Shai or get spooked and continue straight ahead.

If the guy followed Shai into the dead-end road, they would turn around and block his exit. If he didn't turn, they would follow the Chevy until it stopped somewhere and apprehend their target there.

That's why Yamanu was in the car with Onegus. If they had to catch Orion in a public place, Yamanu would shroud the operation, hiding it from human eyes.

The Guardian leaned over to glance at the tablet. "Three minutes to showtime." He chuckled. "Who knew that one day we would be thankful for L.A.'s damn traffic. It's given us time to get ready."

Onegus nodded.

Yamanu crossed his arms over his chest. "Capturing this male should be interesting."

It was, but the uneasy feeling in Onegus's gut reminded him that they were about to entrap a guy with no proper justification.

They had no proof or even a shred of evidence that Orion had committed a crime or posed a threat to the clan. What they were about to do was unlawful, bordering on immoral.

Onegus was a lawman, not just a military commander, and he didn't like being on the wrong side of the divide.

"You look like you ate a lemon," Yamanu said.

"I don't like trapping a man just because I want to get information out of him. He hasn't committed any crimes against the clan, and as far as we know, not against humans either."

Yamanu lifted one shoulder in a half shrug. "It's very much like the situation we had with Kalugal. He hadn't done anything to us, but we wanted to find out what he was up to, so we trapped him."

"We knew that he was involved in illegal activities," Onegus countered.

"We suspected that he was making money from insider information, but as long as he wasn't enslaving humans or physically harming them in the process, that's not the kind of unlawful activity that we are concerned with."

"We didn't know whether he was enslaving humans or not. He had that enormous bunker, and we had no idea what he was doing in there. That's why we wanted Jin to tether him." Onegus sighed through his nose. "That won't be enough with Orion, though. We need to ask him questions, not just observe what he does. With Kalugal, we knew where he came from and who his men were. We know absolutely nothing about Orion."

"There you go." Yamanu uncrossed his arms. "This is a military mission, not a law enforcement operation, and you need to switch your cop cap to a helmet. We need information, Orion has it, end of story."

Onegus cast the Guardian a lopsided smile. "When you're right, you're right."

"I'm always right." Yamanu pointed at the tablet. "Here he comes."

As the circle representing Shai's car was about to turn into Red Canyon Road, Onegus switched his tablet view to the feed from the drone hovering above the intersection.

Onegus watched the cream-colored Chevy as Shai made the turn. When it slowed down to a crawl and then pulled to the curb and stopped, he was sure that the guy had gotten spooked and would keep on driving, but then the car started moving again and followed Shai onto the side road.

"Thank the merciful Fates." Onegus threw the gearshift into drive.

Orion

It was a trap, one Orion hadn't expected, but should have.

The navigation system had clearly shown that it was a dead-end road, but he'd thought that it just hadn't been updated, as it often happened with new housing developments, and that Geraldine's boyfriend was either going home, or to inspect the work in progress.

When he noted the two vehicles behind him, Orion assumed that they were driving to the same development.

But as the car in front of him reached what appeared to be the end of the road, four burly men exited the two vehicles that had been waiting there, and the two vehicles behind him pulled to a stop, blocking his retreat.

Perhaps Geraldine's boyfriend was someone important, someone who for some reason feared for his life.

A criminal perhaps?

Orion wasn't really worried. As long as the men didn't open fire as soon as he exited the car, he would just compel them to leave, and he would have a nice little chat with the boyfriend.

After slowly opening the door, he stepped out with his arms in the air. "I'm unarmed. Don't shoot." He embedded the last part with strong compulsion, making sure that they wouldn't.

"No one is going to shoot you," a man said behind him. "We only want to talk."

Lowering his arms, Orion slowly turned around and assessed the man.

He was tall, blond, and good-looking enough to be a movie star. Perhaps this was a movie set, one that was heavily guarded for some reason.

Except, he had a feeling that it was something much worse than that. The tiny hairs at the back of his neck were tingling in alarm.

"I took the wrong turn." Orion smiled apologetically. "I didn't know that this was a restricted access road. Get back in your cars, turn around, and forget that I was ever here."

The compulsion in his voice should have worked right away.

The blond flashed him a charming smile. "Your tricks are not going to work on us." The guy pointed to his earpieces. "We know who you are and what you can do, Orion."

How could the guy block his voice and still hear what he was saying? And how did they know who he was?

Had Geraldine remembered him? Only a handful of people knew him as Orion, and only one person knew about him being immortal and the powers he possessed.

"Who are you?"

"My name is Onegus." The guy walked up to him and offered him his hand. "You have nothing to fear from us. We only want to talk."

Orion didn't take the man's hand. "Who are you?" he repeated, waving a hand to encompass the entire group. "And what do you want with me?"

"We are immortals like you," Onegus said. "We've been searching for others like us for a millennium."

Orion looked at the men with wonder, his curiosity and excitement overpowering his fear. Without his compulsion, he was defenseless against these people, but he believed Onegus that they meant him no harm. There was no hostility in their eyes or their scents, only curiosity to match his own.

"So have I. For a long time, I thought that I was an anomaly, a lone immortal cursed to walk the earth alone."

Onegus chuckled. "So you got busy creating more?"

Orion frowned. "I've never fathered a child, if that's what you mean. I'm infertile."

"You are not. Our kind has a very low fertility rate, and you should count yourself lucky that you didn't get a human female pregnant. Your child would have been human with a human's lifespan."

"Then how could I have created more like me?"

"By inducing a Dormant."

Orion shook his head. "I have no idea what you're talking about."

"A Dormant is a human who carries the immortal gene," Onegus explained. "They can be induced and transition into immortality."

The guy was contradicting himself. A moment ago, he'd said that a child born to an immortal with a human would be born human. Which meant that the immortal gene wasn't transferable unless both parents were immortal.

But he hadn't scented a lie, so there must be another explanation. "I've never met a dormant carrier of immortal genes. How would I even know that they had them?"

"What about Geraldine?" The boyfriend walked over to Onegus and stood next to him. "Did you induce her?"

"She was already immortal when I found her. I don't even know how to induce what you call a Dormant."

Shai

After getting a pair of earpieces from Alfie, Shai had replaced his fingers with the devices. He'd listened to Onegus and Orion as patiently as he could, letting the chief do what he was good at, but Orion's answers were bullshit.

He claimed that he didn't know of other immortals, and that he'd found Geraldine after she'd been turned. Why hadn't he tried to seduce her?

The least favorable scenario Shai had come up with so far had been missing a few crucial pieces, but they all seemed to have fallen into place now.

It looked as though Orion had somehow found Geraldine after she'd been turned immortal and had compelled her into having a romantic relationship with him. But when he'd tried to get her away from her family, she'd fought his compulsion and refused.

When that hadn't worked, he'd kidnapped her, probably by snatching her up from the water when she'd gone swimming on that fateful day and putting her on a boat. She'd fought him, jumped ship, and when he'd chased after her, the terrible accident had happened, nearly killing her.

He'd managed to save her, but guilt over what had happened prevented him from compelling her to have a relationship with him again. The same guilt had also prompted him to look after her and her family ever since.

"Bastard," Shai hissed.

Onegus stopped him from lunging at the guy with a hand on his chest. "Relax, Shai. We don't know all the facts yet." He turned to Orion. "How did you find Geraldine?"

The guy shrugged. "I found her by chance."

It was such a blatant lie that no immortal special senses were required to detect it.

"Liar." Shai tried to lunge at the lying piece of shit, but once again, Onegus stopped him.

"Calm down, or I'll have to remove you from the situation. If you want to be part of this conversation, behave."

Right now, Onegus wasn't his friend and future son-in-law. He was the chief, and he wouldn't hesitate to order one of the Guardians to stuff Shai into his car and handcuff him to the steering wheel.

Shai nodded. "I'm okay."

"Good." Onegus turned to Orion. "Let's assume that I believe you, and that you happened to meet Geraldine by chance. Where was it? Did you meet her at the supermarket? Did you live in the same suburban neighborhood? Otherwise, I don't see how you could've met a suburban mother who didn't work outside her home."

Orion smiled. "I met her at one of the quilting competitions she attended. I was searching for nice, well-made quilts for an antiques gallery I own."

That could have been true, but Shai knew that it was just another lie.

What was the guy hiding?

If he knew how to detect immortals among the billions of humans, he would have also found clan members and Doomers, but he'd claimed that he'd been a solo operator.

Given the chief's doubting expression, Onegus seemed to share his opinion. "I hoped that you would cooperate and that we wouldn't need to resort to harsher interrogation methods, but regrettably, you insist on lying. Who are you trying to protect, Orion?"

Shai wanted to know that as well.

Orion was good at hiding his fear, and his voice was steady and calm as he said, "I've only ever protected Geraldine and her family."

"Why?" Onegus asked.

"Because she's immortal like me, and she has memory issues. I was afraid that she would get discovered. I had to keep shielding her."

"Why didn't you take her with you?" Onegus asked.

A shadow passed over the guy's eyes. "I travel a lot, and Geraldine was raising a daughter."

"Did you have anything to do with her accident?" Shai asked.

Wincing, Orion shook his head. "I was away when that happened. When I returned and learned that she was presumed dead, I searched for her, hoping against hope that she had survived. I found her three days after her accident. She'd washed up to shore many miles down the coastline."

That agreed with what Geraldine and Annani had told them, so perhaps that part was true.

Onegus smiled one of his cobra smiles. "I assume that Geraldine didn't have memory issues before the accident."

Orion closed his eyes for a brief moment. "She didn't."

"Did you try to take her with you before she was injured?" Shai asked.

"No. She was married and had a child." He winced. "She didn't remember them after her accident. She didn't remember anything at all, not her name, not even how to speak. She had to relearn everything from scratch."

"If you knew about her family, why didn't you return her to them?" Onegus pressed on. "Why didn't you tell her that she had a husband and a child? Did you want to keep her for yourself?"

Orion's eyes blazed with suppressed anger, but his tone remained even as he answered. "I figured that it was a unique opportunity for her to disappear. Geraldine couldn't stay around for much longer anyway, and eventually, she would have had to fake her own death and disappear. I shielded her from the anguish of it by not telling her about the family she'd left behind."

That rang true, and yet Shai's gut still insisted that Orion was playing them all and that he was mixing truth with lies to make his story sound more believable.

Onegus let out a sigh. "As lovely as it is standing out here, I think it's time to move this party to somewhere safer and more comfortable." He snapped his fingers, and before Orion knew what was happening, one of the Guardians stabbed him in the neck with a syringe.

"Don't worry," Onegus said as horror flashed through Orion's eyes. "This is only going to put you to sleep for a little while, and the worst you should expect is to wake up with a headache."

The Guardian caught Orion before the guy slumped to the ground and carried him to Onegus's car.

"Where are you taking him?" Shai asked.

"The keep."

The one nice apartment in the keep's underground was taken at the moment, and Shai debated whether putting Orion in one of the small cells was the right thing to do.

So far, he hadn't admitted to any wrongdoing, and they couldn't prove that he was guilty of any.

"Are you going to put him in one of the small cells or move Vrog to one?" Shai followed Onegus to his car.

"Kian authorized Vrog's move to the village, and he's on his way as we speak. Hopefully, Okidu will be done preparing the suite for Orion by the time we get there. I don't want him to feel like a prisoner." He put his hand on Shai's shoulder. "We might need the Clan Mother to get the truth out of him, so you need to be patient."

Shai nodded. "Should I tell Geraldine?"

"I can call Cassandra. She knows where the keep is, and she can drive her mother there. I'm sure both mother and daughter will want to see Orion as soon as possible." Onegus smirked. "I also have a feeling that he will find it much harder to lie to their faces, especially Geraldine's."

"I'll get them both. I'll tell her what he said on the way."

"Perhaps you shouldn't. Let her come to him with just what she remembers and ask him all the same questions we did. That way he will have to repeat what he told us or change his tune."

Shai ran a hand over the back of his neck. "She'll ask. What am I going to tell her?"

"Tell her precisely what I told you. She'll understand."

Geraldine

Geraldine's hands shook as she applied lipstick. Shai had called, telling her about Orion's capture.

Why had he followed Shai? What had he wanted to do to him?

She was terrified of the answer. What if Orion had killed all of her more serious lovers? Was that why they'd disappeared from her life so completely that she couldn't remember whether they'd actually existed?

No, that was absurd. Orion was kind. He wouldn't have murdered anyone.

Soon she would have her answers.

Cassandra was on her way, and so was Shai, and he would take them both to the keep to see Orion.

Geraldine still couldn't believe that they'd caught him, drugged him, and taken him to the clan's keep.

Hopefully, he wouldn't be too upset with her for allowing that to happen.

Hopefully, he could prove that he hadn't done her any harm.

Hopefully, they would let him go.

"What have I done?"

Her reflection in the mirror looked at her with accusation in her eyes.

"Mom, I'm here," Cassandra called from downstairs. "Are you coming down?"

"In a minute," Geraldine called back.

Taking a deep breath, she squared her shoulders, took her purse, and headed toward the stairs.

Cassandra waited for her at the foot of the staircase with worry in her eyes. "Are you okay?"

"Not really," Geraldine admitted. "But I'm holding up, and I'm readying for a fight."

"With Orion?"

Geraldine shook her head. "With Kian, Onegus, Shai, and anyone else who wants to keep Orion imprisoned. I got him into this mess, and I'm going to get him out of it."

Cassandra put both her hands on Geraldine's shoulders. "You don't have the power to fight for him, but have some faith in those men. They are not going to keep him locked up unless they have to or unless he deserves it. We don't know what part he played in your accident and everything that happened to you before and after."

Geraldine's gut clenched. "Did Onegus tell you anything?"

"No. Did Shai share any details with you?"

"He didn't. He said that Onegus asked Orion some questions and that Orion gave him some answers that they weren't sure were truthful. Onegus doesn't want me to know what those answers were because he doesn't want me to get influenced by them. He wants me to question Orion as if he hasn't been questioned yet."

"It makes sense." Cassandra leaned and kissed Geraldine's cheek. "It's going to be okay, Mom. You'll have me, Shai, and Onegus with you. You can do it."

"Of course I can." Geraldine took Cassandra's hands off her. "And I'm grateful to be surrounded by people I love and who love me back as I confront Orion. But he has taken care of me for decades, and I have to fight for him, even if my loved ones disagree."

As the door opened and Shai walked in, his pinched expression told her more than he'd been willing to reveal. Whatever Orion had told them had either been self-incriminating, untrue, or things she couldn't imagine.

"Just tell me one thing." She walked up to him. "Is it worse than what we suspected?"

"I don't know." He took her hand. "Let's put it this way. If everything he said was true, then his story matches our best scenario hypothesis. But if he lied, all the other scenarios are still possible. He didn't say anything that we haven't considered before."

"That's good to know." She let loose a relieved breath. "You looked as if you'd learned something really bad when you came in."

"I didn't." He wrapped his arm around her waist. "Are you ready to go?"

She nodded. "How long is he going to be asleep?"

"According to Onegus, he should be waking up soon. Kian is probably already there."

Orion

When Orion woke up, he found himself on a plush bed, his head pounding just as Onegus had warned it would.

Nevertheless, he forced his eyes to remain open and look at where he was. It looked like a hotel bedroom, with one door open to a sitting area where he could sense three males and smell freshly brewed coffee.

He desperately needed a cup.

He also desperately needed to visit the bathroom, which was behind the other open door.

At least they hadn't thrown him in a dungeon. Except, a second sweep of the place revealed that there were no windows in the bedroom, so perhaps he was in one after all.

Since there was no point in pretending that he was still asleep, Orion slid off the bed and ducked into the bathroom.

After taking care of his bladder, he washed his face, unpacked the new toothbrush that had been left for him, and brushed his teeth. There was also a new electric shaver, still in the box, a new comb, still in its plastic wrap, and a plush terry robe hung on a hook next to a towel that was the same cream color.

When he entered the living room, Onegus gave him a smile. "How is your head?" He pushed to his feet and walked over to the small bar cabinet.

"Pounding." Orion looked at the other two males sitting next to a round dining table. He recognized them as part of the team that had trapped him earlier. "I could use some coffee."

"Here you go." Onegus handed him a cup. "The boss is on his way, and he wants you sharp and alert."

"Why?" Orion took a long sip, suppressing the urge to sigh with how good it was.

"To answer his questions."

Orion sat down on the couch. "What do you people want with me?"

"Just the truth, buddy."

"And when you get it, will you let me go?"

Onegus nodded.

Orion found that hard to believe. Then again, they hadn't imprisoned Geraldine, who was exactly like him, so they had no reason to keep him.

Unless they'd used her to trap him, and it all had been a setup. Had there been someone else with her in the house? Someone keeping her from leaving?

"How did you find Geraldine? I thought that I made sure she wouldn't reveal her immortality."

"We found Cassandra first." Onegus grinned like a peacock. "She's my mate."

That was a surprise.

"Do you mean girlfriend or wife?"

"Fiancée, in human terms. Immortals mate for life."

"Cassandra is not immortal."

"She is now. I induced her transition."

"I don't understand." Orion put his empty coffee cup on the table. "You said that a child born to an immortal and a human is human. I know who Cassandra's father was, and he wasn't immortal."

"The children of male immortals with human females are born human. The children of female immortals with male humans are born Dormant, which means that they carry the immortal gene in dormant form and that it can be activated with venom."

"Venom? Like during sex? So only the female children carry it?"

"Both male and female children born to an immortal mother carry the gene and can be activated. But the males cannot transmit it to their children."

Orion took a moment to organize the information in his head, which resulted in another question. "How are the males activated?"

"Also with venom, just not during sex. They have to fight an immortal male and spur his aggression enough for him to produce venom."

"I see."

It all somehow made sense.

"How did your people find out about that? Was it trial and error?"

Onegus regarded him with wary eyes. "Let's save the rest of your questions for the boss. He should be here any minute."

"Who is your so-called boss?"

"His name is Kian, and that's all you need to know for now."

Kian

As Kian waited for the cell door to open, he made a mental note to do some remodeling in the underground facility. He'd never expected to be making such frequent use of the place, and this morning he'd had to expedite Vrog's move to the village to make room for Orion.

They needed at least one more apartment-style cell.

When the door finished swinging out, he strode inside, meeting the eyes of the cell's newest occupant.

As per his instructions, Orion hadn't been cuffed, and no one stopped him as he rose to his feet and offered Kian his hand.

"Kian, I assume?"

"Indeed." He shook the guy's hand. "We've been very curious about you, Orion."

"I had no idea you even existed." The guy let go of his hand and looked at Andrew.

"This is Andrew," Kian said without explaining why he was there. "And these are Brundar and Anandur." He turned to the Guardians sitting at the dining table. "You can leave. We are expecting more guests, and there isn't enough room."

Andrew's ability to detect lies didn't work as well with immortals as it did with humans, and the earpieces probably would make it even more difficult for him to read Orion. But it was worth a try.

As the two got up and walked out, Anandur and Brundar took their place.

"Who else are you expecting?" Orion asked.

"Cassandra, Geraldine, and Shai."

Orion tensed, his expression turning hard. "Do you also keep Geraldine and Cassandra imprisoned?"

"Fates forbid." Kian sat down on one of the armchairs. "Cassandra is mated to Onegus, and Geraldine is mated to Shai. They are part of my clan now." He leaned forward. "That is why I want to find out what's happened to her, and I hope you can tell us more than we've managed to figure out so far."

The tension didn't leave Orion's body, but he tried to sound bored. "Tell me what you've figured out, and I'll try to fill in the missing pieces."

Andrew cleared his throat, which meant two things. One was that he could read Orion, which was excellent, and the other was that the guy wasn't being truthful. Translation—he had no intention of telling them anything and only wanted to find out what they knew.

"I'd rather hear the entire story from you first. Everything from the day you met Geraldine to when you induced her transition, and everything that has happened since."

"I've already told your men that I didn't induce her. I just learned from Onegus how it's done."

Andrew didn't clear his throat.

Interesting. The guy had really been clueless. How was it possible?

Onegus also looked at Andrew for confirmation, and when he shrugged, Onegus's eyes widened just a fraction.

Kian debated whether to keep on interrogating Orion or wait for Geraldine's arrival. Perhaps when the guy got confirmation from her that she was indeed free and happily mated, he would be less guarded and start telling them the truth.

Crossing his legs at the ankles, Kian decided to kill time by asking questions that were not pertinent to Geraldine's case. "What do you do for a living, Orion?"

"I deal in antiques. What about you?"

"The clan owns many enterprises. We invest in new technology, building projects, precious metals, minerals, the list is long."

Orion smiled. "I'm small fry compared to you."

"You need to support only yourself. The clan has many more mouths to feed."

"How many?"

It was Kian's turn to smile. "Wouldn't you like to know. For now, that's privileged information."

"When would it become available to me?"

"When you tell us the truth, the entire truth, and nothing but the truth, and we determine that you're trustworthy."

Geraldine

As Geraldine walked down the wide, industrial looking corridor, Shai to her right and Cassandra to her left, her heart hammered against her rib cage. They were underground, in the clan's dungeon, and guilt was swelling in her throat, choking her airway.

She was on the edge of a panic attack but refused to surrender to it.

How was she going to face Orion? What excuse could she give him for bringing him to this horrid place? Was he shackled to the wall with manacles? Were they torturing him?

Shai had laughed when she'd asked that, and Cassandra had assured her that the dungeon accommodations were more like an upscale hotel's than a prison's, but she couldn't help wondering whether they'd been telling her the truth.

"It's that one." Shai pointed to an open door that looked like something that belonged on a bank safe. It was at least a foot thick and made from some kind of metal.

All the doors on this level were like that, built to withstand an immortal male's strength.

Feeling her knees going weak, Geraldine clutched Shai's arm so tight that he winced. She forced herself to loosen her grip and let him lead her into the cell.

It was full of people, but her eyes immediately darted to Orion, who rose to his feet and started walking toward her.

The distance between them was no more than five feet, two steps for Orion, but time slowed, and she saw him approaching her in slow motion.

"Geraldine," he said her name.

"I'm so sorry." Tears streaming down her cheek, she let go of Shai's arm and flung herself at him.

He embraced her gently. "Why are you sorry?"

"You're here because of me," she whispered into his neck.

"Is that a bad thing?" He leaned back and looked down at her. "Are they mistreating you here?"

"No, they are wonderful. I love Shai and he loves me, and I'm very happy. But I remembered you, and I knew that you would come, and I told them about it, and they were lying in wait for you."

He frowned. "Why?"

"To find out what happened to me and also if there are more immortals out there. The clan has been searching for more survivors for thousands of years, but other than those horrid Doomers, they only found one survivor and several Dormants. Are there more out there?"

He shook his head. "I've also been searching."

Behind her, Cassandra cleared her throat. "Hello, Orion. I don't remember you, but I was told that you were a frequent visitor to our home when I was growing up."

He let go of Geraldine and reached for Cassandra. "I'm very proud of the woman you've become. And I'm so happy that you turned immortal. I didn't know it was even possible."

Kian rose to his feet. "Please, let's all sit down."

Geraldine glanced at Shai before joining Orion on the couch, beckoning him to sit on her other side. It was meant more as a reassurance to him than her need for his support.

She was relieved to confirm that she had absolutely no romantic feelings for Orion, but Shai needed to know that as well.

Kian's brother-in-law vacated the armchair for Cassandra, but she declined the offer and joined Onegus and the two bodyguards at the dining table.

Orion took Geraldine's hand. "How much do you remember?"

Shai had warned her not to mention the goddess. "The memories are slowly coming back. I know that you were helping me throughout the years, but I don't remember anything from before the accident."

"You were severely injured. It's a miracle that you're alive."

"Do you know how it happened?"

He shook his head. "I found you three days later. You were already healing, but you had a long way to go. I assumed that you hit your head on a rock or on a boat."

"How did you find me in the first place?" She swallowed. "Did you induce me?"

He chuckled. "You are the third person who's asked me that. I didn't induce you. You were already immortal."

"Then who did it?"

"No one." He smiled. "You were born immortal."

She frowned. "How is that possible? Even two immortal parents can only have a dormant child. No one is born an immortal."

Kian cleared his throat. "If a child is conceived by a god or a goddess with a human partner, it's born immortal."

She heard him, but she wasn't sure she'd heard correctly. "What are you saying?"

"He's saying that you are a child of a god," Orion said.

Feeling all the blood leaving her face, she turned to him. "How do you know that?"

"I know who your father is. He is my father as well, and he is a god."

Orion

"You are both Toven's children." Cassandra said. "And I'm his granddaughter. Oh, wow." She grinned. "Can he also blow things up with his mind?"

It was so much like Cassandra to ask that.

Orion chuckled. "No. This is a talent unique to you. I should have known that you weren't entirely human when your mother told me about the little explosions she thought you were causing. I thought that she'd imagined it."

"Didn't you feel the power swirling under my skin?" Cassandra asked.

He shook his head. "I thought that you had an explosive personality."

When several people chuckled, he glanced at Shai, Geraldine's boyfriend, who was no longer looking at him with murder in his eyes, but rather awe.

Geraldine lifted a hand to her temple and rubbed it. "I can't believe that I'm a demigoddess. Why am I not more powerful?"

It only dawned on him then that Cassandra named his father Toven.

Was that the god's real name? He'd refused to tell Orion who he really was, calling himself Herman, but he'd admitted that he'd used many names since all the other gods had perished.

Orion had studied ancient mythologies though, searching for descriptions that would match the male who had fathered him, but he didn't remember the name Toven mentioned anywhere. Perhaps his father had been a minor god whose name hadn't made it into any of the surviving mythologies.

"Well?" Geraldine reminded him that she was still waiting for an answer.

"I'm sorry." He smiled at her. "You had been suppressing your abilities even before I met you, and I encouraged that throughout the years. I didn't want you to give yourself away."

"Tell us about your father," Kian said. "What do you know about him? Where is he? How did he survive?"

"What I know about him isn't much. I know that he's a jaded bastard who doesn't care about anyone or anything. I don't know where he is because he never stays in one place for long. I didn't even know his real name until Cassandra said it, although I would like to know how she knew that. But I do know how he survived. He told me that he'd been disgusted with the proceedings in the gods' assembly, snuck out, and flew away on some flying contraption that some of the gods possessed. He hadn't known that his people perished along with a big chunk of the ancient world's population until he returned home months later and saw the devastation."

"What did he do once he found out?" Kian asked.

"Flew far away and made a home for himself somewhere else. That was all he told me."

Kian looked at the guy named Andrew, who nodded.

Was he some kind of a truth detector? He hadn't said a word other than clearing his throat when Orion had lied.

"Two more goddesses survived," Kian said. "One is my mother, and the other is her sister."

"So you're a demigod as well," Orion said.

"I'm an immortal, and that's all I am." Kian folded his arms over his chest. "I don't think of myself as a demigod. It seems pretentious."

Orion nodded. "Indeed."

He didn't like the title either, thinking of himself as hard to kill and easy to heal. His powers were useful, but they weren't godly. They were just mind tricks that even some humans could do.

Kian was still regarding him with those intense blue eyes of his. "Now that I've shared with you my clan's biggest secret, I want you to tell me how you found out that your father was a god, and how you found Geraldine. You told her that you discovered your immortality on the battlefield when you recovered from an injury that should have been fatal. Is that true?"

"That's correct. My mother didn't know who my father was."

"What about your fangs?" Kian unfolded his arms and leaned forward. "Your venom glands? Didn't you wonder what those were about?"

"When they started growing, I already knew that I was deathless. It was after that battle." He snorted. "I thought that I'd been bitten by a vampire, and I clung to that explanation for a long time. I didn't tell my mother what was going on and tried to hide those damn fangs."

"How old were you when you got that injury?" Geraldine asked.

"Fourteen."

A tear slid down her cheek. "You were just a boy."

"I wasn't the youngest. Boys as young as ten were drafted. Those were different times, dark times that I'd rather forget."

"How did you find your father?" Kian asked.

"That's a long story." He glanced longingly at the empty coffee carafe. "Can we take a coffee break? I haven't had breakfast yet either."

Kian turned to the redhead sitting at the dining table. "Can you get us pastries and sandwiches from the vending machines?"

"Sure, boss." The giant rose to his feet. "Cappuccinos, anyone?"

"I would love one." Orion smiled up at him. "If it's not a bother, with two sugars, please."

"No problem. Anyone else?"

It had been a test of sorts, to see what kind of people they were, and how well they were going to treat him. So far, they seemed like a decent bunch, and if they'd accepted Geraldine and Cassandra into their clan, perhaps they would accept him as well.

It would be nice not to be so alone, to be among others like him, and perhaps, if his luck held, he might also find an immortal mate to call his own. But he wouldn't give up his autonomy for that, nor would he ever stop searching for Toven's other children.

THE ADVENTURE CONTINUES
ALENA & ORION'S STORY IS NEXT
THE CHILDREN OF THE GODS BOOK 56
DARK HUNTER'S QUERY

Turn the page to read the excerpt—>

Join the VIP Club
To find out what's included in your free membership,
flip to the last page.

Dark Hunter's Query

For most of his five centuries of existence, Orion has walked the earth alone, searching for answers.
Why is he immortal?
Where did his powers come from?
Is he the only one of his kind?
When fate puts Orion face to face with the god who sired

him, he learns the secret behind his immortality and that he might not be the only one.

As the goddess's eldest daughter and a mother of thirteen, Alena deserves the title of Clan Mother just as much as Annani, but she's not interested in honorifics.

Being her mother's companion and keeping the mischievous goddess out of trouble is a rewarding, full-time job. Lately, though, Alena's love for her mother and the clan's gratitude is not enough.

She craves adventure, excitement, and perhaps a true-love mate of her own.

When Alena and Orion meet, sparks fly, but they both resist the pull. Alena could never bring herself to trust the powerful compeller, and Orion could never allow himself to fall in love again.

Alena

Alena, eldest daughter of the goddess Annani, a mother of thirteen, a grandmother of seventeen, a great-grandmother of twenty-three, and a great many times over grandmother of nearly every member of her clan, gazed at her phone's screen and sighed like a besotted schoolgirl.

In her over two millennia of existence, Alena had never reacted so strongly to a male, let alone to a mere depiction of one. The portrait had been created by a talented illustrator, but it hadn't been embellished in any way. The forensic artist had merely given life to a verbal description taken from a human's memory, and Annani had attested to its accuracy.

Annani had hung the framed original in her receiving room, a fond reminder of the male's father—the god Toven, whom she'd greatly admired in her youth. According to her mother, father and son looked so much alike that they were nearly indistinguishable.

Taken by the immortal's striking looks, Alena had captured Orion's image with her phone so she could gaze at it whenever she pleased, which was often. By now, she had every detail of the drawing committed to memory—the intelligent eyes, the chiseled cheekbones, the full sensuous lips, the aristocratic nose, the shoulder-length dark hair, the strong column of his neck—and yet she still felt compelled to pull out her phone and gaze at it.

Despite being an artistic construct, the drawing looked so lifelike, Orion's face so expressive, that it made her feel as if he were looking straight into her soul.

But it was all an illusion, and getting excited over a pretty face was as shallow as it got. She was too old to be blindsided by skin-deep beauty and wise enough to know that the only beauty that mattered was the kind found on the inside.

The male was gorgeous, perfect in the way all gods and the first generation of their offspring with humans were. It didn't mean that he was a good man, or that he could carry on an intelligent conversation, or that he was the truelove mate she'd been secretly hoping for.

Alena was the eldest, and yet the Fates had bestowed the blessing of a truelove mate on her younger siblings first. She wasn't jealous of their happiness and wished them the best their eternal lives had to offer, but she wanted her own happily ever after, and she was tired of waiting.

Except, Orion couldn't be the one for her, and if he was, the Fates had a really sick sense of humor. He was a compeller, and Alena could never be with a male who could take away her will at his whim. Just imagining being so helpless and at the mercy of another made her shiver. So even though his beautiful face evoked a powerful longing and caused a stirring—the kind Alena had never experienced before—and even though she pulled up his damn picture and stared at it numerous times a day, he could never be her truelove mate.

Her one and only probably had not been born yet, or he was making his way toward her while she was letting herself get enchanted by the pretty face of another.

Alena sighed.

Hopefully, the one the Fates chose for her would have longish black hair, piercing blue eyes, and a face that looked like it was lovingly carved from granite by a talented sculptor—precisely like Orion, just not Orion himself.

Could her fated one be Orion's father? Except, Orion hadn't inherited his compulsion ability from his human mother, and Toven was probably a compeller as well.

Maybe Orion had a brother? One who hadn't inherited the ability?

After all, Geraldine was also Toven's daughter, and she wasn't a compeller.

Hope surging in her heart, Alena closed her phone and put it back in her skirt pocket.

She was running out of patience.

Supposedly the Fates rewarded those who selflessly sacrificed for others or suffered greatly with the gift of a truelove mate. Had she sacrificed or suffered less than her siblings? Was that why she was the last one left even though she was the eldest?

Kian had dedicated his life to the clan, so she could understand why he'd been granted a mate first. Amanda had lost a child, which was the worst suffering Alena could imagine, so it was only fair that she'd been the next one in line to find her fated mate. Sari had worked almost as hard as Kian to better the lives of those clan members who'd chosen to remain in Scotland, so it was also fair that she'd gotten her happily ever after.

Alena deserved hers as well.

She wasn't a natural leader like Kian or Sari, and she hadn't suffered a terrible loss like Amanda, but she was the de facto mother of the clan, and she also sacrificed a lot to keep her own mother out of trouble.

Not that any of it had been a great sacrifice or had caused her any suffering.

Motherhood was the best possible reward in itself, and traveling the world with Annani wasn't exactly a hardship either.

As Annani's companion, Alena had been an unwilling participant in her mother's crazy shenanigans, but she had to admit that most of them had been fun and not overly dangerous. She also enjoyed the babies and toddlers who arrived at the sanctuary to be kept safe until it was time for them to transition.

Life had been good to her, but she'd been doing the same thing for two thousand years, and it was time for a change.

Her only solo adventure had been impersonating a Slovenian supermodel in the hopes of luring Kalugal out of hiding.

After the fun time she'd spent with the team who'd accompanied her to New York, it had been difficult to go back to the routine. For a few precious days, she'd enjoyed being different, being her own person and not her mother's shadow.

It seemed like such a distant memory, like it had taken place in another lifetime.

The face she saw in the mirror was the same one she'd been looking at for two millennia.

Gone was the sophisticated hairstyle she'd adopted for the New York trip, replaced by her habitual loose braid, her face was free of makeup, and she wore one of her long, comfortable dresses instead of the fashionable clothes Amanda had gotten her for that trip.

Those had been given away to charity soon after she'd returned from New York.

There was no reason to dress up in the sanctuary, where everyone expected her to look the part of Annani's devoted daughter—the goddess's companion and advisor—a part she'd been playing for so long that no one could envision her doing anything else, including herself.

Not that there was anything wrong with it.

Her position at Annani's side was a duty and an honor that Alena had proudly and lovingly performed for centuries—a position that could not be filled by anyone but her.

Orion

Orion regarded the leader of his captors, noting the hard lines of Kian's face, the stiffness of his shoulders, and the sheer size of him. The guy was big, he was gruff, but he wasn't cold, and that gave Orion hope.

So far, other than the damn tranquilizer they'd knocked him out with, these immortals hadn't treated him too badly. Nevertheless, they were holding him against his will, and even though the apartment he'd woken up in was as fancy as any high-end hotel suite, it was still a prison cell.

Other than having been born immortal, he hadn't done anything to them, and they had no reason to hold him, but he was at their mercy, his compulsion ability nullified by the earpieces they were all wearing.

Without it, he was as helpless as any human, and the only way out of the situation was to cooperate with his captors and give them what they wanted, which was information about his jerk of a father.

No skin off his nose.

If they could find the god, Orion didn't care what they did with him.

Kian put his paper cup down on the table and crossed his arms over his chest. "Now that you've eaten breakfast and gotten caffeinated, I want to hear the story of how you found your father and got him to admit that he was a god."

It was clear that the guy's patience was wearing thin, but Orion needed a little more time to think. The coffee break he'd practically begged Kian for had helped ease the pounding headache he'd woken up with, but his mind was still foggy.

He didn't mind telling them about his father, but there were other things he'd learned from the god that he wasn't sure he should share with them.

Did it matter if they knew that he was hunting for the god's other potential children?

They already knew about his sister and niece and had accepted Geraldine and Cassandra into their clan, but had their motives been pure?

They needed new blood for their community—more genetic diversity. They might try to get to his other siblings first and draft them into their clan.

Was that so bad, though?

Perhaps they could help him with his quest.

Orion had exhausted all of the information he had, but they might have access to resources that he didn't.

Damn, if only his head would clear so he could follow one thought to its logical conclusion instead of all his thoughts jumping around in his head like bunnies on speed.

Were these people trustworthy?

Were they a force for good or the opposite of that?

Was he lucky that they had found his sister and him?

The effects of the tranquilizer were beginning to wane, but he was still having a hard time reconciling what he'd learned from his captors with what he'd been told by his father. Some of it confirmed the god's story, but there was so much more that his father hadn't shared with him.

For nearly five centuries, Orion had been convinced that he was the only immortal, an anomaly, and then he'd met his father who'd claimed to be a god—not a deity, but a lone survivor of a superior race of people who'd been annihilated by one of their own.

Herman, aka Toven, had claimed that the gods from various mythologies had been real people. At the time, Orion had doubted his father's story, had suspected that the guy was either delusional or being deliberately deceitful, but his captors had confirmed everything Herman had told him. The gods hadn't been the constructs of human imagination, and what's more, his father wasn't the only survivor.

Had his father known about the two goddesses who'd escaped the attack and chosen not to tell him?

Had he known that some humans carried the dormant godly gene and withheld the information on purpose?

"Whenever you're ready," Kian prompted.

"Can I bother you for another cup?" Orion cast the guy a pleading look. "My head feels like it's stuffed with cotton. Usually, I don't suffer from such maladies, but the tranquilizer your guy injected me with must have been incredibly potent."

Kian grimaced. "It had to be to knock out an immortal."

"I'll brew a fresh pot," Onegus said. The male mated to his niece was the head of the clan's security forces, and yet he got up to reload the coffeemaker. "It will take a couple of minutes."

Apparently, these people didn't follow strict hierarchy. The guy could have asked one of the guards to brew the coffee but had chosen to do so himself. They acted more like a family or a group of friends than a military organization, which Orion took to be a good sign as to the kind of people he was dealing with.

Next to him, his sister winced. "I'm so sorry."

He patted her knee. "My head already feels much better."

"I didn't mean the headache." Geraldine smiled apologetically. "Well, that too, but what I'm really sorry about is entrapping you. You wouldn't be in this situation if I hadn't dug into my murky past."

"Why did you?"

"Do you mean why did I want to find out about my past or why did I help the clan trap you?"

"The first one."

"As long as I was oblivious about having had another life, I was content with the one I had. But after I discovered that I had a daughter who I couldn't remember, I had to find out how it happened. But I should have just moved on." She sighed. "In part, it's your fault that I didn't. You compelled me not to leave the house for more than a day, so I couldn't start my new life with Shai in his village."

Orion nodded. "Indeed, and that means that my capture is on me, and you have nothing to apologize for." He cast a sidelong glance at Kian. "I've been careful not to get noticed by humans, but I never anticipated other immortals. Although with the advent of the modern era and the proliferation of imaging devices, avoiding discovery by humans is getting more difficult. I can rely on my compulsion ability to get out of tight spots, but I can't compel inanimate objects, and nowadays, there are surveillance cameras everywhere and everyone has smartphones they can use to snap photos with. I had to develop new tactics to avoid getting my image recorded on electronic devices."

Ironically, though, his capture hadn't been the result of technology or even his negligence. Orion had followed the best protocols he could devise. What had gotten him in trouble was precisely the thing his father had warned him against—family, people he cared about, people who could lead others to him.

His sister and her daughters were his Achilles heel.

Next to him, Geraldine shifted her knees sideways and put her hands in her lap. "I have to admit, though, that your compulsion wasn't the only reason I didn't leave the house. As much as I hated the idea of trapping you, I wanted to talk to you and not forget the conversation as soon as you left. We pieced together most of what had happened to me, but there were still so many holes in the puzzle, and I wanted answers. I needed closure."

He put a hand on her knee. "I understand. You don't need to keep apologizing."

Geraldine lifted her big blue eyes to him, so much like his own that it was like looking in the mirror. "You're my brother, but I didn't know that, and I thought that you were my inducer. Do you know how awkward it feels now that I know the truth?" She shook her head. "It gets worse. When I finally recalled our interactions over the years, I was offended that you didn't find me attractive." She chuckled. "Although, I should have known something was up because I wasn't attracted to you either." She waved a hand over his face. "If you were ugly, that would have been understandable, but you are so gorgeous that I can't take my eyes off you."

Orion had never felt comfortable with the looks he'd gotten throughout his life, either covetous from those interested in him sexually or envious and outright hostile from others, but Geraldine was his sister, and her complimenting him on his good looks didn't feel as awkward. It reminded him of his mother and the way she used to regard him with love and adoration in her eyes.

"Thank you." Absentmindedly, he reached for Geraldine's hand and gave it a gentle squeeze. "I'm curious. How did you suddenly recover your memories of me? Did your mate have anything to do with that?"

"The goddess released them." Geraldine shifted her eyes to Kian. "Is it okay for me to reveal that?"

"It's fine."

So that was how she remembered him. Orion had wondered about that, thinking that maybe her boyfriend or one of the other immortals was powerful enough to unlock her submerged memories. But it had taken a goddess to release them, which meant that the others were not as powerful as he was.

He tucked away that bit of information for later use. "Is the goddess here?" He looked at Kian. "Can I meet her?"

Kian chuckled. "The Clan Mother is very curious about you, and I have no doubt that she will want to meet you as soon as possible. She's very fond of your father and speaks highly of him."

Orion grimaced. "He must've changed a lot since she last interacted with him."

"Here you go." Onegus handed him a mug of freshly brewed coffee.

"Thank you." Taking the mug with him, Orion leaned back against the couch cushions and crossed his legs at the ankles. "Perhaps I should start my story at the beginning, many years before I met my father." He took several sips from his coffee before putting the cup on the table.

"Please do," Geraldine said. "I want to know everything about you, or at least the highlights of your life."

Now that Orion's head was clearer and his thought process faster, deciding which information to share and which to withhold became easier.

The coffee break had been a test, and it had allowed him to observe his captors interacting with each other, and more importantly, with his sister and niece.

There was no faking the loving glances between Onegus and Cassandra and between Geraldine and Shai. His sister and niece were indeed happily mated to these clansmen, which made the men his family as well.

Besides, the clan had little to gain from what he could tell them, and he didn't have much to lose.

So far, Orion's query had yielded only one result—Geraldine—and he'd been unsuccessful in locating any of Toven's other children. Perhaps he and Geraldine were the only ones, or maybe he needed help locating the others.

Kian

"As I mentioned before," Orion began, "I was fourteen when I discovered that I was immortal."

"Hold on." Geraldine lifted her hand. "That's not the beginning. I want to know where you were born, who your mother was, and how you ended up on the battlefield at such a young age."

Kian stifled a groan. At this rate, it would be nighttime before Orion reached the part about his father, and Kian had no intentions of staying in the keep for so long.

He called his mother when Orion had been captured, but because the guy had been knocked out cold, he'd had nothing else to report. His mother was no doubt anxiously awaiting an update and getting more aggravated with every passing moment.

Besides, as fascinating as hearing about Orion's life was, he was more interested in Toven's, and even that was not as important or as fun as spending time with his daughter.

Just thinking about Allegra's cute smiles and the adorable sounds she made eased the tension in his shoulders and lightened his heart.

Orion sighed and leaned forward to pick up his coffee mug. "The man who I thought was my father was a merchant in a small town near Milan. I was born nine months after he was killed in what is known as the Great Wars of Italy or the Habsburg-Valois wars. Because of the opportune timing, no one ever suspected that the grieving widow gave birth to a child that wasn't her deceased husband's, and neither did I." He chuckled. "Although even as a small boy, I knew that I looked nothing like that fat, ruddy-cheeked man in the portrait hanging in our home's entryway. What little hair he had was light brown, and my mother was a blond." He lifted his hand and smoothed it over his chin-length raven hair. "As you can see, my hair color is nearly black."

"You have beautiful hair," Cassandra said. "Did no one wonder about the little boy who looked nothing like his deceased father?"

He shrugged. "My mother was smart. She told everyone that I was the spitting image of her cousin, and she repeated it enough times for the fib to become truth. I think that after a while, she started believing it herself."

"Did you believe the lie?" Cassandra asked.

"Why wouldn't I? I adored my mother, and I had no reason to doubt her."

Kian huffed out a breath. "You must have realized the truth after surviving the injury that should have killed you."

Hopefully, jumping ahead to that would shorten the story time.

"Not right away." Orion's lips lifted in a crooked smile. "I came up with several possible explanations, starting with a guardian angel and ending with a good witch."

"What about being bitten by a vampire?" Geraldine asked.

"That came later, after my fangs started growing. I panicked, afraid that I would become crazed with blood lust, so I packed up my things and was about to leave in the middle of the night. My mother intercepted me, and when I admitted my fears, she said that vampires didn't exist but that I might have inherited strange things from my father, who wasn't the man she'd been married to.

She told me that I was old enough to learn the truth, and that if I wanted to live, I needed to keep it a secret."

"How did she manage an affair?" Cassandra asked. "I mean, war was raging, and her husband was gone. And how did Toven find her? Did he just stroll into town and seduce her?"

"I don't know. She didn't divulge any details, only that he'd been a stunningly good-looking man and very smart. I'm not sure that she remembered much more than that. When I started discovering my own powers, I realized that he must have tampered with her memories."

Geraldine tilted her head. "Do you think that Toven compelled her to be with him?"

Orion shook his head. "My father is a jaded bastard, but he's not a rapist. My mother accepted him with open arms. I know that it makes her look bad, but she'd been practically sold to her husband by her family, and the arranged marriage was a disaster. He was a terrible man, or at least that was what she claimed, and when he died, she rejoiced at finally being free and celebrated with a very handsome stranger."

"How did she remember her affair with Toven?" Onegus asked. "Did he leave at least some of her memories of him intact?"

"My mother was an artist." Orion looked at Geraldine. "Our father had a thing for creative women. Your mother was an artist as well."

Her eyes widened. "Did you meet my real mother?"

He nodded. "I did, but I'll tell you about that later. I don't want to jump all over the timeline."

Kian was still trying to understand Orion's answer to Onegus's question. "What does your mother being an artist have to do with remembering Toven?"

"Indeed." Orion smiled. "She told me that she'd drunk a lot of wine after her husband's death, and she didn't remember much about the man she'd celebrated her freedom with, but her artist's eye remembered enough of him to draw a portrait." Orion waved a hand over his face. "When I reached adulthood, I realized that I looked just like him, but that's getting ahead of the story as well. You wanted to know how I found myself on the battlefield at the age of fourteen."

Geraldine nodded.

"Quite simply, I was the only male in the household, and they demanded one from each family. My mother wasn't very wealthy, but she wasn't destitute either, and she tried to bribe the recruiters. They took her gold and drafted me anyway. Back then, a woman alone was powerless. There was nothing she could've done to prevent them from taking me."

Geraldine put her hand on his arm. "I can't imagine how terrified you were."

"I was. I just knew that I was going to die. I'd never trained with any kinds of weapons. Heck, I didn't know how to hold a pike or a crossbow."

As Geraldine's chin started to wobble and tears slid down her cheeks, Kian cast her an amused glance. "But he didn't die. That's not a ghost sitting next to you."

The redheaded guard snorted. "I disagree. We have with us the ghost of Orion's past."

Orion

As everyone laughed, Orion closed his eyes. The horror of that day nearly five centuries ago was still fresh in his mind as if it had happened a week ago.

He didn't remember much of the battle or how he had been gutted. It had all been a blur of terror, and dying hadn't been the worst part of it. He'd been glad that it was over.

Except, he hadn't died.

Sometime later, he woke up with dirt filling his nostrils, his mouth, his throat. He'd been buried with the rest of the fallen. Choking, starved for breath, he'd clawed at the loosely compacted earth, had dug up against the flesh of the dead he'd been buried with, and had blindly inched toward the surface.

When he'd finally broken free, Orion had coughed and spat and vomited, and then lost consciousness again. The next time he opened his eyes, he had patted his stomach, searching for the injury, but other than caked-on blood, no trace of it had remained.

That had terrified him almost as much as regaining consciousness in the mass grave had. He'd thought that he was in hell, and in a way he was. Living was purgatory, and unlike the rest of humanity, his would last forever. He was stuck on this horrid plane of existence with no chance for parole.

"Orion?" Geraldine's soft voice pierced the darkness of his memories. "Are you okay?"

Fighting against the phantom choking sensation, he forced himself to suck in a breath. "Yeah, I'm fine. Nearly five centuries to the day, and I can still taste the dirt in my mouth."

"They buried you alive," Kian guessed. "They thought that you were dead."

Orion nodded. "I think that I was actually dead and was resurrected somehow."

The redhead leaned forward. "Was there water in the mass grave? Did it rain?"

"I don't think so." Orion wiped a hand over his mouth. "I remember that the dirt was dry. Why do you ask?"

"You might have entered stasis, but you could have appeared dead to humans even without going into that deep state."

"What year was that?" Shai asked.

"1525."

"So you were born in 1511," Kian calculated. "Was Orion your given name?"

He shook his head. "My mother named me Orlando. I've used many different names over the centuries, but I chose Orion after meeting my real father."

"When did you find him and how?" Kian asked for the fifth or sixth time.

But unlike before, this time he'd get an answer. It was a relief to jump ahead in the timeline, bypassing hundreds of terrible experiences, large and small, that had each left a scar on Orion's soul.

His body was a perfect machine that healed all injuries without leaving a single mark, but his soul was a different story. It was wounded, scarred, and aching, with no hope of ever recovering.

"Thirty-eight years ago, on Rue de la Jussienne in Paris, a chance encounter brought me face to face with my father. I was heading toward my favorite café when I saw him walking toward me. We both stopped at the same time and stared at each other. It was like looking in the mirror. And yet, it didn't occur to me that he might be my father. Everyone is supposed to have a doppelgänger, right?"

Cassandra snorted. "Not someone who looks like you." She turned to Kian. "Or you. Your godly heritage is unmistakable. No human is that perfect."

Kian arched a brow. "Did Toven also think that you were his doppelgänger?"

"No, he knew who I was, but he pretended that he didn't. He gave me a tight-lipped smile and kept walking. I hesitated for a split second before rushing after him.

"*Excuse me*, I said as I fell in step with him. *I wonder if we are related. Looking at you is like looking at the mirror.*"

"*We are not*, he said. *You don't know me, and you've never seen me. Go away.*"

"That's when I knew he was either the one who sired me or a half-brother of mine. He tried to use compulsion, but it didn't work because I had the same power. I told him the same thing Onegus said to me when I tried to use it on him. *Your tricks don't work on me. I'm just like you.*"

Cassandra grinned. "I would have paid good money to see the bastard's face when you told him that."

"He wasn't happy, and he was even less so when he realized that he couldn't get rid of me. I followed him to the townhouse he was renting at the time, and he had no choice but to let me in."

Kian leaned forward, bracing his elbows on his knees. "How long did it take you to force him to admit that he was your father?"

"Not long. I told him that I wasn't going anywhere until he told me everything I wanted to know."

"Did he?" Geraldine asked.

"He told me a lot, but apparently, not nearly enough."

ORDER DARK HUNTER'S QUERY TODAY!

JOIN THE VIP CLUB
To find out what's included in your free membership,
flip to the last page.

The Children of the Gods Series

Reading Order

THE CHILDREN OF THE GODS ORIGINS

1: Goddess's Choice

When gods and immortals still ruled the ancient world, one young goddess risked everything for love.

2: Goddess's Hope

Hungry for power and infatuated with the beautiful Areana, Navuh plots his father's demise. After all, by getting rid of the insane god he would be doing the world a favor. Except, when gods and immortals conspire against each other, humanity pays the price.

But things are not what they seem, and prophecies should not to be trusted...

THE CHILDREN OF THE GODS

Dark Stranger

1: Dark Stranger The Dream

2: Dark Stranger Revealed

3: Dark Stranger Immortal

Dark Enemy

4: Dark Enemy Taken

5: Dark Enemy Captive

6: Dark Enemy Redeemed

Kri & Michael's Story

6.5: My Dark Amazon

Dark Warrior

7: Dark Warrior Mine

8: Dark Warrior's Promise

9: Dark Warrior's Destiny

10: Dark Warrior's Legacy

Dark Guardian

11: Dark Guardian Found

12: Dark Guardian Craved

13: Dark Guardian's Mate

Dark Angel

14: Dark Angel's Obsession

15: Dark Angel's Seduction

16: Dark Angel's Surrender

Dark Operative

17: Dark Operative: A Shadow of Death

18: Dark Operative: A Glimmer of Hope

19: Dark Operative: The Dawn of Love

Dark Survivor

20: Dark Survivor Awakened

21: Dark Survivor Echoes of Love

22: Dark Survivor Reunited

Dark Widow

23: Dark Widow's Secret
24: Dark Widow's Curse
25: Dark Widow's Blessing

Dark Dream

26: Dark Dream's Temptation
27: Dark Dream's Unraveling
28: Dark Dream's Trap

Dark Prince

29: Dark Prince's Enigma
30: Dark Prince's Dilemma
31: Dark Prince's Agenda

Dark Queen

32: Dark Queen's Quest
33: Dark Queen's Knight
34: Dark Queen's Army

Dark Spy

35: Dark Spy Conscripted
36: Dark Spy's Mission
37: Dark Spy's Resolution

Dark Overlord

38: Dark Overlord New Horizon
39: Dark Overlord's Wife

40: Dark Overlord's Clan

Dark Choices

41: Dark Choices The Quandary
42: Dark Choices Paradigm Shift
43: Dark Choices The Accord

Dark Secrets

44: Dark Secrets Resurgence
45: Dark Secrets Unveiled
46: Dark Secrets Absolved

Dark Haven

47: Dark Haven Illusion
48: Dark Haven Unmasked
49: Dark Haven Found

Dark Power

50: Dark Power Untamed
51: Dark Power Unleashed
52: Dark Power Convergence

Dark Memories

53: Dark Memories Submerged
54: Dark Memories Emerge
55: Dark Memories Restored

Dark Hunter

56: Dark Hunter's Query

57: Dark Hunter's Prey

When Alena and Orion join Kalugal and Jacki on a romantic vacation to the enchanting Lake Lugu in China, they anticipate a couple of visits to Kalugal's archeological dig, some sightseeing, and a lot of lovemaking.

Their excursion takes an unexpected turn when Jacki's vision sends them on a perilous hunt for the elusive Kra-ell.

As things progress from bad to worse, Alena beseeches the Fates to keep everyone in their group alive. She can't fathom losing any of them, but most of all, Orion.

For over two thousand years, she walked the earth alone, but after mere days with him at her side, she can't imagine life without him.

58: Dark Hunter's Boon

As Orion and Alena's relationship blooms and solidifies, the two investigative teams combine their recent discoveries to piece together more of the Kra-ell mystery.

Attacking the puzzle from another angle, Eleanor works on gaining access to Echelon's powerful AI spy network.

Together, they are getting dangerously close to finding the elusive Kra-ell.

Dark God

59: Dark God's Avatar

Unaware of the time bomb ticking inside her, Mia had lived the perfect life until it all came to a screeching halt, but despite the difficulties she faces, she doggedly pursues her dreams.

Once known as the god of knowledge and wisdom, Toven has

grown cold and indifferent. Disillusioned with humanity, he travels the world and pens novels about the love he can no longer feel.

Seeking to escape his ever-present ennui, Toven gives a cutting-edge virtual experience a try. When his avatar meets Mia's, their sizzling virtual romance unexpectedly turns into something deeper and more meaningful.

Will it endure in the real world?

60: Dark God's Reviviscence

Toven might have failed in his attempts to improve humanity's condition, but he isn't going to fail to improve Mia's life, making it the best it can be despite her fragile health, and he can do that not as a god, but as a man who possesses the means, the smarts, and the determination to do it.

No effort is enough to repay Mia for reviving his deadened heart and making him excited for the next day, but the flip side of his reviviscence is the fear of losing its catalyst.

Given Mia's condition, Toven doesn't dare to over excite her. His venom is a powerful aphrodisiac, euphoric, and an all-around health booster, but it's also extremely potent. It might kill her instead of making her better.

61: Dark God Destinies Converge

Destinies converge, and secrets are revealed in part three of Mia and Toven's story.

Dark Whispers

62: Dark Whispers From The Past

A brilliant scientist and programmer, William lives for his work, but when he recruits a young bioinformatician to help him decipher the gods' genetic blueprints, he find himself smitten with more than just her brain.

A Ph.d at nineteen, Kaia is considered a prodigy and expects a bright future in academia. But when William invites her to join his secret research team, she accepts for reasons that have nothing to do with her career objectives. Wiliam's promise to look into her best friend's disappearance is an offer she just can't refuse.

63: Dark Whispers From Afar

William knows that his budding relationship with the nineteen-year-old Kaia will be frowned upon, but he's unprepared for her family's vehement opposition.

Family means everything to Kaia, so when she finds herself in the impossible position of having to choose between them and William, she resorts to unconventional means to resolve the conflict.

64: Dark Whispers From Beyond

The sacrifices Kaia and her family have to make for a chance of gaining immortality might tear them apart, and success is not guaranteed.

Is the dubious promise of eternal life worth the risk of losing everything?

Dark Gambit

65: Dark Gambit The Pawn

Temporarily assigned to supervise a team of bioinformaticians, Marcel expects to spend a couple of weeks in the peaceful retreat of Safe Haven, enjoying Oregon Coast's cool weather and rugged beauty.

Things quickly turn chaotic when the retreat's director receives an email with an encoded message about a potential new threat to the clan.

While those in charge of security debate what to do next, Safe Haven's first ever paranormal retreat is about to begin, and one of the attendees is a mysterious woman who makes Marcel's heart beat faster whenever she's near.

Is the beautiful mortal his one truelove?

Or is she the harbinger of more bad news?

66: Dark Gambit The Play

To get to Safe Haven's inner circle, the Kra-ell leader sacrifices a pawn. He does not expect her to reach the final rank and promote to a queen.

67: Dark Gambit Reliance

Marcel takes a big risk by telling Sofia his greatest sin. Can he trust her to keep it a secret? Or maybe it's time to confess his crime and submit to whatever punishment Edna deems appropriate?

Three miserable centuries of living with guilt and remorse are long enough.

Once the dust settles on the Kra-ell crisis, he will gather the courage to put himself at the court's mercy.

Dark Alliance

68: Dark Alliance Kindred Souls
69: Dark Alliance Turbulent Waters
70: Dark Alliance Perfect Storm

Dark Healing

71: Dark Healing Blind Justice
72: Dark Healing Blind Trust
73: Dark Healing Blind Curve

Dark Encounters

74: Dark Encounters of the Close Kind
75: Dark Encounters of the Unexpected Kind
76: Dark Encounters of the Fated Kind

The Children of the Gods Series Sets

Books 1-3: Dark Stranger trilogy—Includes a bonus short story: **The Fates take a Vacation**

Books 4-6: Dark Enemy Trilogy —Includes a bonus short story—**The Fates' Post-Wedding Celebration**

Books 7-10: Dark Warrior Tetralogy

Books 11-13: Dark Guardian Trilogy

Books 14-16: Dark Angel Trilogy

Books 17-19: Dark Operative Trilogy

Books 20-22: Dark Survivor Trilogy

Books 23-25: Dark Widow Trilogy

Books 26-28: Dark Dream Trilogy

Books 29-31: Dark Prince Trilogy

Books 32-34: Dark Queen Trilogy

Books 35-37: Dark Spy Trilogy

Books 38-40: Dark Overlord Trilogy
Books 41-43: Dark Choices Trilogy
Books 44-46: Dark Secrets Trilogy
Books 47-49: Dark Haven Trilogy
Books 50-52: Dark Power Trilogy
Books 53-55: Dark Memories Trilogy
Books 56-58: Dark Hunter Trilogy
Books 59-61: Dark God Trilogy
Books 62-64: Dark Whispers Trilogy
Books 65-67: Dark Gambit Trilogy
Books 68-70: Dark Alliance Trilogy
Books 71-73: Dark healing Trilogy

MEGA SETS

INCLUDE CHARACTER LISTS

The Children of the Gods: Books 1-6
The Children of the Gods: Books 6.5-10

TRY THE SERIES ON

AUDIBLE

2 FREE audiobooks with your new Audible subscription!

PERFECT MATCH SERIES

Vampire's Consort

When Gabriel's company is ready to start beta testing, he invites his old crush to inspect its medical safety protocol.

Curious about the revolutionary technology of the *Perfect Match Virtual Fantasy-Fulfillment studios*, Brenna agrees.

Neither expects to end up partnering for its first fully immersive test run.

King's Chosen

When Lisa's nutty friends get her a gift certificate to *Perfect Match Virtual Fantasy Studios*, she has no intentions of using it. But since the only way to get a refund is if no partner can be found for her, she makes sure to request a fantasy so girly and over the top that no sane guy will pick it up.

Except, someone does.

> **Warning:** This fantasy contains a hot, domineering crown prince, sweet insta-love, steamy love scenes painted with light shades of gray, a wedding, and a HEA in both the virtual and real worlds.
>
> Intended for mature audience.

Captain's Conquest

Working as a Starbucks barista, Alicia fends off flirting all day long, but none of the guys are as charming and sexy as Gregg. His frequent visits are the highlight of her day, but since he's never asked her out, she assumes he's taken. Besides, between a day job and a budding music career, she has no time to start a new relationship.

That is until Gregg makes her an offer she can't refuse—a gift certificate to the virtual fantasy fulfillment service everyone is talking about. As a huge Star Trek fan, Alicia has a perfect match in mind—the captain of the Starship Enterprise.

The Thief Who Loved Me

When Marian splurges on a Perfect Match Virtual adventure as a world infamous jewel thief, she expects high-wire fun with a hot partner who she will never have to see again in real life.

A virtual encounter seems like the perfect answer to Marcus's string of dating disasters. No strings attached, no drama, and definitely no love. As a die-hard James Bond fan, he chooses as his avatar a dashing MI6 operative, and to complement his adventure, a dangerously seductive partner.

Neither expects to find their forever Perfect Match.

My Merman Prince

The beautiful architect working late on the twelfth floor of my building thinks that I'm just the maintenance guy. She's also under the impression that I'm not interested.

Nothing could be further from the truth.

I want her like I've never wanted a woman before, but I don't play where I work.

I don't need the complications.

When she tells me about living out her mermaid fantasy with a stranger in a Perfect Match virtual adventure, I decide to do everything possible to ensure that the stranger is me.

The Dragon King

To save his beloved kingdom from a devastating war, the Crown Prince of Trieste makes a deal with a witch that costs him half of his humanity and dooms him to an eternity of loneliness.

Now king, he's a fearsome cobalt-winged dragon by day and a short-tempered monarch by night. Not many are brave enough to serve in the palace of the brooding and volatile ruler, but Charlotte ignores the rumors and accepts a scribe position in court.

As the young scribe reawakens Bruce's frozen heart, all that stands in the way of their happiness is the witch's bargain. Outsmarting the evil hag will take cunning and courage, and Charlotte is just the right woman for the job.

My Werewolf Romeo

The father of my star student is a big-shot screenwriter and the patron of the drama department who thinks he can dictate what production I should put on. The principal makes it very clear that I need to cooperate with the opinionated asshat or walk away from my dream job at the exclusive private high school.

It doesn't help matters that the guy is single, hot, charming, creative, and seems to like me despite my thinly-veiled hostility.

When he invites me to a custom-tailored Perfect Match virtual adventure to prove that his screenplay is perfect for my production, I accept, intending to have fun while proving that messing with the classics is a foolish idea.

I don't expect to be wowed by his werewolf adaptation of Red Riding Hood mesh-up with Romeo and Juliet, and I certainly don't expect to fall in love with the virtual fantasy's leading man.

The Channeler's Companion

A treat for fans of *The Wheel of Time*.

When Erika hires Rand to assist in her pediatric clinic, she does so despite his good looks and irresistible charm, not because of them.

He's empathic, adores children, and has the patience of a saint.

He's also all she can think about, but he's off limits.

What's a doctor to do to scratch that irresistible itch without risking workplace complications?

A shared adventure in the Perfect Match Virtual Studios seems like the solution, but instead of letting the algorithm choose a partner for her, Erika can try to influence it to select the one she wants. Awarding Rand a gift certificate to the service will get him into their database, but unless Erika can tip the odds in her favor, getting paired with him is a long shot.

Hopefully, a virtual adventure based on her and Rand's favorite series will do the trick.

Note

Dear reader,

I hope my stories have added a little joy to your day. If you have a moment to add some to mine, you can help spread the word about the Children Of The Gods series by telling your friends and penning a review. Your recommendations are the most powerful way to inspire new readers to explore the series.

Thank you,

Isabell

FOR EXCLUSIVE PEEKS AT UPCOMING RELEASES &
A FREE COMPANION BOOK

Join my *VIP Club* and gain access to the VIP portal at itlucas.com
To Join, go to:
http://eepurl.com/blMTpD

INCLUDED IN YOUR FREE MEMBERSHIP:

YOUR VIP PORTAL

- Read preview chapters of upcoming releases.
- Listen to Goddess's Choice narration by Charles Lawrence
- Exclusive content offered only to my VIPs.

FREE I.T. LUCAS COMPANION INCLUDES:

- Goddess's Choice Part 1
- Perfect Match: Vampire's Consort (A standalone Novella)
- Interview Q & A
- Character Charts

If you're already a subscriber, and you are not getting my emails, your provider is sending them to your junk folder, and you are missing out on **IMPORTANT UPDATES, SIDE CHARACTERS' PORTRAITS, ADDITIONAL CONTENT, AND OTHER GOODIES.** To fix that, add isabell@itlucas.com to your email contacts or your email VIP list.

**Check out the specials at
https://www.itlucas.com/specials**

Manufactured by Amazon.ca
Bolton, ON